BLAZING PASSION

Raven heard Steve coming but pretended not to. She felt his hands fasten on her shoulders to spin her about. Adrenaline surged through her as she prepared to defend herself, for this was the moment she had been waiting for—to make him want her beyond all reason . . . then humiliate him.

Now, however, as she stared up at him, caught in his burning gaze, she trembled not from fear that he would harm her but rather from the beginnings of betrayal of her own body. His eyes captured hers in a fever of sheer desire, and she was powerless to pull away.

Books by Patricia Hagan

Midnight Rose
Heaven in a Wildflower
A Forever Kind of Love
Orchids in Moonlight
Love and War
Starlight
Say You Love Me
Passion's Fury
Simply Heaven

Published by HarperPaperbacks

Simply Heaven

⋈ PATRICIA HAGAN ⋈

HarperPaperbacks
A Division of HarperCollinsPublishers

HarperPaperbacks   *A Division of* HarperCollins*Publishers*
10 East 53rd Street, New York, N.Y. 10022

Cover illustration by Jim Griffin

First printing: December 1995

Printed in the United States of America

HarperPaperbacks, HarperMonogram, and colophon are trademarks of HarperCollins*Publishers*

❖ 10 9 8 7 6 5 4 3 2 1

For Kim and Debbie, welcomed additions to the Hagan family . . . and also for the beloved additions they and my nephews, David and Dwain, brought to our clan: Kelsey and Mary Chandler Hagan.

1

Steve Maddox had the survival instincts of a wild animal.

Though exhausted when he had gone to bed, falling asleep as soon as his head touched the pillow, he came wide awake at the first faint sound of someone climbing up the ladder outside his door.

It was his first night in the room he had built for himself in a corner of the hayloft over the barn. He had not pulled the ladder up after him because he hadn't thought it would be necessary. Now, hearing the soft creak of the wooden rungs, he wished he had.

Slipping quietly out of bed, Steve pulled on his trousers. With the uncanny swiftness of a striking rattler, his hand shot out in the darkness to grab his gun from the bedside table. In the three years he had worked at Halcyon plantation he didn't think he had any enemies, but he was taking no chances, especially since it appeared whoever it was meant to surprise him.

He pressed back against the wall. It was a small room. He had only needed space for a bed and a table and chair, but if his sneaking visitor meant to do him harm and started firing through the door, Steve would be out the way.

As he waited tensely, he dared to wonder if it just might be Ned Ralston's stepdaughter creeping up the ladder. She had returned a few months ago from a fancy finishing school in Paris and had made his life hell ever since. Spoiled, used to getting anything she wanted, she had decided on sight that she wanted *him.*

At first, he'd thought it was just harmless flirting, but she had become bolder. Then, one night when she caught him alone in Ned's study, she had thrown herself at him, flinging her arms around his neck and standing on tiptoe to rain kisses all over his face. He had come close to breaking her arm before she would let go of him, and the very next day he had started building the room above the stable.

He'd felt he had no choice except to move out, although he knew it was a bad time with Ned so sick. The doctor had said it was his kidneys and would only get worse, and Steve would have liked to be close by should Ned need him. He had only been living in the house at Ned's insistence. Ned's wife had died several years earlier, and Ned said he was lonely with Lisbeth and her brother, Julius, away at school.

When he had made the excuse that he wanted to move to the barn to be closer to the horses, Ned had teased him about wanting to have privacy to entertain women. Steve just let him think that and had dared to think he would have some peace, at least until now.

He heard a soft grunt as someone stepped off the ladder and stumbled against the wall. Only a few people knew exactly where he had built his room in the loft. Obviously the person blundering around out there was not one of them.

He thought about calling out but knew if it weren't Lisbeth, and whoever it was did have a gun, he might startle them into shooting and the horses below might panic. He didn't want to chance it.

He sucked in his breath and held it.

The doorknob turned.

He clicked the gun's hammer back, the deadly sound puncturing the tense silence.

"Oh, no. Don't shoot. It's me, Steve. Dear God!"

The words were nearly lost in the whisper, but he recognized the voice all the same. "Lisbeth, damn it, I could have killed you!" He put down his gun and struck a match to the bedside lantern to flood the room with mellow light.

Her blue eyes were wide with terror, and her face was as white as the dress she was wearing. "I . . . I didn't mean to frighten you," she stammered.

"You should know better than to sneak up on somebody in the dark like that. What the hell are you doing here?"

"I was worried about Belle—" she was, momentarily taken aback by the sight of him standing there bare-chested but recovered quickly to finish. "She isn't feeling well. I couldn't sleep, and I thought maybe if I came out here we could talk and you'd make me feel better about it."

"You could have talked to me about it earlier. There's nothing wrong with your mare that foaling won't cure."

The corners of her mouth dropped in petulance. "You've been avoiding me, and you know it."

"And with good reason." He fastened his belt. "Now let's get you back to the house before somebody finds out you're here. I'll help you down the ladder. It's a wonder you didn't break your neck."

With an exaggerated sigh, she plopped down on the bed. "I'm not going anywhere till we talk, Steve. I want to know why you don't like me."

"I do like you," he said, running his fingers through his hair in agitation, "but that's as far as it goes . . . as far as it will ever go. I've told you over and over that I think of you as a little sister, nothing more."

"Just because Ned treats you like his son does not make you my brother. I never felt for Julius what I feel for you. That would be real naughty." She wrinkled her nose.

He held out his hand.

She ignored it. "I'm not going anywhere."

"Would you like for me to throw you over my shoulder and carry you out of here like a sack of feed? I'll do it, so help me."

"And I'll scream, and everyone will come running, and I'll say you dragged me out of my bed and brought me out to the barn to rape me."

"You wouldn't."

"I might. You can't be sure I won't." Her eyes danced mischievously. "Don't dare me."

She was right. He couldn't be sure she would not pull such a stunt. "Good grief, Lisbeth, what is it going to take to make you understand that I'm just not interested in you that way?"

"Don't you find me pretty?"

"Of course I do. But that doesn't mean I want to bed you."

"Because your loyalty to Ned keeps you from it. But you'd better wake up and realize which side your bread is buttered on. He's not going to live forever, you know. What will you do when he dies, have you thought about that?"

He hadn't. He took one day at a time. "I got by before. I'll manage again."

"But don't you see? It doesn't have to be that way. I'll get married, of course, but I already know I'll be bored silly. Not one boy who calls on me excites me the way you do. So I'll have you"—she stood to tap his nose coquettishly with her finger—"for my *paramour*."

He brushed her hand away. "No, thanks. Besides, I don't put butter on my bread anyway."

Annoyance flashed across her face, but she sat back down. "You'd best think about it. Lots of married women take lovers. Why shouldn't they? Their husbands have mistresses. You say you can get by, but you know you've never lived so good." She furrowed her brow to appear concerned. "I couldn't understand why Ned kept in touch with you, but he must have been lonely after Mother died. Who knows? Anyway, he told me he felt sorry for you because you didn't have any family. I must admit the thought occurred to me that you were playing on his sympathy to get his money, but that didn't bother me. Heavens, he's got enough that he can afford to be charitable. But do you really want to go back to your old life of poverty? Haven't you come to enjoy the comforts of the rich?"

"That's never mattered." Steve cared only about racking horses. Ned had the best stock available, the best equine facilities money could buy. When he was gone, Julius would probably let it all go to ruin, and that was a shame, but it was all Steve would miss—except for Ned and the wonderful friendship they shared. He coveted nothing else.

Lisbeth sensed what he was thinking. She was well aware of his affinity for the horses. "You can stay on here. Julius certainly won't care one way or the other. He'll probably move into Mobile anyway. He prefers a more urban lifestyle, you know. And if I decide to marry Barley Tremayne, the only boy I find the least bit appealing, we'll live here. I've no intentions of moving in with his family. Their house doesn't hold a candle to this one."

Steve could not help smiling. "So you've got it all figured out. And you enjoy watching the boys stumble over one another each hoping to be the one chosen, when you've already got young Tremayne secretly picked. You've even decided where you'll live and who your lover will be. Pretty sure of yourself, aren't you?"

She stiffened. She did not like being mocked. "I have reason to be sure of myself, Steve, and you would be wise not to make fun of me if you care about your future."

"Well, let me remind you it's my future to care about, not yours."

Suddenly, sharply, she asked, "Did you move out here so you could sneak another woman into your bed without my finding out about it?"

"No. I moved out here to get away from you."

Lisbeth ignored that and persisted. "Is it Selena

Leroux?" Her eyes narrowed suspiciously. "Is it *your* baby she's carrying?"

He shook his head in disgust that she could be so damned contrary. "You've no right to say things like that." Selena was the daughter of one of the Cajun overseers from Louisiana. She was pregnant, but not by Steve; they were close, but not that way. And while her father was shamed by Selena's condition, she had never told anyone but Steve who the father of her baby was: a married man who had drowned in a boating accident on the river. According to Selena, the two of them had been planning on running away together, but now, with him dead, there was no point in hurting his widow by letting her know her husband had been going to leave her. No good could come of it, so Selena kept silent, despite her father's badgering that she reveal who was responsible for her condition.

"Well, you're the only white man who ever talks to her. The others won't be caught dead near her, because everybody knows she's a whore."

"She's not a whore, and I talk to her because she's my friend—and that's nobody's business, including yours."

"Everybody says you're sweet on her. That's why they think it's your baby."

His patience was wearing thin. "I don't give a damn what people think. Now get out of here."

She giggled. "Well, if you don't care what people think, why are you in such a hurry to get rid of me?"

"You little fool." He yanked her to her feet, itching to shake her till her teeth rattled. "It's you I'm concerned about; not me. Do you think Barley would want to marry you if he found out you'd sneaked into my bedroom? And what about Ned? This would upset him real bad."

She jutted her chin. "Well, maybe I'll just upset him by telling him about you and Selena. Then he'll run both of you off. How would you like that? You don't want to make me mad, Steve Maddox," she warned him.

"No, I don't, but I'm not going to be blackmailed either. Besides, if you go to him with a lie like that, he wouldn't believe you and you know it—not when I deny it. Ned trusts me, and I'll be damned if I'm going to let you or anybody else spoil that."

She pulled back from his grasp, and he let her. She chewed her lip thoughtfully for a moment, meeting his fiery gaze with one of her own. Then, not knowing what else to do, she decided to try tears, which appeared on command to trickle down her cheeks. "Don't treat me like this, Steve," she whispered tremulously. "Please. I care for you, I really do."

He was unmoved. He had seen her cry before. It worked with Ned, who was a gentle man and willing to do anything to avoid unpleasantness, but not with him. "Enough of this, Lisbeth. You're getting out of here now."

Suddenly, with a little cry, she threw herself against him, digging her fingers into his shoulders and delighting in the feel of his naked rock-hard flesh. Her breasts pressed against his chest, and she swayed and clung to him even tighter. "You know you want me. You're just being stubborn. That's your problem."

"And your problem is that you can't stand not getting your way." He tried to pry her fingers loose without hurting her, but she was holding tight as a tick on a dog's ear. Finally, he grabbed her wrists and squeezed so hard she had to let go.

"Damn you, you'll regret scorning me like this."

"I'm not scorning you, Lisbeth. I'm just saying no, which seems to be a word you aren't accustomed to hearing."

"You'll be sor—"

He had heard the creaking of the stable door opening below and moved fast to clamp his hand over her mouth and jerk her against him. Someone was coming. Unlike Lisbeth, this person was not being stealthy, so he did not draw his gun.

She struggled in his arms, but he managed to wrest her to one side and quietly, quickly, close the door. "Damn it, be still," he whispered, pressing his lips against her ear. "Do you want to be caught in here?"

Taking her with him, he doused the lantern. She had stopped fighting him and, instead, tensed against him. He was relieved she had, for it meant that despite all her talk to the contrary, she didn't want to be discovered in an embarrassing situation any more than he did.

Now he could hear footsteps on the ladder, moving purposely upward, and felt the first beads of cold sweat on his forehead as he prayed it was not Ned. Surely, he was too weak to climb up, but if he had, Steve knew the only thing he could do was pretend he had a woman in his room.

Let Ned think he was right about why he had wanted to move out of the house. Let him think anything he wanted except that the woman inside was Lisbeth. Steve would be damned if he was going to open the door and let him find her there.

2

Elijah paused halfway up the ladder. He was old and not used to such exertion. Pausing to catch his breath, he thought maybe if he hollered he wouldn't have to go any higher. "Mister Steve, it's me—Elijah. Please wake up, Mister Steve. I got to tell you somethin'."

Relieved it was not Ned, Steve was still alarmed, because Elijah would not have come so late unless it was important. "I'm awake. What is it?" he answered.

"Master Ned told me to fetch you. He says he's got to talk to you right away."

"Is he feeling worse?"

"He don't seem to be. But he don't seem to feel no better neither."

"Tell him I'll be right there."

Steve waited till he was sure Elijah was gone before letting Lisbeth go. She jerked away, anger flashing. "You nearly smothered me, putting your hand over my face like that."

"Sorry." He quickly lit the lantern again. "All right, you heard him. Ned wants to see me. Let's get you out of here so I can find out what he wants. I'll wait a few minutes to give you time to get inside the house before I leave."

She looked uncertain. She was still mad and wanted him to know it.

"Come on," he prodded. "I don't want you to fall going down. Let's forget this happened and be friends. How about it?" He managed a tight smile and held out his hand.

She slapped it away. "Friends!" She spat the word. "How can you be so stupid as to think I would ever be your friend after you dare to push me aside for white trash like Selena Leroux? I'll never forget how you've treated me, never. I don't need your help. I got up here by myself and I can get down by myself. And if you dare touch me again, I'll scream. I swear I will."

He felt like cheering when she finally stormed out but instead focused on dressing as fast as possible. Ned might be feeling worse and just didn't want to tell Elijah. He would worry about trying to smooth things over with Lisbeth later. Even if she did not want to be his friend, he damn sure wanted to keep her from being his enemy.

He reached for a shirt and glanced around to see where he had left his boots. There was no time to spare.

Lisbeth was not about to go to her room, because curiosity was gnawing at her over why Ned would send for Steve at such an ungodly hour. The house was still. Elijah had left candles burning in the hall sconces, casting eerie shadows. She tiptoed along, finally hiding behind a tall vase in the niche in the wall opposite Ned's room. When Steve arrived a few minutes later, he did not see her hiding there.

He knocked. Ned called for him to enter, and he did so. As soon as the door was closed, Lisbeth hurried to press her ear against it.

"Steve, I appreciate your coming like this. I know it's late."

Ned held out a hand, and when Steve shook it he noticed how hot it felt. Ned probably had a fever. Pulling up a chair next to the bed, he sat down. "You know I'll always be here when you need me. Now, what's wrong? You look worried." And he did. His face was drawn and his eyes appeared dull, troubled.

Ned gave a bitter laugh. "You're damn right I'm worried. Wouldn't you be if you knew you were going to die?"

Steve refused to encourage him. "You old warhorse. You'll outlive all of us."

Ned was not to be coaxed from his gloomy mood. "I'm not stupid, Steve. I know I'm not getting any better. That tonic Doc Sawyer gives me doesn't do any good. I don't feel like doing anything but lay in this bed, and that gives me a lot of time to think about dying."

Once more, Steve attempted to lighten things. "Well, you aren't going to die before morning. Can't all this wait till then? I've had a rough day, and you look like you could use some rest too. Suppose I have Elijah bring you some warm milk, and—"

"Damn it, boy, listen to me!" Ned said, his tone

gruff, which made him start coughing, and that led to wheezing.

Steve bolted for the pitcher on the bedside table to pour him a glass of water and held his head up from the pillows while he drank.

Finally, Ned was able to talk. "I've been waiting nearly eighteen years to get this off my chest," he declared fervently, "and I'm not going to put it off a minute longer. I've decided I've got to get my life in order before I go to meet my Maker. Now sit down and hear me out. Please."

Steve sat, bewildered. Ned was being damn mysterious.

"How long have you known me?"

"Three years." Steve had been working as a horse trainer in Virginia on a farm where racking horses were being bred. Horse lovers all over the south were excited about this animal for its beauty, stamina, and calm disposition, but most of all because its smooth natural gait meant it could be ridden comfortably for hours.

When Ned Ralston visited Virginia to buy horses, Steve had been impressed over how he chose the finest breeding stock available without even asking the price. "Money doesn't matter," he had said nonchalantly. "Not when it comes to horses." Then, when Ned heard Steve was the best trainer around, he'd insisted that Steve go back to Alabama with him and work at his plantation, Halcyon.

At first, Steve was reluctant; he didn't really know anything about this man, except that he was supposed to be a rich planter and shipping tycoon. But Ned kept after him, asking him to name his price, and when he did Ned doubled it. For such a generous amount, Steve was willing to give it a try. He had quit his job in Virginia on the spot, and during the trip back to Alabama the two had become fast friends.

Consequently, the last three years had been the best in Steve's life.

"You've been like a son to me," Ned said now. "Till you came along, I didn't feel like I had any family at all."

"You've got Lisbeth and Julius," Steve reminded him.

"I'm afraid my hunting dogs think more of me than they do, thanks to their mother she never did get over how I refused to marry her when my father first wanted me to. But she didn't let that stop her later, when she was a widow with two small children. We didn't love each other. I can honestly say I tried to make her a good husband and be a good father to her children, but she was as cold as a dead man's handshake."

He paused to take a breath.

"The only real happiness I've had since my marriage was when I got interested in the racking horses—and came to know you," he added, voice cracking. "You've meant a lot to me."

"And you know how I feel about you. But are you sure you want to tell me all this? You shouldn't upset yourself this way. It's just stirring up bad memories."

"I've got to. Because the only way you can help me set things right is to hear me out and hear my sins. A long time ago, I did something real bad, something that has haunted me ever since."

"We've all done things we're ashamed of."

"But I've got a big skeleton hiding in my closet, and you have to help me bring it out in the open so I can go to my grave in peace."

"All you have to do is ask," Steve said—and meant it.

Ned turned his head to stare into the shadows, as though he could actually see the past unfolding there. He was silent for so long Steve dared to hope he would just drift off to sleep and forget all about the conversation in the morning. But then he faced him once more, and Steve could see the anguish that remembering had brought to his eyes.

"My father and I never got along. I worshiped my mother, and we never had a cross word, but my old man and I always seemed to be at odds over something. The final straw came when he got it in his head that I was going to marry Edith White. He liked her family and said she came from good blood to mix with mine to carry on the Ralston name. I refused but he kept on, and things got so bad I had to leave. I hated to hurt my mother, but I just couldn't take it anymore."

Ned went on, describing how, after drifting for a while, he had wound up in Texas to become a follower of Sam Houston, joining him in the memorable battle of San Jacinto in 1836.

"I got wounded pretty bad and was weak from losing blood. My horse took me a long way from the battle site, and a Tonkawa Indian girl found me and nursed me back to health. Her name was . . . Lakoma."

The way Ned spoke her name, hesitating for a second as though savoring the sound, told Steve that Lakoma was the key to what this was all about.

"She was the most beautiful woman I've ever seen, before or since. Her hair was as black and silky as a raven's wing, and her eyes were brown like good rich coffee. And her skin . . ."

Steve noticed the color had begun to come back into Ned's face as he recollected fond memories.

"Her skin was like fine wine. Lord, she was a princess! I loved her and she loved me, I know she did. She nursed me back to health, hiding me from her people, because she was afraid of what they would do if they found out she was helping a white man. Finally, when I was well enough to visit a nearby outpost, I found a message waiting that I had to return home right away if I wanted to see my mother before she died." He was suddenly grim once more.

Steve thought he knew the rest of the story. "So you left her and you never forgot her. But that was a long time ago. I doubt I could find her now."

"She married somebody else."

Steve was puzzled. Ned's story was taking on an unexpected twist.

"I meant to go back. I promised Lakoma I would. But I was always weak when it came to my mother, and when I got home to be told she was dying of a broken heart, all because I had run away, I was struck with guilt. Oh, I wish you could have seen her when she saw me after all those years. You'd understand why it was so hard for me. Her face lit up like sunshine, and she found the strength to sit up in that bed and tell me then and there that if I ever went off and left her again, the day I did she would be dead before the sun went down. And I believed her, Steve. I truly did.

"After that," he continued with a deep sigh, "I let my guilt convince me it wouldn't have ever worked out for me and Lakoma to be together. My parents would never have accepted an Indian for a daughter-in-law, so she couldn't have been part of my world, and I'm ashamed to say it but back then I wasn't willing to give up my world for hers. Especially when I knew it would kill my mother. So I tried to put her out of my mind, but I couldn't. Not a day went by that I didn't think about her. I tried to see she was taken care of. I had a friend out there, an Indian agent named Seth Greer. I wrote him and asked him to see if he could find her and let me know how she was doing. He found her for me, all right—and when he did, he married her," he added with a grimace.

"Then you knew she was taken care of." Steve paused, hesitant to be so blunt but feeling he had no choice. "Ned, you should have tried harder to forget her. I sure hope you aren't telling me all this because you want me to go look for her, not when she's been married to somebody else all this time."

"You don't understand." With a broken sob, his face crumpling with emotion, Ned whispered, "You see, she had my baby. She had my *daughter*, Steve. And I didn't know about it till it was too late. If I had, I swear I never would have married Edith. Nothing would have kept me from going back and doing the right thing by my child, not even my mother."

Steve sucked in his breath. Now he knew why Ned had been unable to get Lakoma out of his mind.

"Seth wrote he was raising my girl like she was his own. I sent money to help out. He took some of it, and once in a while he would write a note telling me they were all fine. A few years ago—" his voice cracked again, and he swallowed hard before continuing—"he wrote me that Lakoma had died. It hurt me through and through, and I wrote right back to tell him how sorry I was, and how I would keep sending money for the girl but time went by and I didn't hear from him again. Finally, my letters started coming back marked UNCLAIMED. That's when I figured there was nothing else I could do. I'd lost trace of him and my daughter. I was afraid if I made a fuss, hired detectives and all, the children would hear about it, and I didn't want that. None of this was their fault. They didn't deserve to be hurt by it. So once again I talked myself into believing it was all for the best. But now, faced with dying myself, I've got to try and set things right. And that's where you come in."

Steve groaned inwardly.

"I want you to go to Texas and try to find her. I know it won't be easy, because the only thing I can tell you is where Seth was the last time I heard from him. He had quit his job as Indian agent and was running a trading post near Fort Inge, west of San Antonio. And all I know about my girl is that her name is Raven. I figure they called her that because she had black hair like her mother," he added wistfully.

Steve realized he had been mistaken in thinking Ned was unhappy merely because he was lonely. The man was haunted by his past. But what could Steve do about it? Even if he did find the girl, surely Ned did not expect him to bring her back?

But that was exactly what Ned did expect.

"I want to meet her before I die. I want to make her see things would have turned out different if I'd only known about her before I married Edith." He paused to blink back his tears. "I'm sorry to say I've never been a praying man, but I'm sure going to be praying now that the Lord will give me a little extra time, that he won't call me home till you get back here with Raven so I can tell her what's in my heart and we can get to know each other. Who knows? Maybe we can even learn to love each other. Most of all, I want to make sure she gets what's rightfully hers."

"Halcyon," Steve murmured.

"Exactly."

Curiously, impulsively, Steve asked, "Where do Lisbeth and Julius figure in all this? They're going to be plenty upset."

"They will for a while, but I think they'll accept it in time. Edith spoiled them rotten, but they aren't all bad. Besides, I've provided for them. Lisbeth will have a generous dowry. As for Julius, he's going to have to learn what it's like to work for a living, and that'll be good for him." He saw no need to explain to Steve the details of his stipulation that Julius would have to work at the docks for a nominal salary till his thirtieth birthday, when he would then inherit the vast shipping holdings if he had not quit. Otherwise, Raven would also get that part of the estate.

"If Raven allows it," he went on, "they can keep on living at Halcyon. There's room for them all to raise families here, but that will be up to her."

"And if I can't find her?"

"You will," Ned said confidently. "You're a good man. You've got grit. I knew that the first time we met. And when you make up your mind to do something, you do it."

Steve noticed that Ned's confession had taken a lot out of him. He had turned pale again and his breathing was becoming labored. He decided to change the subject, hoping Ned would calm down and fall asleep. "Well, I never could ride Starfire, remember? I busted my butt both times I tried."

Ned smiled. Talking about his prize racking horse always made him proud. "Well, that's nothing to be ashamed of. Nobody has ever been able to ride him but me. There's never been another horse with such spirit, and you know it."

The smile faded.

"But let's get back to what we were talking about. You've got to find my daughter and bring her home. I realize she may not want to come. Hell, Lakoma may have poisoned her against me. But you make her do it, whether she wants to or not. If she doesn't want to stay, I won't try to make her, but I'm bound and determined to meet her and have my say."

Steve frowned. "What if she decides to leave after you're gone? What will happen to Halcyon? I'd hate to see her sell it to strangers."

"That can't happen, because if she leaves, everything will be divided between Julius and Lisbeth."

Steve nodded, relieved.

Ned reached to touch his arm, his expression intense. "Don't dawdle. I may not have much time left."

Steve patted his hand and stood up. "I'll leave at first light. I'd better try to get a few hours' sleep between now and then."

"Don't tell anybody where you're going or why."

"You know I won't." He headed for the door.

"Steve?"

He turned warily. Ned had worn himself out. It was time to end the conversation.

"I want you to know I've provided for you in my will, but I'm not leaving you the racking horses, even though I know how much they mean to you."

"You don't have to leave me anything, Ned," Steve was quick to tell him. "I don't expect it."

Ned waved him to silence. "I included the horses with everything at Halcyon, because I'm hoping Raven has enough of me in her to love them like I do. But I *have* seen to it that you'll have enough money to buy some horses of your own and maybe even a little farm somewhere."

Steve felt a lump in his throat. "In these past three years you've given me something money can't buy. And if I ride out of here with nothing more than the clothes on my back, I'll always be grateful to you for making me feel like I was a part of something. You've been good to me, Ned, and that's why I'm going to do my damnedest to find your daughter for you."

Outside, her ear pressed against the door, Lisbeth listened, eyes wide, lips parted in a silent gasp. Frozen with shock over all she had just heard, it was only at the last possible second, when Steve's hand was turning the knob, that she came alive in time to avoid being caught eavesdropping and scrambled to hide behind the vase once more.

Her heart pounding, she waited till she was sure Steve had left the house before daring to move. Then she hurried to the opposite wing of the house, where Julius had a suite across from her own. Some nights he stayed in Mobile, but much to her relief this was not one of them.

His door was locked, or she would have burst right in, so desperate was she to tell him what she had just heard.

It took him awhile to respond to her frenzied knock. "Do you know what time it is?" he asked, sleepy and annoyed.

She pushed by him into the sitting room, waiting till he had closed the door before announcing, "It would have been a blessing for us all if Ned had died when he was wounded at San Jacinto!"

Julius stared at her incredulously. "You came here in the middle of the night to tell me that? Have you lost your mind?"

"No, but Ned has sure lost his if he thinks he can flaunt his shameful past and rob us of what is rightfully ours."

"Is this the aftermath of some nightmare you've had and can't get over?"

"Oh, it's a nightmare, all right." She laughed bitterly. "The worst you could ever imagine." Hastily, she conjured up a lie, not about to admit she had gone to Steve's quarters earlier. Instead, she said she had heard Steve come upstairs and, because the hour was so late, feared it meant Ned had taken a turn for the worse, so she had gone to find out and then could not help overhearing what was said between them. Furiously, she recounted Ned's confession.

Julius turned pale as he listened, and when she had finished, he murmured, stunned, "Mother always claimed he went away to sow his wild oats. Thank God, she was spared knowing they took root and sprouted."

"Well, she might have been spared, but we won't be. We'll be shamed forever. I'll be a social outcast, I just know it." She was waving her arms in a frenzy.

Julius snatched an ivory figurine out of her way and set it on the mantel, beyond her reach. "No one is going to find out. Calm down. I don't think we've got anything to worry about."

"How can you say that? Once Steve brings that half-breed here, everyone will know. You've got to stop him." She leaned forward to clutch the lapels of his robe. "You've got to make him see it'll ruin everything. Listen. We both know how he loves the racking horses. We'll tell him he can have all of them if he'll just pretend to go look for her and then, after a while, come back and say he couldn't find her."

"But you just said you heard Ned tell him he was leaving him enough money to buy his own horses. He doesn't have to make any deals with us." Julius swung his head slowly from side to side. "No, I don't think it's wise to let him know we're aware of any of this."

"Well, we have to do something!"

"No, we don't, and if you'll stop and think about it, you'll realize you're getting all upset for nothing. Steve has to go to some godforsaken place to try and find a half-breed Indian girl known only as Raven that no one has heard anything about for years. The chances of his succeeding are practically nonexistent. As for finding out Ned had a child by another woman, it doesn't matter, and we shouldn't think less of him for it. It happened a long time ago, before he was married to Mother. No doubt he's thinking about it now because he knows he's going to die soon. People faced with death do that. They start trying to make peace with themselves. It's only natural."

"I suppose you're right." Based on what she'd heard Ned say, she knew there really wasn't much for Steve to go on. Still, she fretted. "I can't help wishing he wouldn't even try to find her."

"He has to, because if he refuses, Ned might get mad and snatch back the slice of pie he's carved out for him. Stop worrying and go get some sleep."

Lisbeth left him and tiptoed down the hall toward

her own room, glad Julius had allayed her fears. Now she felt confident that Steve would ultimately fail.

And she would be waiting to gloat when he did, which would give her some revenge, at least, for how he had spurned her.

3

The sun was a shapeless gold flame, toasting the land and parching the chaparral and mesquite that dared to sprout from the rocks and sand.

Since passing through San Antonio and heading farther west, Steve felt as though he were locked in wilderness and would never reach civilization again. The ground swells were long and so equal in height and similar in form that they reminded him of a tedious sea voyage he'd taken years back, when the ship had plowed along, hour after slow hour, without raising a single object to attract the eye.

Everything seemed to blend into the horizon in all directions, with nothing in between save an occasional barren hillock or dry gulch, starkly framed by the distant mountains.

He rode with a bandanna across his nose and the lower part of his face to keep the dust out of his throat.

He had traveled steadily since leaving Mobile, stopping only at night. During the day, he paused to water his horse while he ate a portion of his rations. Time was precious. It was going to be hard to decide when to give up and turn back if he could not find Ned's daughter. And if it came to that, he only hoped Ned would feel some peace to know he had tried his best.

He was alert for any hint of danger, because everyone he had talked to since crossing into Texas had said they lived in constant fear of an Indian attack. Nearly eight thousand soldiers were manning fifty-two forts on the western frontier, but even with all the reservations that had been established, it still wasn't enough to protect the settlers from the Indians, who were enraged over the white man's invasion of what they firmly believed was their land. Steve had not been too concerned till after he reached the other side of San Antonio. Now, alone in the wastelands, he could not help wishing he had a guide with him who would know where Indians were most likely to be and could spot signs he might not notice.

So, ever mindful of his surroundings, he whiled away the hours by ruminating on his own life.

He thought about the money Ned was leaving him and how it really made no difference, regardless of the amount. The fact was, the one thing Steve wanted Ned could not leave him—and that was having a real home. He'd felt that for the first time in his life when he accompanied Ned back to Halcyon, but with Ned gone he would no longer feel at home there.

He supposed sooner or later he would have to move on, because he sure as hell didn't intend to hang around and take Lisbeth up on her offer. Maybe some men would leap at the chance, but not him. If not for that awkward situation, he might have considered staying on to tend the horses.

Ned sometimes nagged him to find himself a wife. Steve would laugh at the notion, not admitting he had no intentions of ever getting hitched. He just couldn't see himself falling in love with a woman and wasn't about to marry otherwise. Love hurt. He had learned the only way to keep from being hurt was not to expect anything from a woman beyond the moment at hand. That way, he was spared disappointment.

His mother had died giving birth to him, and no one seemed sure who his father was. After all, a woman struggling to survive on the Philadelphia waterfront in 1830, as his mother had been forced to do, could hardly be concerned with the names of her customers.

His only known relative, an aunt, had taken him to raise, and when she died before his fourth birthday he was put in an orphanage. Bitterly, he remembered clinging to indifferent matrons' skirts, crying and begging for attention, only to be impatiently pushed away, sometimes even slapped and knocked to the floor. Then, when he was old enough, he was placed in homes to do chores, forced to work hard for long cruel hours and beaten if he dared to complain.

He had learned about sex from girls in the households where he lived. A sixteen-year-old had sneaked into his attic bed when he was twelve and was the first of too many to remember. But there had never been any tenderness, just pleasures of the flesh which became solace amid the misery of his life. As he matured, however, he dared to think there might be more to lovemaking than frenzied coupling in the dark, and stupidly fell in love. The girl had been many years older than he was. Never would he forget how cruelly she had laughed at him when, in the throes of passion, he had blurted out that he loved her. That was when he made up his mind never to expect more than fleeting physical pleasure. He made it good, and the girls—and, eventually, women—always came back for more.

When he was older, there were a few who hinted at marriage and all that went with it, but he was honest with everyone, letting them know he was not interested in commitment. That way, he ensured that he would never be hurt or rejected again. . . .

In late afternoon on the third day out from San Antonio, Steve arrived at Fort Inge. Situated on a hill, it was planned around a spacious parade ground with officers' quarters lining one side and soldiers' barracks and stables on another. On the back side was the hospital, magazine, storehouses, and other support buildings necessary to an isolated post.

He stated his business to the cautious sentry on duty at the gate: He was looking for a man named Seth Greer who had once operated a trading post on the San Antonio trail but had not seen it along the way.

The sentry shook his head. "Sorry, I don't know anything about it. Never heard of anybody named Greer. I've only been here a few months, though. Somebody else might be able to help you." He waved another soldier over. "Take this man to the quartermaster's office."

As they crossed the parade ground, Steve instinctively glanced toward the stables. He made a mental note to stop by later, curious about the stock used by the army. He saw some men lounging around outside wearing the familiar blue uniform of the cavalry, but there the resemblance to regular soldiers ended. Some of them had braids, a couple wore scalp locks, and a few had long hair streaming down their backs. They eyed him warily as he passed, dark eyes set in cinnamon faces. These, he knew, were Indians hired to scout for the army.

One of them caught his eye. He was smaller, appeared younger, and seemed to distance himself from the others. His hair was long but instead of the front part being pulled away from his forehead by a bandanna or leather thong, like the rest of the Indians, it tumbled to nearly conceal his eyes.

Steve also noticed how filthy the boy was. His face was covered with dirt, and the baggy uniform he wore was not particularly clean either.

The soldier escorting Steve saw him staring at the scouts and mistook his interest for aversion. "I don't like 'em either. Can't be trusted, none of 'em. They'd just as soon slit your throat as look at you. But the army says we need 'em to track down the rest of their kind."

"Indians betraying Indians," Steve murmured. "That's a sad paradox in a way."

The soldier glanced at him sharply. "You sound like an Indian lover, mister. Maybe you don't know what it's really like out here. It's hell, thanks to the red man, and the sooner we kill every one of them the better."

Steve responded quietly. "My feelings have nothing to do with being an Indian lover. I just find it pitiful that men are forced to turn against their own kind in order to survive. There has to be another way for everyone to live in peace."

The soldier softened a bit. "Yeah, I know what you mean. I don't like the killing either. Hell, I don't even like being a soldier. I thought I would. Thirteen dollars a month sounded good, along with clothes and shelter and food. But I've seen too many men die in this godforsaken place, and I'm not wanting to join them. I'm not like the scouts. They only want their pay and don't give a damn who gets killed so long as it's not them."

They reached the post quartermaster's office, where Steve met Captain Puckett. "Have a seat, Maddox," the captain said after shaking his hand. "Welcome. We don't get a lot of visitors in these parts. Where are you from and what brings you here?"

"I'm a horse trainer on a plantation in Alabama, just north of Mobile." He repeated what he had told the sentry, how he was looking for Seth Greer.

The captain nodded. "The trading post was maybe a mile or so away. It was owned by the government. The commander before me wanted it moved inside the fort for convenience's sake and got permission to do it. Greer said he wouldn't operate it anymore and quit. That was over a year ago."

Steve felt a rush of excitement to have his first lead. "Do you have any idea where he went?"

"Sorry. That's all I know."

"Is there anybody here who would?"

"Maybe Sergeant Major Wacksmith. He's been here longer than anybody else. I saw him a little while ago, heading for the blacksmith shop with his horse."

Steve thanked him and quickly found his way to the shop, which was situated in a corner of the stables. He saw that the scouts were still watching him, along with the boy, who continued to stand apart from the others.

Sergeant Wacksmith was not in a good mood. A

big barrel-chested man, he was wheezing and sweating in the late-afternoon heat as he attempted to shoe a horse. Bending over, holding the horse's hoof in one hand, he was struggling to hammer in the nails. He glanced up briefly at Steve before muttering, "What the hell do you want? Can't you see I'm busy?"

Steve noted the horse appeared uneasy. "You aren't a regular blacksmith, are you?"

"Damn right I'm not. We ain't got but one, Corporal Gooden, and he's down with a bad leg. Horse kicked him yesterday. My horse threw a shoe this morning, and there's nobody to fix it but me."

"Let me do it." Steve rolled up his sleeves.

Wacksmith was only too glad to let him, and gratitude quickly changed to admiration as he realized Steve knew what he was doing. "I know that's not the first horse you've ever shod, mister."

"The horse knows it too, which is more important. He's not going to stand still if he senses you're nervous, and that's when trouble starts."

Steve nailed the shoe in place, checked the others to make sure they were all right, then stood. "That does it. Now I'd like to talk to you, if you've got a minute."

Wacksmith gave him a pat on the back. "What's on your mind? Better make it quick, or we'll have you in a uniform working here full-time, good as you are."

"Thanks, but I've *got* a job—trying to find a man I hope you know something about: Seth Greer."

"Oh, I can help you there, all right. He used to run a trading post down the road. I knew him real good."

"Do you know where he went when it was closed down?"

"Maybe. Why do you want to know?"

Steve knew if word got out he was searching for an heiress, Indian girls would come from all over claiming to be Raven. "All I can tell you is that I was hired to find him and his daughter, but I assure you I mean them no harm."

"Well, you won't find Seth. He's dead."

Steve was not surprised. He had considered that might be the reason Ned's letters from Greer had stopped. "I'm sorry about that," he responded, "but I'd still like to hear anything you can tell me about him."

Wacksmith figured there was no harm in that. "We was real close, Seth and me. I was about the only soldier he took up with, being I'm older than most. Anyway, he didn't like men around his daughter. You probably already know she was a half-breed."

Steve nodded.

"Well, folks out here don't have no use for half-breeds at all. Breeds are misfits; neither whites nor Indians will accept them as a member of their race. Seth's wife was a Tonkawa. She died not long after he came here. I didn't know him then, but I can tell you he loved that squaw to a fault. Sometimes we'd share a bottle of whiskey, and he'd get to talking about her and start crying. Anyway, he was bound and determined to take care of Raven, and he knew some soldiers don't have no more respect for a breed girl than they do a whore. That's why he wouldn't move the trading post inside the fort. Said he'd rather take his chances with renegade Indians than soldiers creeping around at night."

"Then why did he locate near a fort in the first place?"

"He said he was tired of being an Indian agent. The

job opened here, so he took it. Then, too, his girl hadn't blossomed when he first got here, but he said it was like overnight she turned into a real beauty, and the soldiers started going after her like bees after blossoms. So he really didn't mind leaving."

Steve felt another spark of hope. "You said maybe you knew where he went."

"Yeah. Back to the reservation on the Sabine River, northeast of here, where he used to work. He was friends with some of the agents there and said he might try to hire on again, if he couldn't get another trading post to run."

Steve dared to hope out loud. "Then the girl is probably still on the reservation."

"Hard to say. A ranger passing through told me Seth had died, but he didn't know anything about the girl. She might have got married by now. Pretty as she was, she wouldn't have no trouble finding a husband to take care of her."

Steve hoped that was not the case. A husband would only complicate things.

"Wish I could tell you more."

"You've been a big help. At least I know where to start looking. All I need now is one of those scouts"— he nodded toward the Indians who had gathered in the doorway—"to make sure I don't get lost or stumble into the wrong place. I took the trail from Alabama to Texas along the Gulf, figuring it was safer once I got in rough territory."

"That's for sure, but now you got to go up through Bastro and Nacogdoches, and that's country you sure don't want to wander around in. You'll need a guide, all right, but don't expect the army to cooperate. We need all the scouts we got, what with Washington on our backs demanding we beef up patrols to protect the settlers."

Steve feared the sergeant was right. He glanced at the Indians, who were watching him curiously. "Do you suppose one of them would be willing to come with me for the right price? I'm also going to need help once I get there, so someone who knows the language would mean a lot. I'm willing to pay plenty."

"Well, the fact is, most of them do speak enough English to get by. But they also know deserters are shot if they're found."

As though wanting to avoid suspicion that they would even consider such a grave offense as desertion, the scouts began to move away—all except the dirty-faced boy, Steve noted, who continued to stare from behind the thick curtain of hair across his eyes.

Wacksmith also noticed that the boy had not left, and a thought occured to him. "They might let you borrow Little Crow. He's not much good as a scout. All he does is help with the horses."

Steve had a sinking sensation to think he might have to rely on a mere boy but figured he was better than nothing. "Well, what about it? You want to go with me, Little Crow?" He took a step toward him, intending to put a hand on the Indian's shoulder in a gesture of friendship, but the boy suddenly bolted and ran.

Wacksmith laughed. "He don't let nobody get near him. He's a strange one. But talk to Captain Puckett. He might make him go with you."

Steve returned to the post commander's office, where Captain Puckett was quick to say he would be glad to order Little Crow to be Steve's guide. "As Sergeant Wacksmith probably told you, we only let him hang around because he's good with the horses. He's got an uncanny knack. It's like they actually understand everything he says to them."

Steve thanked him and turned to go.

"When will you be leaving?" Puckett called.

"First thing in the morning. I'm tired; so's my horse. And I need to gather fresh supplies."

"Then have dinner with me and my officers tonight. I'd like to hear more about Alabama and the growing issue over slavery, especially since that book came out that's caused such an uproar, you know, *Uncle Tom's Cabin*."

"I'd be pleased to join you, Captain, but I don't know that I can share much with you in the way of politics. Since I don't own any slaves, I try to stay out of the controversy."

Puckett raised a brow in question. "But this man you work for, who owns a plantation, he has slaves, doesn't he?"

"Yes, but they're treated well," Steve was quick to say.

"But they're still in bondage," Puckett said with an air of disdain. "Well, we can talk more tonight. Besides, I'm curious as to why a man would send someone so far to find a half-breed girl. Maybe I can persuade you to tell me."

"I'm afraid I can't help you there." Steve smiled. "I just do what I'm told." He tipped his hat and left, and Captain Puckett went back to laboring over his paperwork.

Neither man had been aware that Little Crow was crouched outside the window, concealed by scrub brush and listening to everything they said.

Captain Puckett, Little Crow mused with a frown,

was not the only one curious as to why Steve Maddox was searching for Raven.

And now the need to find out burned even deeper.

Alabama. The stranger named Steve Maddox was from Alabama! Long ago, Little Crow had seen letters that came sometimes from that faraway place.

The letters had contained money. Dirty money, Little Crow's mother had said bitterly, from a man trying to buy freedom from his guilt.

But that was in another time, another life.

4

Raven stared at the stranger from behind her long thick bangs. It was early morning, and she had just started feeding the stock when Corporal Gooden called her to the blacksmith shop.

"This here is Mr. Steve Maddox." Corporal Gooden winced as he propped his bruised leg on a barrel opposite the one he was sitting on. "Captain Puckett wants you to see that he gets to the Sabine reservation safely. You *do* know the way, don't you?" Gooden smirked at Steve. "Little Crow is a wizard when it comes to horses, but the few patrols he led out didn't do much. He showed up here about a year ago, said his family was all dead and he needed work and a place to stay, and since he was no trouble and would do anything he was told, we didn't run him off."

Gooden looked to Raven again. "Well, boy, speak up. Do you know the way or don't you?"

"I know the way," she responded, in the deep, husky voice she had developed in hopes of sounding more like a boy. It had worked so far; no one had suspected otherwise. "It is the land of my people."

Steve was surprised. "You speak good English."

Raven merely looked at him.

"Did you understand what was said between me and Sergeant Wacksmith yesterday, how I'm looking for a half-breed girl called Raven?"

She nodded without expression.

"The girl is half Tonkawa," Steve said, in case that made any difference.

"Little Crow is Tonkawa," Corporal Gooden remarked.

Steve was suddenly buoyed. "Then maybe you know something about her."

"I don't think so," Raven said. Then she asked, "Why are you looking for her?"

"I'm not at liberty to say except to assure you I mean her no harm."

Raven shrugged as though it made no difference.

Steve turned to Gooden. "Maybe I'd be better off just going back to San Antonio and trying to hire a guide there." Little Crow seemed hostile, and that could mean problems.

"Suit yourself, but with all the Indian raids lately, you might not find one willing to go if it's just going to be the two of you. They want soldiers along in case of attack. And no matter what trail you take from there to the Sabine, if you don't know how to avoid them, you're apt to run into Indians. If I was you, I'd let Little Crow lead the way. He might be young, but he probably still knows more about that territory than any white man. Indians learn things like that at an early age."

Steve appraised the boy again and saw that his eyes, though barely visible behind the bangs, were unmistakably defiant. He obviously did not like having his ability doubted. "I'm not sure. I still think I'd do better on my own."

Gooden laughed. "If you consider scalped doing better, then take off. But I don't think you've got to worry. In my opinion, I suspect Little Crow only pretends not to be a good scout so the army won't use him, because he'd rather hang around here and help me with the horses than go out on patrol. Wouldn't you, boy?" He gave Raven a playful shove.

Raven stumbled backward but quickly got her balance. Ignoring Corporal Gooden, she assured Steve, "If you will do as I say, I will do my best to get you there safely."

Steve thought a moment. He could not afford to waste time looking for another guide, so he agreed, hoping he was not making a mistake. "All right. Get your things and let's go, but I want it understood we don't drag our feet getting there. I want to move fast."

Raven had conditions of her own. "And I want it understood that I set the pace. I cannot be alert for danger if I am in a hurry."

Steve waved her away. "We can argue later."

Raven was not worried. He would learn soon enough how things would be, and as soon as she found out why he was looking for her, she would leave him to fend for himself.

She reasoned he could only have been sent by her father, but why? He certainly hadn't cared about her before. She knew all about Ned Ralston, and how he had sworn he loved her mother and promised to come back to her and then sent his dirty money instead, to appease his conscience for having lied. Her mother had told her everything when she felt she was old enough to understand, and she knew her mother had been deeply hurt. Not only had Ned Ralston broken her heart, he had also shamed her before her people, because when it became known that she was carrying a white man's baby, the Tonkawas had been furious. They had demanded she allow the shaman to end her pregnancy. When she refused, eventually marrying Seth, she had been banished from the tribe.

Raven did not like to imagine what life would have been like without Seth. A kindhearted man, he had searched for her mother at Ned Ralston's request, only to fall in love with her himself. Lakoma, he swore, was the most beautiful woman he had ever seen. He also felt sorry for her and wanted to take care of her, and Lakoma saw his proposal of marriage as a way to escape the taunts and mistreatment of the Tonkawas.

Seth had been good to them, and Raven had looked to him as a father. But she had sensed her mother had never returned his love. Ned Ralston had taken her heart with him when he abandoned her. That was another reason Raven resented him, blaming him for her mother's inability to let go of the past and return the love that a wonderful man like Seth offered.

When her mother died, Raven had seen a light go out in Seth's eyes. A part of him had died too, and Raven knew he only held on to life for her sake. When he finally let go, after coming down with a fever only a short while after they got to the reservation, Raven could not have grieved more had he been her true father. For the first time in her life, she realized what it meant to be truly alone in the world.

The agents who had been Seth's friends tried to look after her, but life soon became unbearable. Had Seth been alive to see how she was treated, she knew he would have moved heaven and earth to take her away from there. The Indians shunned her as a half-breed; even worse, some of the men on the reservation took the attitude that her kind was good for only one thing, and she was constantly having to dodge their bold advances.

Then there were the not-infrequent proposals of marriage from single or widowed settlers or prospectors wanting someone to warm their bed, cook their meals, and bear their children. Women were scarce. It made no difference to wife-seekers whether they married a full-blooded Indian or a half-breed, and even if it had, once they saw Raven, they wanted her above all others.

But Raven was not about to marry a man just to have security as her mother had done, despite her mother's good fortune that Seth had loved her. So she kept to herself as she had always done. A loner, she found solace working with the horses.

Then came a nasty encounter with a young Kiowa one night when he found her alone in the stable. She was keeping watch over a sick horse when True Hawk made advances to her. When she refused him, he became angry and tried to force her. To defend herself, she had cut him with her knife.

Upon hearing about it, agent Thad Slawson declared that, to keep from having any more trouble, he was going to find a husband for Raven right away, whether she liked it or not. So that very day she ran away from the reservation, with only the clothes on her back and her mustang pony, Diablo.

For a while, she survived by hunting and fishing for food, but she knew she was living on borrowed time. To encounter a band of renegades could only mean tragedy for a young woman traveling alone.

Then one day as she was hiding behind some rocks watching an army patrol pass by, she saw an Indian riding with them. His hair was streaming down to his shoulders and he was dressed in a blue uniform like the soldiers. She knew he had to be an Indian scout; she had seen a few while living at the trading post near Fort Inge.

Suddenly the idea had struck her.

She could do anything those scouts could do, but the army would never take in a female. Then and there, Raven decided to pass for a boy.

First, she brushed her hair down over her eyes and cut bangs to conceal the top part of her face, then rubbed dirt into her cheeks to make her soft skin less noticeable. She returned to the reservation only long enough to steal men's clothing. With loose-fitting shirts and pants, her bosom tightly bound, her feminine shape would not be obvious.

She took the name Crow. Her mother had named her Raven because of the lush color of her hair, and she reasoned that crows were also black.

Wanting to get far away from the Sabine reservation, lest she be recognized, Raven had made the arduous trek southwest, winding up back at Fort Inge, where the soldiers eventually dubbed her *Little* Crow, because she was smaller than the other scouts.

At first, the soldiers did not want her, saying she

was too young, but she kept hanging around anyway, and when Corporal Gooden discovered Little Crow was wonderful with horses, he allowed the youngster to stay.

Of course it was necessary for her to be a loner. She could not allow herself to get caught in intimate situations with men, like bathing and sleeping. But no one suspected anything, assuming Little Crow was sensitive about his size and wanted no confrontation with the others.

Raven did not think about the future, as long as she felt secure where she was. Tending the horses and riding her own beloved mustang was all she cared about. There was work to do to keep her busy, food when she was hungry, and shelter from the elements. Nothing else had mattered—till now.

The sun was not yet high when they rode out of the fort. Raven stayed in front, not wanting to ride next to Steve, as she always tried to avoid close contact with anyone. At first, he made several attempts at conversation but gave up when she answered only in monosyllables.

It was afternoon before they stopped to rest and water the horses. Raven watched Steve from the corner of her eye and noted his powerfully built body. He took off his hat, and the wind played with his hair. It was dark, almost as dark as his eyes, which were the color of smoke. His features were ruggedly chiseled, cheekbones high and wide, jawline firm.

He was undeniably handsome, and Raven was jolted to realize how she could not remember ever having had such reflections about a man before. Men were to be avoided, for they caused trouble, and this one was probably no exception, yet there was no mistaking she felt somehow drawn to him.

They were standing on a creek bank, perhaps thirty feet apart. The horses were drinking their fill when Steve made a sudden move that caught Raven's eye and made her nearly choke on a smothered gasp.

He was unfastening his pants, preparing to relieve himself.

She retreated hastily through the bushes, nearly stumbling in her haste to get away.

Steve heard the commotion and glanced about to see Little Crow was in a hurry and must have his own business to tend to.

Before returning, she smeared more dirt on her face, in case her embarrassment had caused her cheeks to redden. She had not stopped to think that on the trail she would be thrown into intimate situations she had managed to avoid at the fort. She would have to be extremely careful.

It was nearly dark when they made camp for the night. Steve knew, without being told, that it would be risky to build a fire, lest the smoke be seen or smelled by someone in the vicinity. So they had a supper of beef jerky and hardtack and drank water from a nearby stream. Afterward, Raven distanced herself from him to bed down.

"You don't have to go so far away," Steve called after her. "I don't snore. At least I've never had complaints from the ladies."

Raven kept on going. Evidently he was not married, since he'd mentioned ladies, and not a wife. But what difference did that make? She had no interest in his personal life, even if she did find him attractive.

The sooner she found out what she wanted to know and took her leave of him, the better.

Still, as she lay on her blanket staring into the starry night, she felt strangely unnerved. At the fort, Corporal Gooden hadn't cared if she slept in an empty horse stall. Here, she could hear a man's even breathing and was bemused to find it a pleasant, even welcome sound.

Because she was plagued by stirrings she did not understand, Raven lay awake for a long time. As a result, she was very groggy when she was awakened at dawn by the sound of water splashing. It took a few seconds to remember where she was—and who she was with.

Peering through a clump of mesquite bushes, she drew a sharp breath at the sight before her.

Steve Maddox was standing in knee-deep water, his back to her, thank heavens, because he was stark naked.

She felt her pulse quicken as her gaze was riveted on firm molded buttocks and rock-hard thighs. He was bathing, sloshing water over his body, muscles rippling against the cold water touching his flesh.

Her eyes moved to his narrow waist, broad back, and wonderfully sculptured shoulders. He was glorious to look at, even though she told herself she should feel guilty about spying on him. It was starting to feel natural, somehow, to find him appealing, just as it seemed instinctive for her to be having difficulty in tearing her gaze away.

Suddenly, he turned, and she ducked down lest he catch her watching . . . and lest she see something else.

Steve heard the rustling in the bushes. "Are you up, Little Crow? Get on down here and wash so we can be on our way. I want to move faster than we did yesterday."

Raven waited until she heard him come out of the creek, then took one quick peek through the mesquite to make sure he was dressed before daring to make her appearance.

"There you are." Steve was buttoning his shirt as she stepped into the clearing. "Go on and bathe. I'm ready to ride."

"The water is too cold." She did not have to pretend to tremble for emphasis. Just the thought of stripping and washing in front of him was enough to make her shake all over. She hurried to her mustang.

He persisted. "There's nothing like a splash of cold water to wake you up in the morning. You'd probably feel better anyway if you washed some of that dirt off your face."

Raven cringed. Keeping her back to him, she said edgily, "I feel fine. The only thing that should concern you is my getting you to the Sabine, and we are wasting time."

Steve knew that was so. Still, he hated to see the boy so dirty. If he cleaned himself up, it would give him some self-esteem and then he might not be so shy. "All right. Let's ride. But later we're going to have a little talk about your bathing habits—or lack of them," he added with a grin.

Raven dug her heels into Diablo's flanks to move him out in front. The pulse in her temples was pounding frantically to think how she had to hurry and find out why her father was looking for her before Steve discovered she really wasn't a boy. Everything would be ruined then. He would see that the soldiers at Fort Inge heard about her deception. Word would spread and her masquerade would have to end.

Soon, she would have to start asking him questions but knew it was best to do that after dark, when he could not see her face as they sat together. The only problem was, she had begun to dread the night . . . and the way he made her feel in the caressing shadows.

5

Despite her desperation to question Steve, Raven could not bring herself to initiate a conversation, fearing he would wonder why she was so curious.

They would make camp at dark and eat from their own provisions. Steve had brought beans, hardtack, and beef jerky. Raven had been able to bring the same after reminding the current manager of the fort trading post that he still owed her for treating his horse for nettle rash, which had been caused by insect bites. All she had done was apply a bran mash to the raised and reddened skin, but he was so grateful he had packed her a nice bag of food.

After eating, Raven would take her blanket and retreat to the woods, only to toss and turn for hours as she cursed herself for allowing thoughts of Steve, sleeping so close by, to affect her so.

On the trail, she continued to keep a slow pace,

needlessly taking a long route, always alert to pick up on anything he might say that would give her a chance to ask questions without appearing eager or obvious, but his only words had to do with their surroundings.

Opportunity struck on their fourth day together. He drew his horse up beside her, and Raven quickly turned away, to avoid his getting a close look at her face in the daylight.

He seemed to speak more to himself than to her, as though bored with keeping silent company with his thoughts. "I'll be glad when this is over. There's a mare back home due to foal before much longer. I need to be there in case she has trouble. Her last one was born dead. The slaves won't help. They're afraid they might be blamed if she loses this one too."

"So you own slaves," she said tightly, not letting on she already knew from having listened outside Captain Puckett's window that it was her father who owned them, not Steve.

"Not me," he confirmed. "They belong to the man I work for."

"Slavery is wrong."

"I agree with you. He probably would too, but he has a large plantation to run."

"Why doesn't he pay them to work for him? People shouldn't be forced to labor for nothing."

Patiently, he endeavored to explain. "Actually, Mr Ralston *does* pay them, Little Crow—in food, clothing, and shelter."

Raven was glad her face was turned, for surely it was now the color of the sun scorching down on them as his words burned into her brain. Mr. Ralston, he had said! Now she knew for certain. He was talking about her father.

Steve did not notice her reaction, how rigidly she sat on the mustang's back, her knuckles turning white as she gripped the reins. Quietly, she asked, "Is Mr. Ralston the one who is looking for the girl?"

"He is."

"Why?" She held her breath.

"I can't tell you that."

She decided to try a different ploy in hopes his expected denial would include the information she was after. "Does he want to make a slave of her too?"

Steve shook his head and laughed at such a ludicrous idea.

"Then what reason would he have? Maybe I shouldn't help you until I know what he wants with her. After all, you say she has the blood of my people in her veins, so therefore I should be loyal enough not to betray her if this man means to harm her."

"You don't have to worry about that."

"Then why would he send someone so far to find her?"

Steve supposed the boy had a right to be suspicious but he was not about to confide the truth. "I have no idea. He just paid me to do a job. Like I'm paying you," he added, to change the subject. "How far to the Sabine? This trip seems to be taking a lot longer than I thought it would."

"We have to go slow. I have to watch for every sign of trouble. Didn't I keep us from being spotted by two Kiowa yesterday?"

Steve remembered how they had hidden behind some rocks till the Indians passed. The Indians had not looked warlike, but Little Crow said he would take no chances, and Steve had agreed. "You did get us through that," he conceded finally, "but I still want to move as fast as we can."

Raven continued to probe. "Tell me about this Mr. Ralston. I am curious as to what sort of man would keep slaves."

Steve saw no harm in talking about Ned, especially if the boy did know something about Raven and was holding back out of concern for her welfare. "He's a good man. Kind. Generous. He owns a lot of land, with a mansion overlooking the river. He grows wheat, rye, oats, and corn, but cotton is his biggest crop. He's also in the export business and owns ships that export goods to places like New York, Cuba, Gibraltar, and London."

Raven's teeth clamped together so hard her jaws hurt. No wonder he could send his dirty money; he obviously had plenty. Big plantation, a mansion, ships—he had it all, and if he hadn't abandoned her and her mother they would all have enjoyed a life of comfort and wealth. "You still haven't told me why he wants the girl," she reminded him. "So even if I do know where she is, I won't tell you, because he cannot be a good man if he owns slaves."

Steve was equally snappish. "I'll find her without your help if I have to, Little Crow, so quit dragging your butt and get us to the reservation where I can hire a guide who isn't so hard to get along with."

The heat was becoming unbearable. Steve took off his shirt and stuffed it in a saddlebag. The sun was brutal on his back, and he dared not be unprotected for long, but for a little while, at least, he could feel the breeze on his skin.

Raven darted a glance at him and caught her breath. His hand moved to rub his chest, and she could see how the mat of hair there glistened with perspiration as it trailed across his flat belly to disappear out of sight below the waist of his tight trousers. His fingers moved slowly, kneading the flesh as though the muscles were taut, begging to be massaged. She was mesmerized and could not look away. He was, without a doubt, the finest figure of a man she had ever seen, and being so close to him this way was taking its toll on her nerves.

Suddenly, she felt a wave of dizziness and realized her eyes had locked. With a shake of her head, she focused once more on the trail, swallowed hard, and felt an almost hysterical urge to talk, to say anything to dispel the tortured thoughts she was experiencing. "This man, does he have a large family?"

He looked at her and laughed. "Still nosy, aren't you?" He noticed how she was sweating. "Your shirt is soaked. Take it off for a while like me. You'll feel better."

Raven felt another dizzy wave. "No, I"—she faltered, groping for a reason to decline—"I don't want my skin to burn."

"I didn't think Indians worried about things like that. Most of the ones I've seen are half naked. That shirt you've got on is way too big for you anyway. You're bound to be miserable with all that cloth wadded up around you."

"No. I'm fine." Dear Lord, make him stop!

Steve chuckled. "What's the matter? Ashamed of your scrawny body? Come on. There's just us, and it doesn't make a damn to me what you look like naked."

Yes, it would, she thought with panic, oh, yes, it would.

"Does he have a family?" she repeated, feeling desperate now, her voice high-pitched and frightened.

Steve gave up. If the boy wanted to hide his body and swelter, so be it. "His wife is dead. He has a son and daughter." No need to explain Lisbeth and Julius weren't really Ned's. He was only making conversation to pass the time.

Raven fumed inwardly. So he had married. That was why he had not kept his promise. Maybe all along he had a wife and children and had just used her mother to help him get well so he could go back to them—used her in many ways, damn him.

"It's my turn to ask questions," Steve said, suddenly curious about a few things himself. There was something almost eerie about the boy, like the way he wore heavy clothes in the hottest weather and allowed his hair to fall down over his face as if he didn't want anyone looking at him. "How is that you speak such good English? How old are you anyway, fifteen? Sixteen?"

"Eighteen. Before my parents died, I was educated at a mission school." That was true, but there was no need to add that Seth had also made her learn to speak his language flawlessly.

"So why don't you do something with your life besides go around smelling like a horse and letting your hair grow down over your face like a wild animal? Get some clothes that fit and take a bath. The way you look, you're never going to find a wife."

"I . . . I don't want a wife," Raven said shakily. He was really upsetting her now.

"Well, I can understand that. I don't either. But what about a woman in your bed once in a while? Even a whore likes a man who's halfway clean. When's the last time you had a bath?"

"I bathe," she replied chokily. "You just don't see me."

With a chuckle, Steve shook his head. "You really baffle me, Little Crow. Why are you so ashamed for anybody to see you naked? A man is a man, for God's sake. It doesn't matter if you aren't big in certain places. Hell, I've always thought that was ridiculous anyway. It's not size that counts with a woman—"

"Can't you find something else to talk about?" Raven could feel beads of perspiration running down her cheeks and swiped at them, seeing the grime on her fingers and knowing her face would be streaked.

Steve was wickedly enjoying how the banter made the boy squirm. Obviously, he was not experienced in the ways of manhood. "I'll wager you've never even had a woman, have you? Well, I'll tell you what I'm going to do for you. Surely there are some whores on the reservation—women willing to give you a tumble for a few dollars. I'm going to make you a present of one when this is over. I'll bed you down for a whole week with the wildest little filly we can find. She'll make you so glad to be a man you'll want to run around naked and show off your—"

"Shut up!" Raven cried, kneeing the mustang into a gallop. She would not listen anymore. In the past, when the scouts or soldiers would say such risqué things she had just gone away. Here, it was different. She could not escape.

Steve did not immediately catch up. He was too lost in thought, wondering what caused Little Crow to be like he was. Something had sure made him shy. He needed to get over it if he was ever going to make anything of himself, especially since he could speak English so well. And while the men at the fort seemed to regard him highly when it came to horses, he didn't need to hide in the shadows of a stable the rest of his life. It was also wrong for him to go around so dirty and unkempt all the time. Steve made up his mind that before their time together ended, he would try to reach him, somehow, and make him understand all that.

Raven saw Diablo was working up a lather, which he didn't need in the sweltering weather. Spotting a creek up ahead, she reined him in to drink.

Steve followed. He was thirsty himself, and, after splashing cool water over his chest and face, he put his shirt back on, because he could feel his skin starting to burn.

"That's a nice horse," he said, making his first attempt to ease the tension between them. "Where did you get him?"

Raven experienced a rush of pride. She was only too glad to talk about Diablo. "He was rounded up and brought in to the reservation. I knew right away he was special, because the best riders tried to break him and couldn't. The braves were getting angry and threatening to beat him to break his spirit, but the Indian agent would not allow it. He said it was wrong to beat a horse into submission."

"I certainly go along with that."

She was glad he felt the same. "The agent decided that the man who could ride him without whipping him would own him."

"And you were the one to do it?"

Raven smiled. "Just because I'm little doesn't mean I can't ride. Besides, that had nothing to do with it."

He was amused. "Really? Then how *did* you break his spirit?"

"I didn't." She wished she could look at Steve full in the face and see his reaction to her statement, but she did not dare. Keeping her head turned, as though watching Diablo drink, she explained, "He still has his spirit. You see, he was able to sense from me that it wasn't my intention to take it away from him and that I was determined he wouldn't take mine from me. We understood each other. We still do. And that's the way it should be for animals and humans, to give each to the other without taking anything away."

Steve was impressed and could well understand what Captain Puckett had meant when he said Little Crow seemed to have an uncanny way with horses.

"Would you like to try to ride him?" Raven could not resist challenging.

If what the boy said about the horse was true, Steve was not about to give him the satisfaction of being thrown. "No, thanks. I've known horses like that. As a matter of fact, Mr. Ralston has one that nobody has ever ridden except him. The horse has almost killed anyone who tried. He threw one man up against the barn and broke his shoulder and tried to trample another one. But he's never thrown Mr. Ralston. Who knows? Maybe he's got the same gift you have."

Raven felt a chill to think the ability she was so proud of might actually have been handed down by the father she loathed. Grudgingly, she had to admit there might be something about him to admire.

Since Little Crow seemed to be warming up a little, Steve wanted to keep the rapport between them growing. He began explain the attributes of the racking horses. "Starfire is a stud. He's sired some real beauties, and—"

A demoniacal shriek exploded around them, and

they both whipped about to see the Indian running toward them. He had dropped from an outcrop bordering the creek, where he had been hiding. Steve reached for his gun, but Raven was faster, grabbing his wrist and whispering, "Don't." Steve had seen the rifle the Indian was pointing and figured to drop him before he could pull the trigger. Now he condemned Raven with a fiery glance for ruining his chance.

Raven saw he was a Lipan Apache, dressed in breechclout, leggings, and moccasins. The hair on the left side of his head had been cut off even with the top of his ear, and the hair on his right side hung to his waist. He was a large man, and only a trace of warpaint was still on his face, but nonetheless it made him look fierce. Noting the strip of bloodied rabbit fur wrapped around a wound on his left arm, she had a good idea of why he was alone and how they happened to stumble upon him and quickly explained to Steve. "He's been shot, probably during a raid, and lost his horse. The other braves had to leave him behind, so he's hiding here, near the water, hoping they'll come back for him. Let me try to talk to him. Keep your hand away from your gun."

Grimly, Steve fired back, "If I do, he's going to kill both of us."

"If he wanted us dead, we already would be, but he didn't shoot for fear he might hit the horses, and the horses are what he's after, so he can get out of here and try to catch up with his band. Now he's probably wondering whether he can get both of us before one of us gets him, because he's only got the full use of one arm."

"Then try to get his attention so I can make my move. I won't miss."

"Don't," she commanded sharply. "Gunfire will bring the others if they're anywhere near." She focused on the Lipan and swallowed against fear. Seth had not only insisted she learn to speak English well, he had also made sure she understood the language of all the Plains tribes. Now she was grateful that he had, for it might be her only chance to save them.

Speaking in the Lipan tongue, she began. "Your women did not have a victory dance when their men returned to your camp last night. But if you will listen to me and do as I say, tonight they will chant while you undergo the Lipan ceremony to cleanse you from the contamination of the enemy." She knew of the tradition of his people.

While still wary, his expression softened, but only a little. "How is it that you know the ways of my people and speak our language? You are not Lipan. And why do you wear the blue leg pants of the pony soldier?" He nodded scornfully to her clothes.

"I work as a scout, but I am Tonkawa, and I know how my people and yours have always had peace between them. I also know of how your great Lipan chief helped us many years ago when there was much trouble with the white chief, Sam Houston. I have always considered the Lipan Apaches my friends, and it will bring much grief to me and my people, and shame to you and yours, if you harm either me or my companion."

The Lipan sneered. "You care about the life of a white man?"

"He saved mine once," she lied, then added, "as I am trying to save yours now."

He hooted. "Save *my* life? I am not the one in danger. As you can see, I hold a long gun."

"And if you fire it, the soldiers will hear it and come, because they are not far away. You see, my friend here is also a scout, and we rode ahead of the soldiers to look for Indians. Obviously"—she paused to force a shallow smile—"the Lipan has proved to be smarter than the Tonkawa and the white man this day."

While the Indian puffed up with pride, obviously pleased over whatever Little Crow was saying to him, Steve was beside himself. Finally he growled under his breath, "What's going on? How do you two find so much to talk about, for God's sake? Just get him out of here, or so help me I'm going for my gun and blast him to hell."

"Be patient. If you make a move for that gun, we're both dead." To the Lipan, she said, "Let me help you. Take my pony and go quickly, before the soldiers get here."

The Lipan was still leery. "It is the bluecoats you help. That makes you a traitor to your people."

"No." Fighting to keep her knees from knocking together, Raven managed to smirk. "I lead the army in circles and make them look like fools, as I am doing now. Why else would I tell you they are close by?"

He matched her smirk with one of his own. "To save your life."

"Perhaps. But if you heed my warning, you will save your own. Now go. Quickly." She motioned to Diablo. "He is faster than the white man's horse."

The Lipan thought a moment and decided the Tonkawa was right. It was best there be no shooting. With a nod towards Steve, he ordered, "I do not trust him. Bring me his gun. Hold it backward, pointed toward you."

Raven braced herself. The Lipan might laugh in

her face for asking, but she had to try. "If I help you, if I hand over his gun to you, will you swear on the souls of your children that you will not harm either of us?"

He gave a slow but sure nod.

Raven breathed easier. She knew the Lipans did not give their word easily, and when they did it was kept. But convincing Steve was another matter. "Please listen to me carefully. He wants me to give him your gun."

"No way." Steve kept his eyes on the Lipan.

"You have to let me take it. If you don't, he's going to kill us both."

"Are you crazy? He's going to do that anyway once he has my gun."

"No, he won't. He gave his word. He won't harm us."

"And you believe him?"

"Yes, and you've got to believe me too, when I say this is the right way."

"This is what I get for depending on a boy to get me anywhere safely," he grumbled as he allowed Little Crow to remove his gun from the holster and carry it to the Lipan. He had another in his saddlebag, but that wasn't going to do him any good when his horse was about to be stolen.

The Lipan, meeting Steve's steely gaze, ordered Raven to get a rope and tie him. "I have a bad arm, as you can see, and he might try to attack me as I mount. But you are scrawny. I do not worry about you." He snickered.

Doggedly, Raven took the loop of rope hanging from the saddle on Steve's horse.

Shaking with fury, Steve said between tightly

clenched teeth, "If I get out of this mess, so help me I'm going to break your neck with my bare hands, Little Crow. I should have known you'd turn traitor. Hell, why don't you ride on out of here with him? Indians are all alike anyway."

"Trust me." She quickly bound his hands behind his back.

Steve bit back a torrent of curses amid a sudden flare of hope as he saw the Lipan walk toward the mustang. "Did you tell him to ride Diablo?" It seemed prudent to whisper, even if the Lipan could not understand English.

Raven nodded proudly, fighting to keep a stern expression on her face, rather than beam with joy.

"Then untie me," he cried, struggling futilely against the rope. "I can grab him when Diablo throws him. Why did you tie me so tight, damn it?"

"So you won't do something stupid that will get us killed." She stepped away from him, not liking the way he was looking at her. Now was no time for him to discover the truth of her gender. She prayed he never would.

Steve continued to rage. "God, I wish I'd followed my instincts and never left the fort with you. Don't you realize once Diablo throws him, he's going to know you tricked him and come up shooting, you idiot?"

Raven ignored him, intent on watching the Lipan hoist himself painfully up on the horse's back.

Steve also watched and waited, tense with dread for the instant when the mustang began to rear and buck. All he could hope for was that the Indian would be sent flying through the air to land head first on a rock and die instantly.

Otherwise, he and Little Crow would be the ones to die.

But nothing happened.

Diablo was completely docile, obediently waiting for his rider to indicate what he wanted him to do.

The Lipan raised his rifle in a grateful salute to Little Crow and reined Diablo about. Once he was past the trees and the rocky bluff bordering the stream, he dug in his heels to urge the mustang into a full gallop.

Raven went to untie Steve's hands. She could feel the blistering fury emanating from him as he stood, rigid, waiting to be freed, and she leaped back as he whirled upon her menacingly, his wrath exploding.

"Now you're going to wish you'd gone with him, damn you!"

He lunged for her.

6

Raven stepped backward, then up on the rock cropping where the Lipan had hidden. Steve went right behind her, but she was wearing moccasins, which made her sure-footed, enabling her to feel for a grip with her foot, while he slipped and slid in his boots as he tried to climb after her.

"You lied about how you came by the mustang, claiming you're the only one who can ride him. Hell, you probably stole him from an old lady who rode him to church every Sunday."

Raven kept going. There was no time to argue with him, and he was beyond reason anyway.

He slipped again, scraping his hand and cursing. "Damn it, get back down here or I'll turn you over my knee and give you the thrashing a lying kid like you deserves. And you're going to walk the rest of the way to the Sabine, you hear me? I'm not about to weigh my horse down in this heat by making him carry double. You didn't have to give yours away. I could have shot that blasted Indian right between the eyes if I hadn't been fool enough to let you give me orders."

"You probably could have," she yelled down to him, relieved the distance between them was increasing. He obviously knew nothing about rock climbing, because for every step he took, he slid back two. "So could I, with my knife, but why kill somebody if you don't have to? There's too much killing in this world. You must have a thirst for blood, Mr. Maddox."

"That's not so, but when it comes down to my life or somebody else's, I'll do my best to make sure they're the one that goes in the ground."

"You're still alive. I don't know what you're so mad about."

"Because he could have killed us, damn it, and also because I can't stand liars. What else have you lied about? You don't even know the way to the Sabine, do you?"

"Yes, and I'll get us there in good time. Trust me." She inched higher.

"If you do anything else stupid, so help me, I'll ride off and leave you. Now stop this foolishness and get down. You've got a long walk ahead of you, Little Crow."

At last Raven reached the top. Shading her eyes against the glaring sun with her hands, she could see Diablo galloping away. "I won't have to walk," she declared happily.

"Well, you're not riding double with me. I told you—"

He was interrupted by the sound of a long, loud, piercing whistle. Looking up, he saw that Little

Crow stood with feet apart, head held high, two fingers of one hand at his mouth as he whistled again.

Seeing that Diablo had heard her, Raven grinned, watching as he gave one mighty buck and toss to send his rider hurtling through the air. The Lipan hit the ground and did not move. Diablo then obediently whirled about, and, ears back, nose high, dug his hooves into the earth to run as fast as his legs would carry him, straight back to where Raven waited.

With Steve watching, open-mouthed and wide-eyed, Diablo came to a stop just below the rock. Raven had climbed halfway down but jumped the rest of the way to land on his back. Taking the reins, her face beamed like sunshine as she said, "He hates the sound of me whistling, even though he always comes when I do. But he also bucks anybody off who happens to be on him at the time."

Steve was speechless.

"Come on." She kneed Diablo into a trot. "Let's get out of here. We don't have to worry about that Lipan, because he won't be moving around for a while, but his friends might be close by."

For the rest of the afternoon, Steve rode in back, brooding as he tried to convince himself it made no difference that he had been bested by a boy. They were both alive. Everything had turned out all right. Still, it needled.

It was dark when they stopped for the night. Raven had remembered where there was a small pool made from an underground stream and wanted to camp there. She had not had a chance to bathe since they had left the fort and looked forward to slipping quietly into the cool water once Steve fell asleep.

Still irritable, Steve dug down into his saddlebag

and took out a canteen of whiskey he kept for times when he needed a drink. This was one of them.

Raven licked her finger and held it to the sky. "There's no wind and plenty of clouds. Smoke would blend in with them and not drift and smell. It's safe to have a small fire if we cook quickly."

"Cook what?" He scowled. "I don't see a rabbit around anywhere waiting to jump on a spit."

"Maybe I can take care of that." Raven went to the mustang and unfastened the small bow and arrow she always kept laced to his neck. Her mother had taught her that Tonkawas kept their tools and other possessions to a crude and simple minimum. The most important weapon, however, was the bow and arrow, and Raven had practiced till she seldom missed. She had even made her bow herself, using the sinewy tendon from a bison for thread and strings.

She left Steve with his whiskey and his grumbling and went a short distance to wait patiently for an unsuspecting rabbit to come hopping along in the moonlight. When one did, she felled him with a single arrow and then returned to camp to skin him and set him roasting on a spit.

Later, between delicious mouthfuls, Steve said humbly, "Little Crow, I guess I owe a lot to you after all."

Raven suppressed a smile. She did not want to appear to gloat and could sense he did not find it easy to admit when he was wrong. But, to his credit, he was willing to set things right, which was, in her estimation, the true mark of a man. She admired him for it and offered her own concession to making peace between them. "I'm sorry I wasn't able to tell you about my plan, but there wasn't time. I knew I had to get him out of there before he got suspicious and decided to kill us both and be done with it."

"I understand." Steve held out the canteen. "You behaved like a man today. You deserve a man's drink."

She waved it away. "I don't like whiskey. I've seen how it makes some people crazy."

"A few sips won't hurt, and it will make you relax. We've had a rough day. We're both worn out." He continued to hold out the canteen as he went on to say, "I can't believe a young boy like you isn't eager to try it."

And since Raven feared he might wonder about it too hard, she took the canteen, tipped it to her lips, and drank, then grimaced as it burned her throat, finally hitting her stomach like a hot coal.

Steve threw back his head and laughed as he slapped her on her shoulder. She instantly drew back. Thinking she did so out of fear, he told her, "You don't have to be afraid. Pounding somebody on the back is a good-natured gesture among white men."

"I just don't like being touched." She handed him the canteen. "And I really don't like your firewater."

"What *do* you like, a boy like you?" His eyes narrowed thoughtfully. "You've got no friends. No family. No home. Just you and your crazy mustang, who obviously doesn't want anymore to do with people than you do. You can't have a very happy life, Little Crow."

She had learned in the past that the best way to steer the conversation from her was to respond to questions with one of her own. "What about you? Is your life happy?"

He thought a minute, then shrugged. "I guess so— till now. Frankly, it's not very pleasant being out here in this wilderness worrying over maybe getting scalped. I don't mind saying I'd rather be back in Alabama tending horses."

Raven seized the opportunity to try again to discover something, anything, that would reveal why her father was looking for her. "So why are you here searching for the girl you call Raven? You speak highly of the man you work for, but he must not feel the same for you if he would ask you to come out here, knowing you might run into danger."

"Because he's desperate to find his—" Steve caught himself just in time. The whiskey was making his tongue loose. He had almost said *daughter,* and that would be a big mistake. Little Crow might have proved he had spunk and grit and could think clearly in the midst of a crisis, but he had also exhibited how wily he could be. Steve had revealed that Ned was a very rich man, so it stood to reason that Little Crow would be sure to grab an opportunity to help some Tonkawa girlfriend claim to be heiress to the fortune.

"Find his what?" Raven managed to ask in a normal tone of voice, although her pulse was beating wildly. If he would say *daughter,* that would lead to other questions, and eventually she would pry the real story out of him.

"Never mind. We weren't talking about me or the reason I'm here, anyway. It's you I'm curious about." He took another drink. "But I suppose it doesn't matter, since we won't be together much longer. I think once we reach the reservation I'll try to hire somebody older who might remember Greer or the girl. You obviously don't—unless you're keeping something else from me," he could not resist innuendo.

"No, nothing." It had become so easy to lie since her deception as a boy had begun. "But you might have a problem finding anyone who'll help unless you tell why you're looking for her. You say you mean her no harm, but how can anyone be sure?"

"The man who sent me has business with her. That's all you or anybody else needs to know. If I succeed, everyone will realize she's in no danger."

He settled back, using his saddle for a pillow. Raven knew she would get no more information out of him this night and was starting to think she would never learn why her father was looking for her. What difference did it make anyway? He had nothing she wanted, and she certainly had nothing to offer him. Steve could go back to Alabama and tell him his daughter could not be found, so he would let the past finally be as dead and buried as her mother and her stepfather.

With that resolve, Raven knew it was time to put her curiosity aside and return to her life, such as it was. She had never thought much about the future but supposed she should start. Sooner or later, someone would discover her pretense, and that could mean big trouble. Maybe she should go to Mexico and try to find work there. The vaqueros might not mind a young and capable girl helping them once she proved she could herd cattle and break horses like a man. And she would also let them know quickly not to get any ideas about her.

The fire was almost out. Smothering the remaining embers with dirt, she took her blanket and retreated to make her bed, as usual. Steve did not notice. His eyes were closed. He was worn out, as he had said.

She bathed in the pool but did not linger, fearing he might wake up.

At last she lay down, but, as on every other night since they had been on the trail together, she could not fall asleep. She knew having Steve so close by was the reason.

Before she had become Little Crow, her experiences with men had not been pleasant, so she had not given them much thought as a woman. But she also had never met one like Steve, who made her feel as though baby birds were fluttering around in her stomach. Something about him seemed to warm her all over. Maybe it really was time for them to part, before she forgot to concentrate on passing for a boy and made a mistake that could lead to discovery.

With her mind made up to leave him, she allowed herself the pleasure of fantasizing as to what he was really like.

When he casually relieved himself on a creek bank, not knowing a woman was watching him, she always turned away but could not help being tempted to peek, because she had never seen a man naked below the waist. She had never wanted to—till Steve.

Sometimes she would look at him from behind her thick layer of bangs, focusing on his mouth and how appealing it was when he smiled, wondering how his lips, so tender, would feel against her own. She looked, too, at his hands and felt a warm rush deep down in her belly to think of them on her body.

She knew how babies were made, and thinking of her and Steve coupled that way made her feel tingly all over. What did it mean? Would she ever know? Dear God, what was this dangerously handsome man doing to her by just his presence?

Finally, fitfully, she drifted away, intent on waking before first light. She would leave one of her arrows on the ground beside Steve, pointing in the direction he should ride and confident he would understand the meaning. Then she would head south, eventually making her way to Mexico. . . .

Dawn came, the sun leaped eagerly into the sky to begin another blazing assault upon the earth, and Raven slept soundly. It was only when she heard singing in the early morning stillness that she awoke with a start.

Cursing because she would have to wait another day before sneaking away, she crept irritably through the bushes to see why Steve was so happy. Then, hearing a splash, she crouched behind a bush and peeked through the leaves. If he was bathing again, there was nothing wrong with spying for a few seconds. One more day, and she would be gone and never see him again anyway, and she couldn't help being curious and—she gasped.

He was swimming in the pool, so clear and inviting. As he sliced through the water with firm, sure strokes of his muscular arms, now and then his bare buttocks would break the water's surface. She could see his firm thighs, the tautness of his legs.

He reached the other side and stood, his back to her, and she could not tear her eyes away, drinking in every magnificent part of his body. She leaned closer to afford a better look, wanting to memorize every detail, knowing she would probably never witness such a sight again.

And then he turned.

Raven caught her breath and held it.

He was running his fingers through his wet hair, pushing it back from his face, standing with his legs wide apart.

She saw him then in all the glory of his manhood and could not stop staring, and when he began to run his hands over himself to wash, she became even more mesmerized as her mind betrayed her in the worst possible way. She began to imagine it was actually *her* hands rubbing his rock-hard chest, moving to caress his broad shoulders and on down the sinewy arms. It was *her* fingers playing upon his thighs, moving between to cleanse, then dipping down into the pond to splash more water upon his most private parts.

Raven could hear the pounding of her own heart and suddenly wondered if he could too, because he was lifting his head, glancing about, like an animal sensing danger. He stood very still for a moment, alert, letting his senses take over to guide him. Then, satisfied he had heard nothing, he dove once again into the water.

Raven licked her lips nervously, for they were dry from her ragged, harsh breathing. She felt dizzy and her insides churned; she wondered if she was going to be sick. Then she angrily chided herself for how she was reacting.

With a wild shake of her head to deny what she was so helplessly experiencing, she summoned every shred of self-control she possessed to make herself turn away. But feeling waves of emotion that seemed to overwhelm she missed her footing, tripped over a clump of mesquite, and pitched forward, landing with a thud and a cry of surprise.

Steve heard the noise as he stepped out of the water. Without pausing for his clothes, he headed in the direction it had come from. "What's wrong, Little Crow, did you fall?"

In panic, Raven tried to stand, but her foot was still caught under the branch. Turning, she tried to free herself, but that was the precise instant when Steve came through the brush, still naked. She took one look at him and gave a soft moan and promptly rolled to burrow her face in the dirt.

Steve saw Little Crow was trying to hide his face and laughed to think he was embarrassed over falling. He squatted down long enough to yank the foot free, then straightened. "Don't you know you can break a leg by not watching where you're going? What were you doing anyway?"

"I wasn't spying, I swear," Raven babbled.

Steve knew then he had been. Lord, he was a strange one, all right. But enough was enough. It was time for him to get over his shyness. "Come on and take a swim. The water feels good, and it's going to be another scorcher today. You'll be glad later that we took the time."

"No!" Raven knew she had spoken more forcefully than she should have, because as she scrambled to her feet she saw the gleam in his eye. He had taken her refusal as a challenge.

"Oh, yes, you are!" he cried, determined to break the boy out of his shell. "We're taking a swim together."

Raven yelped in protest as he threw her over his shoulders. Kicking her legs frantically, she beat on his back with her fists, but then she looked down to see how close her face was to his bare bottom, groaned, and squeezed her eyes shut.

Reaching the edge of the pond, Steve pulled her into his arms, then sent her sailing through the air to land in the middle with a splash.

Raven hit on her back and sank, immediately

stretching out her legs so as soon as she touched bottom she could spring quickly back to the surface. With broad strokes, she swam for the opposite side, intending to scramble out and hide till he tired of bedeviling her.

But he was right behind her, diving to land only a few feet behind. "Oh, no, you don't. You're not getting away that easy. Now I've got you in here, you're going to have a bath if I have to give it you myself." His hands clamped on her shoulders to push her under.

Flailing at him with her fists was useless below the water, but when he yanked her to the surface she managed to land a sound punch to his right cheek.

"Well, that merits another dunk," he bellowed, unhurt by the blow but fast becoming annoyed that Little Crow continued to fight him. "Can't you relax and have some fun?"

Down she went again.

This time Steve's hold slipped and he also went under, but when his hands reached out, it was not Little Crow's narrow shoulders he felt but two well-rounded . . . *breasts?*

He burst to the surface. "What the hell?" he spat out around mouthfuls of water.

Raven tried to get away from him, but his fingers were clamped firmly on her torso, and she cried fiercely, "Let me go, damn you!" She swung at him again, but he dodged the blow.

Nearly struck dumb with wonder, he released her to yank her arms behind her back. Then, with his free hand, he quickly explored the body beneath the clinging army shirt, astonished to positively identify breasts, a narrow waist, and, plunging downward—the final shocking realization that he did not have hold of an Indian boy at all.

He was holding a *woman*.

7

Raven felt Steve's touch and knew it was over.

Her mind frozen in horror, she was unprepared for him to let go of her so abruptly. When he did, she sank again.

This time, he did not pull her up. Instead, he swam out of the pond, not trusting himself to say or do anything till he could sort out what it meant.

Raven came up sputtering. She was also mad, fighting mad. If he had just left her alone, it wouldn't have happened. She could have gone her own way, and he would have forgotten all about Little Crow. Now he would tell everyone. Word would spread. She would have to get to Mexico right away, lest some of the men she had fooled be so angry they would want revenge—in the worst possible way for a woman.

"You should have kept your hands off me," she said as she stepped out of the water.

Steve had pulled on his trousers, strapped on his

holster, and now sat on the ground, waiting for her. "I wish I'd dunked you sooner." He was tight-lipped and grim. "Then you wouldn't have made a fool out of me for so long."

"If you had minded your own business, you would never have found out."

"What I want to know now is why you did it, why you wanted me and everybody else to think you're a boy."

His eyes dropped to her bosom. The wet clothing was like a second skin, and now her shape was obvious, her nipples distinct. She folded her arms across her chest and wished she had dry clothing to change into.

"Tell me, you conniving little liar. Hell, I ought to wring your neck."

"Why?" she challenged fiercely. "I saved your life yesterday, didn't I? And I was able to provide fresh meat for us last night. I haven't gotten us lost. So all in all, I'd say you don't have anything to gripe about, mister, and you won't be bothered with me anymore anyway, because I'm getting out of here and you can go to hell for all I care."

She started to walk away, but he grabbed her ankle to bring her sprawling down beside him. He caught her wrists and yanked her arms above her head to restrain her. "Now listen. You aren't going anywhere except to the Sabine reservation. And then *you* can go to hell for all *I* care."

"I won't go, because you'll tell everybody about me when we get there, and then it will be like it was before, with the young bucks wanting to bed me and the old geezers wanting to marry me. That's why I pretended to be a boy, so they'd all leave me alone."

Tears stung her eyes, and she blinked furiously, determined not to cry. "And you can't make me take you, because I'll do what I've been doing ever since we left Fort Inge, lead you in circles, and first chance I get I'll leave you, and then you'll be lost. Let me go now, and I swear I'll point you in the right direction and you can make it on your own."

She had absently pushed her wet bangs back from her face, where they fell in with the rest of her hair. The dunkings had washed the dirt from her cheeks, and Steve got his first really good look at her. With a bit of doing, she would be pretty. And as he thought that way, leaning over her so close he could feel her nipples against his chest, he cursed himself to experience a stirring in his loins. He shook her arms, as though trying to shake away the emotion, allowing her taunting words to provoke him. "You mean to tell me you've deliberately delayed us? I told you I'm in a hurry to find that girl. The man who sent me may not live long." He released her. "Oh, to hell with you. I'll get there without you. You'd probably lead me into a nest of Indians anyway."

Raven felt no reaction to hear her father might be dying. She had never known him; she had no reason to care. But enraged at Steve's accusation and overcome by the intensity of the moment, she lost control and cried, "I wouldn't do that to you or anybody else. Go your own way, I don't care. And I don't care about Ned Ralston either, so go back to Alabama and tell him you found his daughter and she said she hopes he rots in hell."

Jolted, Steve stared after her as she walked toward the mustang. "What . . . what did you say?" he stammered, sure he had not heard her right.

She turned to repeat her venomous decree, watching his eyes grow wide with astonishment. "Yes, I'm the one you've been looking for. Your search is over. Good-bye."

He was after her in a flash, but she heard him coming and was ready, whipping to face him, her knife drawn in warning. "Don't try to touch me."

Steve eyed the weapon warily. He knew how well she could ride and shoot a bow and arrow and had no reason to doubt her skill with a knife. "There's no need for that," he said gently. "I'm not going to hurt you—Raven." It felt strange to call her that for the first time, and now he wondered how he could have been so blind, but he had not been the only one she had fooled. She was a very intelligent and clever girl.

"Did my father send you to kill me?"

"Good God, no. Why would you think that?"

"Maybe he was afraid once my mother and stepfather died that I might go looking for him and try to make him take care of me, and he didn't want his *wife*"—she sneered—"to know he had fathered a bastard, especially by a lowly squaw."

"That's crazy. Aren't you forgetting I asked first about Seth Greer? Ned didn't know he was dead. He was just trying to find out what happened to you after Seth wrote him that your mother died, because there were no more letters after that and all of Ned's came back."

"He waited a long time to worry about us—eighteen years."

"He sent money."

"To try and buy freedom from his guilt over deserting us. Now he wants to do away with me so no one will ever know the despicable thing he did."

"I swear to you that's not so. He only wants to make amends before he dies. He's a sick man. That's why he sent me to find you instead of coming himself."

Her smile was sardonic. "Has he been sick for eighteen years?"

"I'm not going to try to understand out why he waited so long, but sometimes it takes contemplating his own mortality to make a man want to set things right. That's why he wants to make sure you get what's rightfully yours when he's gone. That's also the reason I couldn't say why I was searching for you. I was afraid, once word got out, Indian girls would come from all over claiming to be you. Keeping quiet made my job harder, but it had to be that way."

Raven had backed all the way to where Diablo was tied to a tree, lazily nibbling chaparral. She was not about to take time to go back and get her blanket and would have to ride completely bareback. She nodded to the knife. "I don't want to hurt you, so stay away from me."

"Come back with me," he begged. "What have you got to lose?"

She laughed coldly. "What about his wife? How will she feel about his bastard claiming anything? And do you really think I want to come face to face with the woman he was married to at the time he planted the seed for me in my mother?"

"They weren't married then, Raven."

Her eyes narrowed. "That makes it even worse, because it proves everything he ever told my mother was a lie. He just used her to nurse him back to health, used her to take his pleasure the way men do with a woman, then tossed her aside. Through the years, I tried to make myself believe maybe he really did love her when they were together, and something happened to keep him from coming back. Now I know I was only fooling myself. He never intended to return."

"You're wrong. Something did happen, and he'll explain it all to you himself, but I think you should know his wife is dead. She passed away several years ago, before I went to work for him. According to Ned, they were never happy together, but that's for him to tell you about, not me."

Raven was unmoved. "Liars and cheats seldom find happiness." She managed to untie Diablo with one hand while still holding the knife and keeping an eye on Steve, lest he make a move toward his gun. And if he did, she would send the blade slicing into his hand before he even touched his holster. She was just that good. "So now his children can have his money."

"They're his stepchildren. His wife was a widow when Ned married her. Ned's wealth is rightfully yours."

She felt a flash of satisfaction to think he'd never had any other children of his own. Still, she wanted no part of him or his wealth. "It doesn't matter. I was doing fine before you came along. I wish now I had refused to be your guide, but no, I had to be nosy and try to find out why you were looking for me. I shouldn't have given a damn—because I don't." She gave a curt nod.

It was Steve's turn to sneer. "You call it *fine* to rub dirt on your face to keep anyone from wanting to look at you and see you're really a girl? And what about having to wear your hair over your eyes so that you're almost blind? That's a miserable way to live."

"That's over now. I'll go somewhere else and be me."

"What makes you think it will be any different anywhere else? I've got a feeling those young bucks gave you a hard time because you're a half-breed. I've heard how they frown on mixing blood."

"Well, I doubt I'd be welcomed in Alabama either."

"Nobody would dare look down on Ned Ralston's daughter," Steve countered, hoping it was true but fearing Lisbeth and Julius would never accept her.

"It makes no difference, because I'm not going. I've had enough of prejudice to last me a lifetime. I'm sick of feeling like I'm supposed to apologize for being born or having to pretend I'm something I'm not. So you can go back to my father"—She rolled her eyes—"God, how it sticks in my craw to call him that, and tell him I refused to help ease his conscience before he dies. I think he deserves to suffer for what he did. Or say you couldn't find me. I don't care.

"Now," she instructed, "I want you to take your gun from your holster very slowly and toss it in those bushes over there so you won't get any ideas about trying to wing me. I'll get on Diablo and ride out of here, and nobody gets hurt. Otherwise, I swear I'll put this knife through your hand before you can slap leather."

He knew she meant it, and something told him she could do it. He did as she said.

She swung up on the mustang, took the reins in one hand, and with her other pointed the knife toward a distant rise. "If you keep in that direction, you should make the Sabine in about three days, riding steady. The way I was going would have taken six. Try to have eyes in the back of your head. Take cover if you see dust rising; that means horses, probably Indians. Don't make any fires, and don't chance traveling by night. You'll only get lost."

She reached and untied his horse.

"Hey, what are you doing?" He started toward her, but she held up the knife. He froze but protested, "I can't walk all that distance. Are you crazy?"

"I'll let him go when I've gone far enough that you won't have time to run him down and come after me. I really don't want to kill you."

She could not deny the warmth of desire that spread through her body to remember the sight of his naked body, and, yes, how despite the terror of the moment it had felt so good when he had held her, touched her.

It was that sensuous longing that provoked her to admit, "Now that we will never see each other again, I don't mind telling you that you made me feel very strange. You made me"—she drew a deep, ragged breath, wondering if she should go on, then recklessly did so—"you made me want to be a woman for the first time in my life." She fell silent for a moment, then she said with a faint, sad smile, "Go with God, Steve Maddox. I wish you well."

She dug in her heels to send Diablo into a clattering gallop, holding on to Steve's horse to take him with her.

Steve quickly retrieved his gun, put it back in his holster, and stood with his hands on his hips to watch her ride away. He smiled at the sight of her firm, rounded buttocks rising up and down on the mustang's back. He had never noticed before, but then why would he have cared what an Indian boy's butt looked like?

He grinned to think of how she had all but

admitted he had aroused her and remembered all the times he had been immodest, unaware a woman was around. How embarrassed she must have been, but he felt no embarrassment himself for he was blameless.

Raven Ralston, he knew beyond all doubt, was unlike any female he had ever known in his life. He admired her for her spunk and grit and could think of no other woman who could do what she had done— passed for a boy, an Indian scout. But he also felt sorry for her to know the hell she must have gone through to make her go to such desperate means to deny her own gender.

He supposed he could understand why she felt the way she did about Ned. It must have been a lot to swallow all at once, his wanting to step into her life, unannounced after so many years. She'd had plenty of time to harden her heart toward him and no reason at all to feel anything good for him anyway.

As for Ned, while Steve had heard his explanation as to why things happened as they did, it wasn't up to him to judge whether it was right or wrong. And whether or not Ned had actually deceived Lakoma and lied to her, as Raven believed, one thing was for certain: Ned Rolston had suffered. Steve suspected the only happiness Ned had ever really known since his days in Texas was after the two of them had met and his racking horses became such a vital part of Ned's life.

But regardless of whether Ned needed atonement before dying or whether Raven was justified in wanting no part of him and the life he offered, Steve was determined that each of them would have a chance to find out.

He put his fingers to his mouth and gave a long, loud whistle.

Raven had said Diablo hated the sound of a shrill whistle.

He saw she had been right.

Diablo didn't care who was responsible. All he knew was that he couldn't stand the sound. With a wild kick, he bucked, and Raven, caught unawares, flew up and over his head.

Steve took off running. She was still dazed by the time he reached her, and he was able to snatch her knife from the sheath at her belt before she rallied enough to go for it.

Her eyes looked like burning coals as she glared up at him. She sat on her bottom, arms stretched out behind her, palms flat against the ground, legs wide. "Damn you, Steve Maddox. You'll be sorry."

"Probably." He gave a lopsided grin and held out his hand to her. "But don't blame me. Blame Diablo. He's the one who goes crazy when he hears a whistle."

She knocked his hand away and got to her feet, her back feeling sore. She had landed hard.

She walked over to Diablo and cursed him for the traitor he was, but he merely quirked an ear and stretched to gobble a dandelion, as though he had nothing to apologize for. After all, she was the one who had told his secret.

"This doesn't change anything. I'm still not going." She prepared to mount again, but Steve yanked her back.

"You're going if I have to hog-tie you and throw you across that mustang's back like a sack of potatoes, because I intend to do what Ned Ralston asked me to do—bring you to him. He's dying. The least you can do is hear him out and let him go to his grave in peace. After that, I don't care what you do."

She could tell by the fire in his eyes and the set of his jaw that he meant what he said. "Well then, I guess I don't have much choice," she said coldly, evenly. "You've got my knife."

"That's right. Now let's ride. Thanks to you I've wasted a lot of time, and I intend for us to make tracks for Alabama now as fast as we can. And I *don't* intend to listen to any whining about how tired you are."

She swung up on Diablo and met his determined gaze with one of her own. "You won't hear me complain, mister, but like I said—you'll be sorry."

She didn't know it, but he already was. As he headed for his own horse he found himself wishing he had refused Ned after all.

Because something told him life at Halcyon, a word he knew meant peaceful and calm, was never going to be the same. It might, he mused wryly, even be necessary to change the name once Raven got there.

8

Raven refused to talk to him, no matter how hard he tried to engage her in conversation. She had held a tiny hope that, once they reached the reservation, she could enlist help from one of the agents by telling him she was being taken to Alabama against her will. But Steve obviously anticipated her plan, for when they finally reached the Sabine River, he turned south instead of heading north toward the reservation. Realizing what he was doing, she grudgingly spoke to remind him they were short on supplies.

Steve knew it, just as he knew she had probably been planning to scream for help if they went to the reservation. He tossed her a complacent smile. "Well, I'll give your bow back to you long enough to shoot us another rabbit, but I'll make sure to stand behind you, in case you get any ideas about misdirecting the arrow."

"Don't bother. I'm not finding any more food for you. You can starve for all I care."

"You'll starve right along with me."

"I'd rather starve than go where you're taking me."

"You know, you really should be ashamed of yourself," he told her. "Your father is dying, but you don't care. You're so bull-headed you won't even give him a chance."

"What chance did he give me and my mother? He didn't care what happened to us. He went back to his rich life and married another woman."

"He's got a side to the story too, Raven, and whether you want to or not you're going to hear it. But now hear *me*. We can have a nice trip, and I can tell you what it's like there and answer any questions you've got, or you can keep on pouting and be miserable. It's up to you."

She gave an indignant sniff. "You mean to tell me I suddenly have a say in things?"

"Act like a brat," he said curtly. "I don't give a damn."

Raven lapsed back into her angry, brooding silence.

The road along the river went through a district of poor and sandy soil thickly wooded with pine. They passed abandoned farms for a day, then sighted cotton growing on the riverbanks, a little corn, and soon a farmhouse came into view. The occupants were glad for company and obliged them with the best meal Steve had had since leaving Fort Inge. Raven likewise enjoyed the meal of boiled crayfish but was not about to say so, maintaining her stony silence. Before they rode on, however, she did whisper her gratitude to the farmer's wife.

Steve overheard her, and after they had ridden away he said, "That was nice of you, Raven. I'm glad you realize there's no need in being rude to others because you're mad at me."

She ignored him.

They reached a settlement town in Louisiana. After buying a simple muslin dress and undergarments for Raven, even though she grumbled, he sent her to a bathhouse to clean up while he waited outside to make sure she didn't try to run away. He was tired of her disheveled appearance, and when she finally came out, freshly scrubbed, her black hair washed, silky soft, and brushed free of all tangles, he couldn't help telling her how pretty she was. "What a waste for you to pretend to be anything but what you are, Raven—a lovely young woman."

She glared at him and stuck out her tongue.

He thought about loading up with supplies and riding straight through to Alabama but decided instead to take the necessary time to illustrate to Raven that people could be nice. He had come to the conclusion her past experiences with society had not been pleasant for her.

There was no shortage of hospitality on the trails. People were glad for company.

They stopped at another house, where they were served supper by the light of pine knots blazing in the chimney, with their hosts apologizing for the absence of candles. The jug of blackberry wine served with the fresh Gulf shrimp more than made up for any inconvenience, however. Steve noted Raven also seemed to enjoy it, and before the meal had ended, she had opened up a bit and begun to talk to the couple's daughter.

When it was time to sleep, the man of the house, Judd Hannibal, assuming Steve and Raven were married, said, "You two can have that bed in the corner. We ain't got but one other room built on the back, but the kids can sleep in there with me and their ma for tonight."

Steve looked at Raven, expecting her to protest. When they camped at night, he always knotted a rope around her ankle, looping the other end around his arm. That way he woke every time she turned over, so there was no chance of her trying to run away. But he did give her a long enough rope that she could sleep on the other side of bushes, for her privacy. Now, however, they had been offered a bed to share, and he was expecting her to declare they weren't man and wife. Instead, he was surprised to hear her thank Mr. Hannibal sweetly for being so kind.

When they were alone, the room alive with golden shadows playing on the walls, Steve said, "You can have the bed, and I'll take the floor. But I'll be right in front of the door in case you get any ideas," he added, annoyed to see her looking at him so smugly.

"That's nice of you, Mr. Maddox. And since I'm so tired, I think I'll turn in right now."

He took a blanket from the bed and spread it before the door. Then, as he began to unbutton his shirt, planning, as usual, to sleep only in his trousers, he was startled to see that Raven had taken off her clothes and stood naked. His eyes locked on her breasts, which reminded of ripe golden apples in the shimmering firelight, but there was no time to allow his gaze to travel downward, for he had only one brief, tantalizing glimpse before she turned away.

He stared, pulse racing, as she stretched her arms high over her head and faked a prolonged yawn before saying nonchalantly, "It's really hot in here, but since it's not my house, I certainly can't say anything if they insist on not drowning the fire in the grate."

His gaze riveted upon her buttocks, high, firm, and round, and he felt a quivering within as she moved sensuously, sassily, to pull back the blanket on the bed. When she finally lay down, uncovered, he sucked in his breath to see how her breasts were outlined in the fire's dwindling light.

Raven felt him staring and was glad he could not see her face, for surely her cheeks burned with embarrassment. But she had to do it, she told herself over and over, in order to make her scheme work.

Steve watched, fascinated by the rise and fall of her bosom. And was it his imagination, he wondered, a bit wildly, or were her nipples hard? He gave himself a vicious shake, along with a silent admonition for acting like a horny young boy. He knew she was just trying to tease him, arouse him, make him miserable with wanting her. Hadn't she promised he'd be sorry for making her go with him? It was all part of her threat, and he'd be damned if he would let her get to him.

"I know what you're trying to do," he said finally, harshly. "Just make sure you cover yourself before old Hannibal comes in here in the morning. You might give *him* ideas," he added to make her think he was not impressed.

But Raven was not fooled. She had seen the way he reacted, had heard his rapid breathing. He would be miserable all night long, thinking about her naked only a few feet away. She wanted him to suffer, wanted him to feel the same stirrings she had experienced when he'd thought her a boy and unknowingly enticed her. Let him agonize as she had. And if he lost

control and tried to force himself upon her, so much
the better. Here, she would scream and bring Mr.
Hannibal running, and then she'd tell the truth and
accuse Steve of rape. But if he waited till they were
back on the trail to attack, then she would best him in
another way, for he was not yet aware of how profi-
cient she was in hand-to-hand combat. Some of the
young braves on the reservation had been glad to teach
her all she needed to know to protect herself against
white men when her body was her only weapon.

Steve was miserable. Being alone with her since
discovering her ruse had not bothered him till now,
when he knew she was deliberately teasing him. So he
was a long time falling asleep, and when he awoke,
the sun was full in his face. Bolting upright, it all
came back to him: where he was, what he was doing
there, and, with a jolt of panic, the memory of how he
had positioned himself in front of the door to keep
Raven from escaping. But now the door was wide
open and the bed she'd slept in was empty.

He hurried out to the porch, only to stop short to
see her, fully dressed and sitting in the wood swing.
She turned to smile at him sweetly, innocently, as she
pushed against the plank floor with her toes to make
the swing move ever so gently to and fro. "The door
opened out instead of in, Mr. Maddox, so I didn't
have to wake you in leaving after all."

He stuck his hands behind his back so she couldn't
see how they were clenched in frustration. "Why didn't
you run away?"

Wanting to annoy him even more by not answering
his question, she changed the subject. "The horses are
fed, watered, and ready to go. Shall we wake up the
Hannibals to thank them or just be on our way?"

"We ride," he said snappily. "The sooner I deliver you to your father, the quicker I can be rid of the responsibility for you." He went to gather his things, bristling all the while.

As they rode farther into Louisiana, Raven was impressed by the beauty of the land. They were no longer in uncivilized territory, and she marveled at roadside fences made by flower hedges.

"Cherokee rose and sweetbriar," Steve said grudgingly when she asked what kind of blossoms they were.

She could tell he was still mad, because now *he* was the one who wanted to sulk. She decided to irritate him with more questions. "It looks as though they were first planted by the side of an ordinary rail fence, which must have served as some kind of trellis, and as they got bigger, they matted together and became a thicket. What are those other flowers?" She pointed.

He bit out the names. "Trumpet creepers, grapevines, and some sugarcane. How do you know about fences and trellises? I didn't see any around the fort."

"My stepfather told me about things like that. He saw to it I could read, and he provided me with books. He wanted me to know about the genteel side of life"—she winked at him—"because, after all, I'm only *half* savage, remember?"

He fumed to realize she was trying to be as obnoxious as possible. Well, two could play that game. "You're right. You're only half savage, and that's the half we've got to clean up before you meet your father."

"What do you mean?" Something told her she was not going to like his answer. She'd already had a bath and wore a dress. What more did he want?

"We have to get you a really nice traveling outfit.

And a hat. Maybe I'll even hire a carriage in Mobile, to carry you home properly."

Silently she swore she would not let him make her lose her temper. "I don't want to wear a hat, and I don't want to ride in a wagon."

"I didn't say wagon, I said carriage."

"It's all the same."

"That shows what you don't know, Raven. You're no doubt used to open buckboard wagons, like the army uses, with mules to pull. I'm talking about a nice carriage with a top, velvet or leather seats, and good horses."

"Diablo is good enough for me. So are the clothes I have on."

"I disagree. We'll do as I say and really clean you up, whether you like it or not."

Then and there, Raven made up her mind to go one step farther in tormenting Steve into wanting her so desperately she could catch him off guard and escape.

It happened when they were a half day's ride out of Baton Rouge, camped alongside one of Louisiana's many lakes. Steve had managed to catch several nice fish, thanks to Raven's producing the necessary tackle from her saddlebag—hooks carved from bone and line made from Diablo's tail.

As she helped clean and skewer the fish for cooking, she was amused by how Steve very carefully avoided touching her as they worked side by side. She had deliberately unbuttoned the front of her dress low enough to display her cleavage. He was trying to ignore her, but she saw him stealing quick, furtive glances every so often and knew her plan to provoke him beyond the limits of his willpower was working. She did not like doing it, for it made her feel immoral, but if that's what it took to get away from him, so be it.

It was still daylight when they finished eating. Raven stood and began to undo the rest of buttons as she made the casual announcement, "I'm going to go for a swim and take a bath."

Steve stumbled in his haste to get to his feet and walk away.

"Hey, aren't you afraid I'll run away?" she called after him.

"I won't be that lucky," he yelled over his shoulder, careful not to turn around, for out of the corner of his eye he could see her pulling her dress over her head and tossing it aside. Although sorely tempted, he did not look.

She called to taunt him. "That's not very nice of you, because if I decide to stay and claim my inheritance, you'll be out of a job if you aren't nice to me."

He could have told her he had already come to that conclusion, regardless of who eventually took over Halcyon. But what irked him at the moment was what she was trying to do to him. He'd abandon her, if not for his promise to Ned, but he had come too far now and would somehow manage to put up with her the rest of the way. After they reached Baton Rouge, it would take four days of steady riding to reach Mobile, maybe less if they could pick up the pace a bit. Meanwhile, all he had to do was ignore her and not let her get under his skin, not let her make him do something he would later regret.

Thrashing through some weeds and brambles, he found a clearing and sat down. He would not go back where she was until he could be sure she had her clothes on. Maybe he would sit there till after dark to be on the safe side.

She was singing. He could not make out the words, for it was an Indian song, but he couldn't help thinking it was pretty. Her voice was pretty. *She* was pretty, damn it.

He dug his heels into the soft earth, making tiny ruts in his frustration. In a nice gown, hair coifed, body oiled and perfumed, she would have men flocking after her like crows to a cornfield. Sure, Lisbeth, with her big blue eyes and golden curls, had her share of beaus, but she was the kind men wanted mostly for a wife, mistress of their manor, mother of their children. Raven, on the other hand, evoked delicious thoughts beyond standard fare. With her dark, seductive eyes, husky, throaty voice, and the supple way she moved, a man couldn't look at Raven and think beyond what it would be like to have her moaning and thrashing in his bed.

Despite her cold facade, there was something about her, Steve had sensed, that promised passion untold to the man she favored with the pleasures she had to offer.

But Steve knew she did *not* wish to bestow her treasures upon him. She didn't want him—she just wanted him to want her, so she could make him look like a fool when she ultimately rejected him. Maybe she hoped to catch him unawares, best him again, and escape. But he was not going to fall into her trap.

He tried to turn his mind to other matters to pass the time and thought of Ned, hoping he was still alive, knowing if he was how pleased he would be to see his daughter at long last.

He thought, too, about the racking horses and how he was looking forward to working with them again . . . if only for a little while. Maybe, after Ned died, he would return to Virginia, to the ranch where he had worked before. He was good with horses, could probably get his old job back, and—

Suddenly it dawned on him how quiet it was. Raven had stopped singing, and there were no sounds of splashing. Maybe she hadn't been joking, he thought in a panic as he scrambled to his feet. Maybe she had made that crack about running away to throw him off guard, and right now she was riding away on his horse, instead of Diablo also, so he couldn't whistle and get her thrown again. But she would take Diablo also, so there'd be no way for him to go after her.

"Damn the vixen," he cursed, pushing through the brush.

He stopped short.

Raven was still there, standing waist deep in water as she washed her hair. But then she turned, her fingers moving through the long tresses.

Steve watched, mesmerized.

Cupping her hands, she reached down and scooped up water to splash upon her breasts, then began to gently knead them with her fingers as she washed. Her face, turned toward the sky, was bathed in the peach and lavender glow of sunset.

After a few moments, she began to walk out of the lake, and more of her body was revealed with every step she took. Steve could not tear his heated gaze away, though every nerve within him commanded otherwise.

His gaze dropped, and he had one quick glimpse of

the dark crowning *V* of hair above her womanhood before she turned to reach for her clothes.

He had seen her, all of her. She was beautiful, and glorious, and never had he wanted a woman more.

9

Steve ungrily shoved his way back through the bushes. Raven heard him coming but pretended not to, quickly buttoning her shirt. She was almost done when she felt his hands fasten on her shoulders to spin her about. Adrenaline surged as she prepared to defend herself, for this was the moment she had been waiting for—to make him want her beyond all reason and then humiliate him by overpowering him.

Now, however, as she stared up at him, caught in his burning gaze, she trembled not from fear that he could harm her physically but rather from experiencing the beginnings of the betrayal of her own body. His eyes had captured hers to imprison them in a building fever of shared desire, and she was powerless to pull away.

Steve could see how unnerved she was and found himself wondering whether she had deliberately made him want her or if she actually was so naive as not to comprehend the effect she had upon him now that she no longer had to pretend to be anything other than what she was.

He could see her pulse beating in her throat, heard the quick, ragged breaths she drew, and saw how her breasts rose and fell as he held her tight against him. He fought against smiling to realize that she was shaken by his nearness, and the angry clutching of his fingers melted into a gentle caress.

"Damn you," he whispered huskily, hoarsely, as he drew her against him. "Damn you for making me do this, Raven." His mouth closed over hers.

The kiss ran passionate and deep, and, despite herself, Raven could not fight it. Her lips parted beneath his gentle assault, and she could only yield to the delicious wonder of his exploring tongue. His hands moved to her back, trailing up and down her curves, pressing her yet closer, until they seemed molded together. Through the haze of desire that had entrapped her, she was startled to feel his hardness against her. It was the clarity of desire she had sought to create, but in so doing she had unwittingly caused her own. And now she melted against him in submission as his touch fed the flames within, making them leap higher and higher till she was consumed, devoured, and ready to yield to his every wish.

His hands moved to her breasts, to cup and squeeze, and his hardness against her began to throb, ever so gently, and she thrilled to it, and unconsciously leaned into it, but at the same time knew she had to pull away, lest there be no turning back. It was madness, weakness. She prided herself on never being weak.

Her hands had been clutching his shoulders, and it was all she could do to move, for they seemed to have become leaden, refusing to budge. With all her strength, she was finally able to place them against his chest and get ready to push him away.

But at that precise instant, Steve released her.

She blinked in stunned disbelief to see his mouth spread into a slow, taunting grin and his eyes no longer glazed with rapture but mocking, instead. "This isn't what you had in mind, is it, sweetheart? You weren't supposed to want it too, were you?"

"I . . . I don't know what you're talking about," she stammered and began backing away from him.

He made no move to stop her. "Sure you do. You've been teasing me so you could laugh in my face, only you didn't figure on catching the fever yourself."

As the distance between them widened, her bravado returned. "You're crazy. I didn't know you were going to spy on me when I took a bath, and I didn't enjoy what you were doing just now. You took me by surprise for a minute, that's all."

"You wanted me to see you bathing."

She shook her head wildly. "That's not true."

"And last night you wanted to make me crazy thinking about you lying there half naked, hoping I'd try to crawl in bed with you so you could scream rape, bring the Hannibals running, and tell them how I forced you to pretend we were married. That would have made me look like a prize fool in front of everybody. Only it didn't work, sweetheart, not there and not here, where you were probably going to catch me in a weak moment, bust my head with a rock, and take off. You're quite a little actress, you know that?

You pretend to be so shy and innocent, but actually you're a scheming little witch."

Raven could have told him he was wrong. It wasn't to make him look foolish that she had tried to make him want her, it was to get back at him for all those nights she had lain awake wanting *him*. Only now it didn't matter, because desire had turned to loathing.

"You started all this. You came into my world, I didn't go to yours. And you forced me to come with you, and I told you when you did you'd be sorry. And you will.

"But hear this," she continued furiously. "I didn't want you just now. I could never want a . . . stubborn oaf like you." She finished with a curt nod.

Steve cocked his head to one side. "Now is that a fact? Because I'd have sworn you wanted me just now as bad as I wanted you. Let's find out."

He took a step toward her, but Raven threw up her hands and made ready for combat. She was weak no longer, and anything she had felt for him had dissolved amid humiliation and indignity. "Don't come any closer."

Steve paused and bit down on his lower lip as it came to him what she had actually been planning. The little vixen probably knew every Indian trick there was and could fight like a warrior. She had no doubt hoped to get him in a vulnerable position and then beat the tar out of him before he knew what happened.

And suddenly it all seemed hilarious, and he threw back his head and laughed long and loud.

"You'll regret treating me this way," Raven warned.

"Well, if kissing me like you just did is a sample of

revenge, I'll be looking forward to it. Meanwhile, I suggest a truce so we can get where we're going." He walked away to leave her standing there glaring after him.

They endeavored to ignore each other. Steve was intent on traveling as fast as possible, while Raven focused on her surroundings.

She found the countryside beautiful and adequately populated, so there was no shortage of places to stop for food and rest. When meeting someone, and given the opportunity, she would ask questions, wanting to learn as much as possible about her new world but determined not to engage in conversation with Steve unless absolutely necessary.

She kept her distance, riding behind him most of the time. It was understood they couldn't stand each other, but still she was incited by the memories of how he had held her, kissed her. She had only to glance at his mouth to remember how delicious he had tasted, and at his hands to think how they had cupped her breasts and kindled sweet hot fires within her. And sometimes she would dare glance down at him and think of him pressed hard against her. Then she would chide herself and return to concentrating furiously on the scenery.

They passed plantations, and Raven marveled at the huge mansions, set far back, the roads leading to them lined with tremendous live oaks. As they passed one, curiosity got the best of her, and she asked, "What is that hanging from the tree limbs?"

He followed her gaze to the phantasmal cascades descending from the huge serpentine limbs of the oaks. "It's called moss. You'll see plenty of it from now on. It's all over the trees at Halcyon."

"Beautiful," she whispered, awed. "Just beautiful."

Steve turned to look at her and saw the wonder on her face. It occurred to him then how strange she must feel after the life she had led, suddenly thrust into a different civilization. And with so much more yet to be seen and experienced, he knew she was either in for a delightful treat or the greatest despair she'd ever known. It remained to be seen just how her new life was going to affect her, but he sharply reminded himself it made no difference to him. He would soon be through with her. Eventually he would leave Halcyon, and never see her again, much less give a damn what happened to her. Still, despite the raging within, he could not dismiss the reality that he was drawn to her . . . which was all the more reason to get her out of his life as soon as possible.

Raven marveled at fields of cotton that stretched as far as the eye could see, with black people dressed in rags bent double as they crept between the rows, dragging huge picking sacks behind them. She knew they were slaves and thought it terrible but said nothing. It was a culture new to her, a way of life she did not understand and wanted no part of.

Now and then they would pass open carriages with finely dressed ladies out for an airing on a sweltering hot afternoon. Always the horses were driven by a black man dressed in a bright red coat. The ladies would look at Raven and Steve from the corners of their eyes but never turn their heads. Once, on impulse, Raven waved and called gaily, but the women pretended not to notice.

At the inns where they stopped to eat, Raven was

introduced to new foods, which she found she liked, such as chicken that had been rolled in flour and fried; big green leaves called mustard, boiled with hunks of fat from a hog; potatoes mashed and fluffy and covered in a thick brown sauce called gravy; and big chunks of a baked crispy bread made from ground corn. Most of all, however, she liked the foods known as desserts, especially a light and fluffy cake covered in fat juicy strawberries and topped with a dollop of whipped cream, made from the risings of fresh milk.

So far, Raven had not felt anyone was looking down on her but then she realized Steve was not stopping at the fancy places, where the ladies she had seen riding in the elegant carriages would go to eat. The furnishings where they went were sparse, and they ate off chipped dishes and drank from glasses with tiny cracks. It was only when they passed a place where the customers dined outdoors beneath little umbrellas to shade the sun that Raven noted there were nicer restaurants.

"I suppose you don't take me to places like that because they won't let me in," she remarked. Then, not giving him time to either confirm nor deny, went on to sadly reminisce. "One time when Seth took me with him to San Antonio to get supplies, we passed a café that had a big chocolate cake in the window. I wanted a piece so bad. I had a little money in my pocket, so while Seth was busy in a store, I went back to the café and went inside, but some men threw me out. Seth got mad at those men when he found out about it and said maybe I could finally understand why he tried to keep me away from white people."

"Were you dressed like an Indian?"

"Of course. My mother always dressed me in a

pretty beaded dress made of nice soft deerhide. She wasn't ashamed of the Indian part of me. Neither was Seth."

"Well, here, wearing the kind of dress you've got on, folks will never suspect you're part Indian."

"Do you really think so?"

She looked at him with so much hope it made him feel guilty. She did have dark skin—cinnamon-colored skin. There would probably be a little prejudice, but something told him she had the spunk to cope with it, especially with Ralston money backing her. "You'll do fine," he said, turning away so he wouldn't have to see the doubt in her eyes, and adding, "and the reason I haven't taken you to the fancy restaurants is because neither one of us is properly dressed for them right now."

She settled back and felt a little better about everything.

Raven's first sight of Mobile was the huge waterfront, with its docks and wharves and warehouses.

"See those?" Steve pointed to a row of brick warehouses. "They belong to your father. Ten of them. They're capable of storing over seventy thousand bales of cotton. He also owns presses that can compress a million bales in six months. He owns fourteen wharves that can be reached by a channel twenty-two feet deep.

"Over there"—he pointed again—"you can see some of his steamers, which operate between here and Montgomery. The trip takes two days, and the boat stops about two hundred times to load and unload passengers, grain, flour, meats, lumber, liquors, tobacco, cotton, and corn. Every possible sort of household item and luxury finds its way upriver to consumers."

"Is my father here somewhere?" Raven glanced around uneasily. She did not want to meet him unexpectedly, she wanted time to prepare herself.

"No. As I told you, he's sick at his plantation upriver. But even if he weren't, he wouldn't be here. I can't remember the last time Ned came to Mobile. He's got people to run things here, and he'd rather devote his time to the racking horses."

"Racking horses." Raven sniffed with disdain. "A horse is a horse, but he thinks he has found something special."

"When you see them, you might think so too," Steve remarked fondly. "Especially Starfire."

"Starfire?"

"Your father's horse. I told you about him, how no one has ever been able to ride him except your father. He's the most magnificent animal I've ever seen. And he doesn't throw him when somebody whistles," he added with a grin.

Raven ignored him. She was getting good at that, she realized, lifting her chin and turning her head in dismissal of his sarcasm. "He's still just a horse," she muttered under her breath. "I could probably ride him if I wanted to, which I don't."

The town lay at the head of an open bay and ran along the edge of the water north and south. The streets were long and broad, paved with oyster shells. The main avenue, Government Street, was lined with shops offering the latest goods from New York, London, and Paris.

Steve could see Raven was impressed, but not overly so. "Seems to me," he said hesitantly, "that a girl raised like you were would be shaking all over with excitement to think about having all this handed to her."

She blinked uncertainly.

"All this," he repeated with an exasperated wave of his hand. "With Ned's money, you can buy anything you want."

"*His* money. Not mine."

It could be hers, Steve thought, if she'd quit being so stubborn, but he was tired of arguing, glad his job would soon be over.

He reined up and dismounted. Raven did the same. After securing their horses to a hitching post, he led the way to the door of a shop with a sign above that proclaimed BONHEUR BOUTIQUE. Motioning for Raven to precede him, he said, "I don't speak French, but I happen to know this place is called Happiness Shop. We're about to find out if that's true—thanks to your father's money."

Reluctantly, shyly, Raven stepped inside. The air was sweet with the smell of perfume, and as she glanced around she knew she had never been anywhere so elegant. She sank to her ankles in the thick purple rug and thought the walls, covered in a paper of pink and peach-colored roses, looked like a garden that stretched forever. There were tufted white velvet chairs and settees and ornate vases and flowers and more flowers.

Steve stood back and watched, pleased by her reaction. She would find out soon enough how money could open a lot of doors, though he personally had never worried about having any. As long as he had a roof over his head when it was raining, food in his belly when he was hungry, a good horse to take him where he wanted to go, and a firm-feeling woman when he had a yen, he needed nothing else—except, he was struck with a sharp pang to admit, there were times when he wished he had roots. Once Ned was gone, he knew that longing would intensify.

A tiny silver bell above the door had tinkled when they entered, and a few seconds later the lace curtain at the back of the shop parted and a woman appeared. She wore a blue taffeta gown, and her dark hair was pulled back in a snood. Little round glasses perched on the end of her pointed nose. Her expression, at first, was pleasant, but, seeing Raven, her hand fluttered to her throat and she said, "I believe you are in the wrong shop."

"I don't think so." Steve gave her a lazy smile. Removing his hat, he walked over to settle on one of the pink velvet settees. "We're here to buy some happiness, like your sign says. And I'd like for you to fix this little lady up with a few nice gowns."

"Uh—" The woman hesitated to say it but finally blurted out, "Sir, this is a very expensive shop."

"Money is no object."

The woman looked as if she might faint.

Raven turned to Steve and said, "Let's go."

"Not till you get your clothes." He frowned at the woman. "Maybe we'd better talk to the owner."

Stiffly, she informed him, "I *am* the owner, Madame Bonet, and I assure you, sir, that I have nothing that the young"—she nearly choked on the word—"*lady* would be interested in."

"Well, you never can tell. Bring out what you've got, and we'll decide."

"But you don't understand, monsieur. We don't cater to"—she lowered her voice to a scornful whisper—"*quadroons*. I will appreciate your taking your business elsewhere."

"She's not a quadroon. And I don't think you know

whose money we're spending here. Does the name Ned Ralston mean anything to you?"

"Of course," she said uneasily. "He owns this building."

"That's what I thought. Now will you please do as I ask, or would you like Mr. Ralston to come in so you can refuse him personally."

She paled. "That won't be necessary. I'll be glad to help you." She fled back through the curtains.

Raven started to protest again, but Steve waved her to silence. "She'll break her neck serving you now, so relax."

"But what did she call me? What is a quadroon?"

"A woman of color. One quarter Negro. Your skin is darker than most, and she made a mistake. So you see?" He winked. "I told you no one would guess you're half Indian."

"But—"

"Relax. I'm going to go have a beer or two, and when I come back I'm sure *I* won't even know who you are."

And when he returned a few hours later, he almost didn't.

Raven was standing in the middle of the pink and white room but easily outshone the magnificent surroundings. Her hair, washed and styled in ringlets by a coiffeur hastily summoned by Madame Bonet, shone like the raven's wing for which she was named. She was wearing a *pardessus*—a jacket—of green silk taffeta over a separate skirt. A satin ribbon of the same color adorned the jacket and the flounce of the skirt. The upper arms were embellished with a false cuff of net with fringe, and she was carrying a lace scarf and a parasol to match the fabric and lace edging of her costume.

"Do you like it, monsieur?" Madame Bonet rushed forward to dust away a tiny piece of lint from Raven's skirt. "The vivid green color is the latest from Paris and popular because of the recent invention of aniline dyes.

"Mademoiselle found several things she liked," she hastened to tell him. "There are a few alterations to be made, but I have two of my best girls working on them now."

"Have everything finished and delivered to the hotel by tonight and send the bill to Mr. Ralston. Here's a deposit." He threw down some bills.

Raven had already left the shop, wanting to enjoy the beautiful blue and gold day dressed in such a fine outfit.

He was about to follow after her when Madame Bonet touched his sleeve and said, with a faintly conspiring smile, "I am sorry I misunderstood when you first brought the lady in, monsieur. Mr. Ralston has good taste. He has the ability to see the rose among the thorns. Feel free to bring his mistresses to my shop anytime."

Steve tipped his hat and grinned. "Oh, she's not his mistress, she's his daughter. But I'll be glad to give him your message."

This time, Madame Bonet did become faint.

And Steve just continued on his way.

10

Raven was determined not to let her excitement show, but it was hard. After all, she had never owned more than one dress at a time in her life, much less even dreamed of wearing such creations as the ones from Bonheur Boutique. And, of course, she'd never had her hair styled either.

But even more delights were in store.

Her eyes nearly popped out of her head when she saw her hotel room. The bed was huge, with a covering stretched above it on poles like a giant flattened tepee but made not of animal skin but a pretty fabric as soft as the gown she had on, in a shade of pink to match the cloth covering the bed.

Slowly, she walked about to marvel over the table draped in dainty ruffles of white lace with a mirror edged in gold hanging above. One wall was nearly covered by a huge piece of furniture she assumed was supposed to be used for hanging clothes, although she wondered who would ever have enough to fill it.

There were rugs on the floor, and fresh flowers sitting on the washstand next to the pitcher and bowl. Two large windows looked out on the street below. In the distance, she could see the waterfront, with large ships anchored offshore and smaller ones at the docks.

It was a busy place, with people scurrying about, and Raven felt a thrill to be a part of it—if only for a little while. Soon she would go back to Texas, then on to Mexico, but while she was here she wanted to see and do everything, for it was a world she could visit . . . if not embrace.

She found herself wondering about the kind of life she might have lived had her father not abandoned her. While she had not yet seen his plantation, she was sure she would prefer it to the city. There would be horses and wide-open spaces, which was all she needed to make her happy. Fancy gowns and fancy restaurants had their place, but she could not imagine going about dressed every day in finery and spending her time sewing or reading poetry and doing other feminine things—like riding a horse sideways; she wrinkled her nose in disgust to imagine that. She'd seen women riding that way and thought it ridiculous.

Looking down at the ladies walking along the boardwalk, she knew beyond doubt that, if left to their own resources in the wilderness, they could not survive. Not a one of them, she wagered, could defend herself. In the face of danger, they would scream or faint or do both. And certainly they did not know how to make a rabbit snare or carve fishhooks and make fishing lines.

Feeling smug, she dropped the lace curtains and turned to glance again around the room. She would enjoy sleeping in the big soft bed, if only for a night. Steve had said they would get an early start in the morning and hope to arrive at Halcyon by midday. She would then meet her father and, as politely as possible, hear what he had to say. Then, after resting a day, she would put on her scout uniform, which was tucked away in her saddlebag, leap on Diablo, and ride away to leave her father and the life she might have had behind.

Putting Steve out of her mind, however, was going to take some doing.

He had left her in the hotel lobby, saying someone else could see her to her room because he was going to get a bath and a shave. He had suggested she rest a spell, because he was taking her out for a nice dinner. "At one of those places we couldn't go to before," he had added with a wink.

Raven often wondered what he would think if he knew the effect he had on her in those light, teasing moments. Sometimes she had to turn away, lest she start to tremble at his nearness.

A knock on the door tore her from reverie. She hurried to answer. Then, blinking at the stranger standing there, she whispered uncertainly, "Steve?"

He was wearing a new outfit—a blue silk shirt with a string tie, navy blue coat, matching trousers, and a new felt hat, which he removed in a sweeping gesture. "I'm afraid so. I should apologize for letting all the trail dust cake up and make me look like a field hand."

"No, no. You always looked fine, really." She fell silent, embarrassed to be so ill at ease, but he was more handsome than ever, and the warm ripple quickly became a hot wave that rolled from her head to her toes. "You didn't have to go to so much trouble."

"Of course I did, because I wanted to take you out for a nice evening." He held out his arm to her. "Ready?"

Hoping her hand would not start shaking, she slipped it in the crook of his arm and nodded past the nervous lump in her throat.

All eyes were upon them as they entered the hotel dining room, and Raven tensed. "I knew it. They can tell I'm a half-breed and they don't want me here."

"Will you stop it?" With his free hand, he squeezed her fingers that were digging into his arm. "You don't look Indian at all. French Creole, maybe. But that's not why they're staring."

"Then why?" She found it terribly unnerving. Most of the men had a smile on their lips, while the women seemed almost hostile. "Do they think I'm your *quadroon*?"

"A quadroon isn't a thing," he corrected her, amused. "It's a woman who's one-fourth Negro, remember? And it's nothing to be ashamed of, at least not in my opinion. As for these folks, the men think you're ravishing, and the women are justifiably jealous."

A waiter in a white coat and black trousers showed them to a linen-covered table. A bowl of fragrant gardenias was in the center.

Raven was still unnerved by all the attention, but gradually that faded. Then her unease came from being faced with having to get through the meal without making a fool of herself. There was a bewildering number of glasses and dishes and silverware on the table, and she did not know what any of them were for. All she had ever needed in the past was a plate, a spoon, and a mug. She knew nothing of glasses with long stems and eating utensils of different sizes and types. She would have to watch Steve and imitate him.

As they ate they made small talk about the city. He told her that Mobile was outranked as a cotton port only by New Orleans, Savannah, and Charleston. She pretended not to care when he bragged about her father and how he owned a regular line of packets, ships of the first class, to run monthly back and forth to New York. She felt like telling him that the fact her father was rich and successful made him no less a liar and scoundrel in her eyes.

When they were served dessert—a chocolate and cream concoction that made Raven's mouth water just to look at it—Steve asked bluntly, "Well, so far how do you like what could be your new life?"

Snappily, she informed him, "It's not going to be my new life. Quite frankly, I can't help thinking how my mother might have liked living here, had my father kept his promises."

"Do you really think she would have adjusted? Remember, while you've grown up in a white man's world, she was raised Indian."

"My mother was a very intelligent woman. She could have adjusted to anything. If my father thought otherwise, it's because he wanted to."

Steve had not wanted the conversation to go this way, but since she had brought up the subject, he dared ask, "But didn't she love the man she married at all? From what little I've heard about Seth Greer, it appears he was good to her."

"He was. He was also good to me. But goodness doesn't always make up for love, and my mother just loved my father so much she was never able to put him out of her mind. She died calling his name," she added, made bitter by the memory. "I'm just glad Seth wasn't there to hear it. It would have hurt him deeply, because even though he had to know my mother still loved my father, he didn't deserve to hear her confirm it with her dying breath."

"I guess not. But your father did have reasons for what he did, and he'll tell you what they were."

"I'll hear him out, but that's all. Then I'm leaving."

Steve pushed the chocolate concoction away and reached for the after-dinner brandy the waiter had just brought. Thinking of Raven and Ned's first meeting made him need a drink.

He hoped it would go well. He could understand Raven's resentment, but for Ned's sake he hoped she would not be too rough on him. "You know he wants you to have almost everything he's got. The least you could do is think about it instead of cutting off your nose to spite your face, as the saying goes."

Raven also pushed the dessert away. It was no longer appealing. Nothing was—except getting the meeting over with and leaving afterward. "Hating him as I do includes hating his money and everything he owns. I only came because you made me, remember?"

Steve set his jaw as ire rose. "What Ned did in the past doesn't matter. Maybe he shouldn't have made promises to your mother that he didn't keep, but that's over and done with and he can't undo any of it. All he wants now is to try and make things right with you before he dies. If you want to turn your back on him and walk out on everything he's offering, that's your loss. But I'm not going to let you hurt him, understand? For whatever time he's got left in this world, you're going to leave him in peace. Keep your mouth shut and let him tell you how sorry he is. Let him tell you he loves you. And when he dies, you can go, but while you're here, swallow your bitterness and hatred, understand?"

"I told you I have no intention of staying. He could live for months."

"He won't, but you aren't leaving while he's alive, because he doesn't deserve to have you walk out on him in his final days."

She jutted her chin stubbornly. "I'll run away."

His smile was almost sinister. "No, you won't."

"And what makes you think so?"

His tone softened. "Because I know Ned and I think I know you, and you're not as tough as you want people to think you are. Frankly, after you meet him, I don't think you'll be able to keep on hating him."

"You're real sure of yourself, aren't you?"

Steve didn't answer. He was not sure of anything anymore, except that he wanted Ned to have a peaceful death, if possible. That, and the fact that he needed to get away from Raven before he yielded to temptation and found himself embroiled in a situation it might be difficult to get out of. Something told him that if he ever made love to her, he would not be able to walk away. He needed to get her off his mind, stop thinking about how good it had felt to kiss her, how nice the feel of her body was against his, and the way to do that was to pay a visit to the waterfront. He knew lots of women there who could easily distract him.

"Are you finished?" he asked, an annoyed edge to his voice as he got to his feet.

Raven also stood. "Yes. I'm tired, and I'd like to go

to bed. I'll find my own way to my room, thank you."
And with a swish of her skirts, she breezed out, this
time oblivious to the stares.

She hurried across the lobby and up the stairs to
her room, slamming and locking the door, her heart
pounding fast, but not from exertion. It was Steve's
changing his mind about letting her go that agitated
her. It wasn't fair. But at least he did not suspect he
was actually the reason she wanted to get away as
quickly as possible. And she could not let him know
that, could not let him even suspect how he made
her feel.

A sound at the door made her jump, startled, and
she whirled about in a mixture of fear and anticipation. If it were Steve, it meant he had a key to her
room, which would then mean that his behavior at
dinner had all been an act and he was now coming
to   what? If he'd had any untoward intentions, they
would have surfaced on the trail, out in the wilderness. Certainly not here, where she could scream and
be heard. No, it was not Steve fumbling with a key in
the door. It was someone else, someone who meant
her harm.

Glancing about for a weapon, she wished she had
fired up one of the lanterns, but then her eyes fell on
the water pitcher. Snatching it up, she held it high,
ready to send it crashing down on the head of whoever dared walk through that door.

"Are you having trouble, Nonnie?"

Raven heard a man's voice, followed by a woman's
response. "I'm afraid so. The manager keeps promising me a new passkey, but he never seems to get
around to it. This one just doesn't like to fit in certain
doors—like this one."

"Here. Let me."

There was a click, and the door swung open.

At the sight of the young woman in a white uniform and blue apron, Raven quickly lowered the pitcher.

"Oh, goodness!" The maid gasped to see Raven standing there. "I'm sorry. I forgot to knock. I thought you were still out for the evening. I'll come back later."

She turned, but Raven said, "No, it's all right. Come in, please. But the room is clean. I haven't mussed it at all."

"I was just going to turn down the bed. My name is Nonnie. If there is anything I can do for you, just let me know. And I'd appreciate it," she added hopefully, "if you won't tell on me for bursting in like I did. It could cost me my job, and this hotel is the nicest in Mobile. In fact, it's probably the only one that hires maids. The rest only have cleaning stewards, and that doesn't pay as much."

"Of course I won't say anything." Raven was just glad the girl had not seen her standing behind the door ready to bring the water pitcher crashing down on her head.

Nonnie went to the bed and carefully pulled the spread back. "You're pretty." She smiled over her shoulder. "Where are you from?"

"Texas. And thank you," she added self-consciously. No one had ever told her she was pretty before except Steve. Her mother had been a no-nonsense kind of woman who had no time for such things as being concerned with how someone looked. Seth had been the same way.

The maid regarded her curiously. "Are you staying all by yourself? Surely not. You must be married."

"No, but there is someone traveling with me, and we aren't married, so he has a room of his own."

"Oh, I see." She nodded approval.

Raven did not want to continue talking about herself, so she pointed to the bed. "That is really a beautiful tepee, isn't it? I've never seen one like that before, made out of material instead of skin, and certainly not above a bed, but I guess you don't need tepee walls in a room," she added, with a nervous little giggle.

At first Nonnie thought the guest was just trying to be funny, but by the expression on her face she could tell she was serious. Looking at her warily, she said, "That isn't a tepee, ma'am. It's called a canopy, and I can't imagine one being made of anything except fabric." Her eyes narrowed. "Where did you say you're from?"

Raven turned away, embarrassed. "Texas," she mumbled. "We . . . we don't have beds like that out there." She went to the window, keeping her back turned. She did not want to talk anymore, afraid she'd make an even bigger fool of herself.

Nonnie decided she was just a country girl come to town, and that was nothing to be ashamed of. She was straight out of the fields herself and grateful for a better job. "Well, I've heard Texas is rather uncivilized, so I'm not surprised they don't have canopies. This one isn't as nice as the ones in some of the other rooms. They've got netting to keep away mosquitoes."

Raven didn't care about mosquitoes or canopies or anything else. All she wanted was to leave, and as she stared down at the busy street below, she wondered how far she could get before Steve discovered she was gone and trailed after her.

"Anything going on down there?" Nonnie asked as

she plumped the pillows. "It's usually quiet this time of night. Most of the noise is down at the waterfront."

"All I see are men, and they all seem to be walking in the same direction." Raven thought that was odd. "They all seem to be in good spirits, too."

Nonnie gave a scornful sniff. "You can bet they are. They're going to buy whiskey and women, both plentiful at the wharves. Makes me sick, it does, how a whore can sell her body to a man. They don't care if a man is married or not. All they're interested in is the money."

Raven made no comment. It was not a topic she was interested in discussing. She knew about bawdy houses, because the soldiers, thinking she was a boy, had had no reason to watch what they said around her. When they did start talking about women and sex, she had taken her leave as quickly and discreetly as possible, but sometimes not quickly enough, and the descriptions became pretty explicit. She had learned more than she wanted to.

Nonnie went on. "I tell you one thing, miss, when I get married, I'll keep my man satisfied so he won't have no call to go looking for another woman, no matter what it takes. I know some women would just as soon their man take a whore and leave them alone, but not me. I'll keep my husband's bed warm, to be sure. Say, it's getting dark in here. Should I fire up a lantern?"

Raven declined and was relieved when the maid finally left, even though she was lonely, for it was the first night in weeks that Steve had not been near. It was an experience she'd never had before, having a man so close by, and she could not deny she had enjoyed it.

As her thoughts drifted while the shadows of night crept into the room, she was struck to think maybe the women in the restaurant had not been jealous of her looks at all, but envious because she was with Steve. He had looked so handsome—clean-shaven, hair neatly trimmed, clothes neat and well-fitting. What woman would not be proud to be at his side? And she even more so, for she knew of his rugged, almost feral side, which was exciting in a different way. She knew the smell of him, the feel of him, and her skin prickled deliciously to remember the intimate moments they had shared.

She crossed her arms over her chest, as though to steel herself against regret for how the evening might have ended had tension not sprung between them. Would they have gone for a walk, dappled by moonlight filtering through the moss-draped trees? Would they have maybe even held hands? No one had ever held her hand. Raven could almost feel the warm strength of his fingers laced through hers. And if she allowed herself to, she could yet taste his lips.

"Stop it," she commanded herself aloud. This was foolish. This was insane. She was tormenting herself for nothing. The kiss had been a mockery. He had seen through her ploy, knew she was teasing him into wanting her, and laughed in her face. Instead of shivering deliciously to remember, she should be quaking with fury that he could be so callous. Not that she condoned her own behavior, far from it. She had felt common, debased, to flaunt herself as she had. But her way of punishing him had turned against her, and now she was paying the price by feeling absolutely terrible about it all.

She started to turn away from the window but then

looked again. It couldn't be, could it? But it was! She clutched the lace curtains in her hands and stared down at Steve as he walked along so eagerly. He was whistling, smiling, and she bit down on her lower lip to realize he was on his way, like the other men, to buy his evening's pleasure.

Don't you dare cry, she commanded herself. Don't you dare cry, and don't you dare care. She had no right. It was none of her concern. She meant nothing to him and never would, and now she knew that, even if they hadn't wound up sparring with other, he had never intended to spend the evening with her. He'd had it in his mind all along to go to a whore.

"Walk in the moonlight indeed!" she cried furiously, picking up a pillow and slamming it back down on the bed, only to fall on top and burrow her face in it. What she should do was yank off her fine clothes, pull out the scout uniform, and go to the stable, get Diablo, and ride out of here this very night. But she knew she would not do that. She had come too far and was too curious about her father to leave now.

But she would go, she promised herself, blinking back frustrated tears, just as soon as possible, and to hell with Steve Maddox. Somehow, she would make herself forget him.

But, as always, when sleep took her away, Raven was betrayed by her own dreams, and once more she was helplessly in Steve's embrace, yielding to his hot, sweet kiss.

Hedda Bowers told herself she might be a whore but she had her pride. "I'm not taking your money," she said.

Steve looked at her, bemused. They were upstairs over Pegleg Jack's Tavern, where Hedda had a room like the other prostitutes who worked for Pegleg, giving him a cut of their night's take. The room was not much, but it was adequate, with a double bed and a chest where he supposed Hedda kept her things. He was leaning back against the pillows, a glass in one hand, an almost empty bottle of rye whiskey in the other. Hedda was an old friend, easy to talk to, and the time had slipped by without his realizing it.

"Do you know how long we've been up here? Nearly an hour. And all you want to do is sip that liquor and talk. You ain't interested in a tumble in the hay, Steve Maddox, so I got to get back downstairs and get me a customer. Pegleg is going to raise hell with me for being up here so long anyway. He don't like his girls to take more than half an hour on a busy night like tonight.

"But like I said," she added, moving from where she had been sitting next to him, "I ain't taking your money. Now you gotta go, unless"—she looked at him slyly, lashes lowered provocatively—"you've got a yen after all."

He didn't. He knew now he never had. He'd only wanted companionship, and Hedda had provided it. The fact was, though he'd never admit it, he just didn't want any woman right then except Raven, and he was wasting his time pretending.

He watched as Hedda immodestly stripped in front of him. She had put on a red satin robe, trimmed in white feathers, but peeled out of it to change into a fetching purple gown to wear downstairs in hopes of enticing a paying customer. She had a good body: full, rounded breasts, narrow waist, and cushy, wide hips. He always enjoyed her—but not this night.

When she was dressed, she tousled his hair and said, "You come back when you're in the mood, you hear? I hate to rush you, but if I'm lucky, I'll need this room in about ten minutes." She gave him a quick kiss and left.

Steve did not tarry. Hedda would have no problems finding someone else. He was still dressed. All he had to do was pick up his hat and walk out.

He paused, peeled a few bills from his wallet, and tossed them on the bedside table. After all, it wasn't Hedda's fault that for the time being the only desire he could feel was for Raven.

11

Raven was waiting in the hotel lobby when Steve came downstairs the next morning. She stood with her head held high, ignoring the admiring glances of people around her. She was stunning in her new travel outfit, and he said as much in greeting, but she ignored him. Fine, he thought resolutely. Let her pout. A few more hours and she'd be Ned's responsibility—if Ned were still alive. If not, he would turn her over to Ned's lawyer and let him deal with her.

He could tell she was trying hard to pretend she didn't care about anything, but when he helped her into the fine carriage he had hired for the remainder of the trip, he noticed how she ran her fingers over the plush velvet seats, the way her eyes took in the team of fine white horses with their bright red harnesses. Then, after glancing about to make sure Diablo was secured to the rear of the carriage, she settled back with an exaggerated sigh, as though bored with it all.

Steve bit back a smile at her pretense, knowing she must have lived a hand-to-mouth existence all her life. Seth Greer's wages, either as an Indian agent or as the manager of a government trading post, had doubtless been just enough to survive on. Whatever money Ned had sent would have gone for bare essentials, with nothing left over for luxuries. And while any other girl would probably be drooling over the opportunity that awaited, Raven was so stubborn she'd sooner die than take advantage of it.

Nothing would have suited him better than to ignore her all the way to Halcyon, but thinking how she was about to meet Lisbeth and Julius, he felt sorry for her and decided to prepare her a little, at least. "Remember I told you Ned's wife had two children when they married."

She shrugged, as though it made no difference.

"Maybe you'd like to know something about them."

"I won't be around long enough to care."

"You might. Seeing you could give Ned a new lease on life. Maybe he'll live two or three years, who knows?" Steve had no idea that would happen, but he wanted to give her something to think about.

She looked at him sharply. "You can't make me stay that long. Nobody can."

"Don't worry. If you're as bratty to him as you are to me, he'll probably run you off by sundown."

"Good." She folded her arms across her chest and lifted her chin just a wee bit higher. "Then everyone will be happy."

"Lisbeth and Julius are spoiled, used to having their own way and hard to get along with under the best of circumstances. They'll probably both fly through the roof when they find out about you, because they planned on inheriting everything Ned's got. I want you to let me know if they give you any trouble. I'll do what I can to smooth things over, but don't let Ned know if they do. He doesn't need the worry."

"There won't be any. They'll soon learn I have no intention of taking anything from them." She closed her eyes and wished she could just fall asleep. Being with Steve was, as always, upsetting, especially when all she could think of was how the night before he had kissed someone as he had kissed her, had held another woman in his arms. . . .

Shaking her head to dispel the image, she tried to focus on the countryside, but it was just more of what she had already seen since they had reached the low country of the deep South. The land was flat, with moss-draped trees clustered in dark, swampy marshes. Now and then she had a glimpse of the lazy, muddy river, ever so often a ramshackle hut. There were no fields of green, and finally she remarked with a touch of scorn, "You talked about Halcyon as if it was paradise. All I see is swamp. How much farther till we reach my father's land?"

"You're on it."

She sat up straight to stare at him in disbelief.

"You have been for the past half hour."

"But—" She glanced about wildly. They were on a narrow road, hardly wider than a cow path, and marshes loomed dismally on both sides. "This is a wilderness."

He chuckled. "That's all any of it was before Ned's grandfather cleared some fields. His father cleared even more. Evidently Ned was satisfied and didn't extend the farmland any farther. That's something *you* can do, if you like."

Just then, they rounded a bend, and any response Raven might have been about to make was swallowed in her awed gasp at the seemingly endless landscape that came into view. Everywhere, as far as the eye could see in any direction, the earth was covered in a blanket of green. White, fluffy balls dotted one side, while, on the other, golden silks danced in the wind atop stalks stretching skyward.

"Cotton and corn," Steve confirmed. "The fields go on for several miles."

"But where is the house?"

He pointed to the river, barely visibly beyond the cornstalks. "The land follows the river. The house is two bends away. Ned said it took over a year to build it, because his grandfather was afraid that the flatlands would flood. So he dug lagoons in from the river and used the dirt to build a big hillock. It was a lot of work, but the spring floods have never been a threat to the house."

Raven noticed how so many of the workers paused to wave as they passed, apparently glad to see Steve was back. He called a few by name. She also saw how they stared at her. "I guess they don't know who I am. Didn't anyone know you were going to look for me?"

"Only Ned. He wouldn't have told anyone."

"I guess not. He'd be too ashamed." She could not resist the barb.

"Oh, that wouldn't have anything to do with it. He doesn't have to apologize to anyone for anything. He just wouldn't figure it was any of their business."

They rounded another bend in the road, and Raven saw different crops. She could identify tobacco plants, because some Indian tribes grew tobacco, but she was unfamiliar with the shorter leaves in another field.

"Collards. Cabbage. Lettuce," Steve told her. "It takes a lot of vegetables for so many slaves, because Ned makes sure they're well fed. Over there"—he pointed—"beyond those trees, are the hog pens. Then there are pens for chickens and cows, and also a small dairy. You can't see the buildings from here, but there are all kinds of artisans at work—craftsmen for bricks, pottery, weaving; leather workers for saddles and bridles and shoes; even a greenhouse, because Ned likes to have fresh flowers in the house year-round. There's also a small winery.

"Anything anyone could want is right here," he finished in admiration. "Halcyon is a town in its own right."

Raven could not help but be impressed. "And my father runs all of it?"

He laughed, not in ridicule but only at the idea that any one person could physically oversee such an operation. "Hardly. Like his grandfather and his father before him, Ned insists on competent overseers. There are parts of this place he probably hasn't visited in years. There's no need. He knows the men in charge are doing a good job, because they report once a week and give him a full report."

"But if he's sick—"

"Julius should be looking after things now," Steve said, "but I'm sure he hasn't lifted a finger. Thank goodness, most of the overseers can be trusted to carry on."

"Where are the horses you talked about?"

"Closer to the house. They're the only thing Ned

sees to himself. He won't let the stable hands do a thing except clean the barns and feed them, under his direction or mine. I do all the training. That's another reason I was anxious to get back. Ned's not strong enough to look after the horses by himself."

Raven was so engrossed in seeing everything that she did not hear anyone shouting to Steve. It was only when he abruptly pulled back on the horses' reins and leaped down from the carriage that she saw a woman waving as she came out of yet another cotton field. She was white, while the other workers were all black, and although her face was smeared with streaks of sweat and dirt, Raven could tell she was pretty. Her hair was hidden beneath a bright-colored bandanna, and even though her dress was loose, it was quite obvious she was going to have a baby.

Selena Leroux threw her arms around Steve. "Thank God, you're back! I've missed you so."

Raven noticed Steve didn't seem to mind how filthy the girl was from scrambling in the dirt to pick cotton to stuff in the big burlap bag that she had dropped to run to greet him.

He hugged her, then held her at arm's length. "You shouldn't be working in the fields, Selena. It looks like you're getting close to your time."

She laughed and patted her round tummy proudly. "Oh, I've got a little while to go yet, and you know Poppa. Everybody at our house works, no matter what."

"But there's easier work you could be doing." He took her hands and turned them palm up. Raven winced to see the bloody blisters.

Selena drew back self-consciously. "They haven't toughened yet. It takes awhile after picking starts."

"You need to wrap those blisters before they get infected."

"Enough about me." Framing her eyes against the sun, she looked beyond him to Raven. "Who's that you've got with you? Is she the reason you ran off without telling anybody?"

"I'll explain everything later. Right now I want to know about Ned. Is he still alive?"

"Barely, from what the house servants say. The doctor visits every day now; I see his carriage coming and going. Who is she?" She continued to stare at Raven.

Steve put his hands on her shoulders and kissed her on her forehead. "I'll come see you tonight. And when you talk to your pa, tell him I said to let you work indoors from now on."

She snorted. "And he'll tell me to go to hell in a wheelbarrow—if he doesn't give me a beating first." With another curious look at Raven, she walked away.

As soon as Steve got back in the carriage, he asked, "Did you hear? Your father is still alive, so we made it back in time after all."

She did not want to talk about her father. "Who was that?"

"Selena Leroux. She's a friend of mine."

"Why is she working in the fields when she's white? The only other whites I've seen are those on horseback, and you said they were overseers."

"Selena's father is one of the overseers, and he wants all his children to work. There's nothing wrong with that, but she shouldn't be picking cotton in her condition. Ned doesn't even allow the Negro women in the fields when they're expecting babies."

"Then why does her father insist on it? Doesn't her husband have a say?"

"She's not married."

"But—" Raven fell silent. She had been about to ask why Selena was not married when she was pregnant, then decided not to. After all, like everything else on the vast plantation, it was none of her concern. She was merely passing through.

They were almost to the next bend when Steve again yanked back on the reins, this time so sharply that Raven pitched forward and gave a little cry of surprise. But he didn't notice as he dropped to the ground and started walking swiftly toward a man on horseback on the other side of the split rail fence. The man had seen them approaching but, unlike the others they had passed, had turned his back and did not wave. Raven had thought that odd, and now, watching the scene unfold, saw that Steve was angry, and the man was obviously trying to ignore him.

"Masson Leroux, I want to talk to you."

Leroux. Raven strained to hear. He had to be Selena's father.

Masson gave his horse a nudge. "I don't have time."

Steve reached out and yanked him from the saddle to the ground. "Take time."

"Hey, you got no call to do that." Masson scrambled to his feet, fists doubled, face twisted with rage, but made no move to fight. "You coulda hurt me, slamming me down like that."

"And Selena and her baby can be hurt by you making her work in the hot sun every day. You know how Ned feels about pregnant women working the fields."

His mouth twisted in scorn. "Them women aren't

having their babies in shame and disgrace. They got husbands. They aren't whores. Nobody cares about whores."

"Selena is no whore, and you know it. She made a mistake, that's all. You've no right to punish her this way."

Masson retreated a few steps, knowing he was treading on dangerous ground but too mad to care. "If you're so concerned about Selena, why don't you marry her and give her bastard a name?"

Neither heard Raven's soft gasp.

"Don't think I'm not tempted, if only to get her away you. If I see her in those fields again, you'll answer to me, you got that?"

Masson forced a sneer of bravado. What he wanted to do was knock Steve on his butt, but he was not about to risk getting whipped in front of all the workers who had stopped to watch. Instead, he spoke loud enough for them to hear. "I take orders from Mr. Ralston, not you. He hasn't give a damn about nothing but those fancy horses of his for the past four years, and we both know it. The last thing he'd care about right now is me making my pregnant slut of a daughter work for her keep, and if you don't like it, you tell him and then let him tell me. Have *you* got *that?*" He glanced to the workers for their murmurs of agreement. They knew if they showed any signs of loyalty to Maddox, they'd feel Masson's whip on their bare backs as soon as the carriage was out of sight.

Steve's hands snaked out to grab him by his throat and lift him up until he was dancing on his toes and clawing at Steve's squeezing fingers, eyes bulging. "Don't let me see or hear of Selena's being in the fields anymore. I won't warn you again."

He released him with a shove that sent him sprawling to the ground once more, then turned and went back to the carriage.

He got in, said nothing, and popped the reins. They rolled along in silence for a few moments, and then Raven bluntly asked, "Well, why *don't* you marry her?"

Steve glanced at her, unsure he had heard her right. "What did you say?"

Telling herself she was a fool to ache because another woman was carrying his child, she said, "I asked why don't you marry her? Her father asked you the same question."

"Because it's not my baby."

He said it so simply that Raven found herself believing him and hoped he could not see how relieved she was. "Then why did he say that?"

"It's his way of telling me that if I want to look out for her I should marry her; otherwise, to keep my mouth shut and stay out of his family's business. But she's my friend. . . . I do try to look out for my friends, but that doesn't mean I have to marry them," he added with a laugh.

"Why aren't you married?" She cursed herself the moment she asked. Now he was looking at her with a twinkle in his eye, and dear God, she didn't care about his personal life at all—did she?

He thought about it a moment. "I could lie and say I've never met the right woman, but the truth is, I've met lots of women who would have made good wives. The fact is, I don't want to be married. I like my freedom. I suppose"—he nodded toward the pasture they were approaching, where Ned's beloved racking horses were grazing—"I'm like a stallion running free that's never been caught or broke. I've still got my spirit. I want to keep it."

"And you believe marriage takes a man's spirit?"

"Absolutely. A woman breaks a man just like a horse and works him to death. If he's obedient to her every command, she rewards him with a pat on the head once in a while. If he resists, she makes him wish he'd never been born. No, thanks. I'll keep my spirit—*and* my freedom. What about you?"

Intent on absorbing all he'd just said, his question took her by surprise. "Me? I've never thought about it."

"Seems to me it would have been a whole lot easier to find yourself a husband to take care of you than pretend to be a boy."

Raven bristled. "I don't need a man to take care of me. I feel the same as you. I'm not willing to give up my spirit, either, and that's what a man expects of his—"

She broke off as they rounded the last bend in the road and Halcyon, in all its stunning glory, came into view.

Wanting her to be impressed, Steve described the true marvel of what she was seeing. "The house is unlike any other in the state. It sits on a brick foundation, and those arches are over twelve feet high. Like the walls, they were plastered and carved by the most expert European craftsmen money could buy. The brick steps are covered with imported marble, and the doorknobs and keyhole guards are made of silver.

"Those columns," he continued, "are called Corinthian in style, and those fancy scroll designs you see all the way to the top are called capitals. There are no windows on the first floor, only narrow doors made of small panes of glass so they can stand open in the warm months and allow the river breeze to flow through the house. There are forty rooms, and those not used for anything else store all the furniture, paintings, tapestries, and other things that Ned's grandfather imported from Europe but never got around to unpacking."

"It . . . it's three times bigger than the hotel where we stayed last night," she stammered in wonder.

"There's an L-shaped wing out back. The kitchen is on its first floor, the house servants live on the second. The only improvement Ned made to the house itself was to the basement. He was trying to do something about sanitary facilities, so he had a large stone basin to hold water built on the second floor, with a small furnace beneath. Copper pipes run hot water from the basin into the bedrooms when the servants light the furnace. Real nice for shaving." He grinned and rubbed the stubble on his chin.

"So you live there too," she said quietly.

He dared to wonder if she hoped he did. "No. I live above one of the stables. You can see it on the other side of the pecan grove." He pointed.

She told herself to be relieved they would not be under the same roof and changed the subject. "There are so many pretty flowers everywhere."

"Ned loves them. Those vines you see on the upstairs railing are wisteria, but it's the gardens he prizes. There are all kinds of roses and other flowers I can't name, but he can tell you each and every one. There's a grotto with a pagoda and bells, and exotic birds like peacocks. The lagoons are stocked with fish and swans and pelicans, and there's a fenced area for deer and rabbit that are so tame you can pet them. Then there's an area for hunting several miles from here."

Raven thought it all lovely, but it only served to feed her resentment over how her mother might have enjoyed such grandeur.

Her stomach gave a hungry rumble. She hadn't eaten all day, declining breakfast to keep from being around Steve anymore than she had to. "Do you think we could postpone my meeting my father till after I've had lunch?"

He thought she was just stalling, which annoyed him a bit. "That's up to you," he said coolly. "I'll just introduce you to Julius and Lisbeth. They can see you're fed and then take you up to him."

She did not like that idea at all and quickly changed her mind. "Maybe I can wait to eat . . . if you'll stay with me," she added hopefully.

He realized then she was just nervous, which was understandable, and he softened. "I'll be glad to, but then I've got things to do, so you'll be on your own. And besides, you've taken up enough of my time."

But Raven was not about to be bested. "Well, it's nice to know you won't be watching me like a hawk anymore, and I can just jump on Diablo and ride out of here any time I want."

"No, you can't," he said matter-of-factly. "Remember? All I've got to do is whistle."

12

Julius and Lisbeth were having lunch on the glass porch, one of their favorite places in the entire mansion. It had been their mother's idea to enclose the veranda outside the formal dining room, where there was a nice view of the river and the gardens. They could also see a portion of the drive, lined with great live oaks, and the lawn, with its checkerboard design that had been achieved by planting different kinds of grass.

The furniture was white-painted wicker with peach and blue floral cushions and a glass-topped table. Baskets of lush ferns and fragrant flowers were abundant, making the atmosphere appear cool, even on a stifling day.

Noting how cheerful Lisbeth seemed, Julius asked, "Do you have a secret I don't know about? Has Barley Tremayne finally proposed?"

"No, but he will," she replied airily. "Actually, I'm

happy because Steve's been gone so long, which means any day now he'll be back to tell to Ned he couldn't find that girl."

"I told you there was nothing to worry about." He patted her hand.

Mariah walked in, carrying bowls of fresh peaches for their dessert. She had not only been their mammy when they were babies but had actually run the household ever since Ned had married their mother, for Edith had cared nothing about such responsibilities. She'd left them to Mariah so she could spend all her time socializing instead.

Hearing Julius, Mariah asked, "Who's worried? Is there something going on I don't know about?"

Julius laughed. "Impossible. You know everything."

"I know it might be nice to invite Mr. Barley for Sunday dinner," she said, patting Lisbeth's shoulder as she set down her bowl of peaches. "That young man does love my fried chicken."

"Who doesn't?" Lisbeth smiled at her. "That's a lovely idea."

Mariah looked to Julius. "Are you sure there isn't a special lady friend you'd care to invite?" She was anxious to see them both married and raising a family, so the mansion would come alive with the laughter of children.

"No, Mariah, I'm afraid the dining room isn't big enough to hold them all," he teased. "So it will just be the three of us, since Ned doesn't come downstairs anymore."

"That's true, that's true," Mariah said with a sympathetic shake of her head. "He's just wastin' away. It's like he's gone to bed to die. If only Mr.

Steve would come back, that might cheer him up, but don't nobody know where he's gone, and if Master Ned knows he ain't saying."

Julius exchanged a knowing glance with Lisbeth. "Well, it doesn't matter. We'll enjoy your chicken. Maybe you'd better tell that boy of yours to wring an extra neck."

Mariah had gone to the serving cart where she had left a bowl of cream for the peaches. Now, looking toward the road, she let out a whoop of joy. "One extra chicken won't be enough. I'm gonna tell him to wring three necks, maybe four!"

Julius laughed. "Barley doesn't eat *that* much."

"But Mr. Steve does. And as long as he's been gone, he's bound to be starved for my cooking."

Lisbeth and Julius looked at each other, not understanding, and when she turned and ran for the door, Julius called after her, "What's got into you, Mariah?"

She kept on going. "It's Mr. Steve. He's coming up the road."

They started to get up at the same time, collided, and fell back in their chairs. They tried again, only to have the same thing happen. Then, hearing Mariah's last words they slumped back and paled.

"Looks like he's got somebody with him too, a young lady. I'll just bet that boy's finally done gone and found himself a wife."

"Sit," Julius commanded Lisbeth brusquely, holding her as she started to rise. "We can't go rushing out there like maniacs. We have to calm down and think about this."

"Think about *what?*" She stared at him in horror. "If he's got a woman with him, she's not his wife, and we both know it. He's found her, that's what he's done. He's found Ned's bastard!"

"Maybe. Maybe not."

"But—"

"Let me think, please."

"There's nothing to think about. Don't you see? She's *here.*" She grabbed his arm. "And we've got to do something fast!"

"Well, I'm afraid the only thing we can do for the moment is walk out there and act properly surprised when we're introduced to our stepsister and try to be polite till we figure out what we're going to do about it."

A horrible thought struck. "She's an imposter. She has to be. When he couldn't find Ned's real daughter, he got someone to pretend to be her. Then, when Ned dies, she'll divide everything with Steve. It's a scheme, don't you see? They'll kick us out and have everything. We've got to stop him."

"Steve is too smart to try something like that. Ned will ask questions only his daughter could answer."

"What if it *is* her? What if Steve persuades her to marry him, so *he'll* be the one to inherit everything? I wouldn't put it past him."

"We'll talk about it later. There's no time now. Let's go. Remember what I said and don't make a scene."

Doggedly, she knew she had no choice but to follow after him.

Raven was sitting ramrod straight, clenching her teeth and praying her clasped hands would not start shaking as she and Steve drew ever closer to the

grandest house she had ever seen. The father she had
loathed and resented as long as she could remember
was in that house, she thought with a flash of panic.
She was about to meet him face-to-face, and though
she'd had weeks to prepare for it, she was not ready.
What could she say? What *was* there to say? That she
hated him? That she didn't care if he lived or died
and wanted nothing from him and never had? Could
she be that vindictive? She had always thought so but
was now uncertain.

Steve slowed the horses to a walk, and Raven
looked at him quizzically. He cleared his throat,
pushed his hat back from his forehead, looked at her
long, hard, and searchingly, and finally said, "It
won't hurt you to be easy on him, Raven. Hate can be
like a poison, eating away at you inside. You'll feel a
lot better later on if you let him make peace now."

"But you're going to make me stay till he dies.
Maybe I could pretend for a day or two, but—"

"Look, I'm surprised he's lasted this long, and I'm
sure the only reason is because he's been clinging to
the hope that I'd be able to find you. It means everything to him."

"But he's going to think the only reason I came was
because you told me about my inheritance."

"So what if he does? Ned is no fool. He's got sense
enough to know you wouldn't exactly be jumping
with joy at the idea of meeting him after the way
things happened."

Bitterness stirred in her. "He just wants me to make
him feel good. That's why he sent money all those
years, to ease his conscience, like my mother said."

"Damn it, Raven, you have got to be the most
stubborn filly I have ever run across in my entire life.

You don't know that's why he did it. Maybe he felt a genuine responsibility for both you and your mother. Oh, to hell with it"—he popped the reins to start the carriage rolling—"I just hope you've got enough decency not to beat a dead horse."

"What's that supposed to mean?"

"It means it's pointless for you to condemn him for something he's probably already suffered for more than you and I will ever know. But if that's what you want to do, I can't stop you. And I suppose if you really make him miserable, I'll be glad to let you ride out. But for the time you're here," he added hesitantly, as though uncomfortable with the words, "I want you to know I'll be around should you need me."

"That's . . . nice," she managed to say around the sudden lump in her throat.

"And there's something else."

She dared not ask him what it was.

"What happened between us on the trail. . . ."

"Yes?" she prodded, burning to know what was on his mind.

"No hard feelings." He flashed a broad grin. "We'll forget about it, all right?" Lord, he thought, heat rising within, he hoped she didn't notice how his voice shook a little and how he was trying his best to cover up what he was really feeling. But something had to be said. They had experienced a lot of crazy emotions along the way, some of which would doubtless nag him for a long time . . . maybe forever. He had never met anybody like her before and knew, somehow, he never would again.

Raven managed to say she agreed, careful to keep her face turned away. When they'd first met, she had refrained from looking at him lest he see something to make him suspect she might not be a boy after all. Now she could only pray he would not see she was more of a woman than she'd ever been, and he alone was the reason why.

"Those people standing on the porch," she said nervously. "Who are they?"

"That's Julius and Lisbeth, and the Negro woman is Mariah. She's been their mammy since they were born. She's also the housekeeper."

"Mammy?" Raven was confused. "You mean like a mother?"

"Sort of. She took care of them, wet-nursed them. Don't Indian women nurse each other's babies?"

"Only if the baby's mother dies, or has no milk. Was that why she nursed them?"

Steve hesitated. Raven was naive about so many things, and while sometimes he found it refreshing, she could also make him feel damned uncomfortable. Like now, when she was waiting for him to explain about mammies. Since this was all a new world to her, a new culture, he figured she had a right to have her questions answered, albeit on a delicate subject. "Well, the truth is, some women would rather not nurse their babies themselves. So if they're wealthy enough to have slaves, they get one who has a nursing baby of her own to feed theirs, too."

"But why?" Raven persisted.

"Different reasons. They're too busy, some of them. Others, I've heard, fear it will ruin their, uh"—again he faltered—"shape. And they don't want to be disturbed during the night. Things like that. So they let slave women do it for them."

Raven was amazed. "I think that's terrible. I can't

imagine an Indian woman handing over her baby to another woman to feed just because she's busy or worried about her shape." She made a face. "I'll probably never get married and have babies, but if I did, I'd never let anyone else nurse my baby unless it was absolutely necessary."

With a surreptitious glance at her ample bosom, Steve secretly doubted she'd have a problem. "Well, it might be best if you keep your opinions about such things to yourself."

"It doesn't matter anyway," she retorted grumpily. "I won't be here long enough for it to matter what I think."

Mariah could wait no longer. She lifted her gray skirt and petticoats so she wouldn't trip and ran down the steps. She loved Steve and got down on her knees every night, praying he would stay at Halcyon after Master Ned passed on. He was good and kind and all the slaves loved him, and maybe if the pretty young thing sitting next to him was his wife it meant he was going to settle down.

"Thank the good Lord you're back, Mr. Steve," she called as the carriage finally rolled to a stop. "We've missed you so much."

"And I've missed you, Mariah." He avoided looking at Julius and Lisbeth. There was no telling what they were thinking right then, probably that he had brought home a wife. But they would have to wonder awhile, because he planned to leave it to Ned to tell them about their stepsister.

He lifted Raven down from the carriage. He knew she was scared. "Just remember what I told you," he said, so low that no one else could hear. "I'll be around if you need me."

"I'll remember," she murmured, thinking how

his touch was always reassuring, his nearness calming. When the time came to go, she would miss him terribly.

She smoothed her skirt, swallowed hard, took a deep breath, tucked her hand in the crook of his arm, and prepared to face whatever lay ahead.

Steve waited till they reached the porch. Then, steeling himself, he announced, "I've brought someone to see your stepfather. He can make the introductions later." He paused, wondering how the hell he was supposed to present her, then simply said—"This is Raven."

13

Her hair was the color of midnight. That puzzled Ned. He had always thought angels had golden hair. And he had to be dead and seeing an angel, because when he had been shot, a fire exploded in his chest and blood seemed to be everywhere. There had been scant seconds of consciousness, filled with indescribable anguish, just long enough for him to offer a prayer of contrition. Then he had faded away. He was sure he had died and the beautiful young woman bending over him was receiving him into heaven, and he was relieved to have mercifully achieved salvation.

Ned stirred, smiling in his sleep as his dreams continued to take him to happier times.

When he had finally rallied from his delirium, weak from loss of blood, he had realized Lakoma was an angel only in the true sense of the word and had then proceeded to fall in love with her as she nursed him back to health.

She had spoken a few words of English, and he taught her more, but eventually the omnipotent language of love stripped away any barriers of communication that remained between them.

She had found him slumped on his horse, which had lumbered along to take him many miles from the battle site at San Jacinto. Days blended into weeks, weeks faded into months, but he hadn't cared about the passing of time, for each moment spent with Lakoma was a kind of heaven all its own. He never knew he could be so happy.

But then the message from home reached him: his mother was dying. He had to go back to Alabama. And in his dream he was holding Lakoma against him, saying good-bye and promising to return.

"I fear you will not come back to me," she whispered. "I feel I will not see you again until you cross the rainbow bridge." Ned asked her what she was talking about, and she told him of the tale handed down by her people. "They believe the rainbow is actually the bridge to the spirit world, and those we love who have gone before us will be waiting to take our hand and lead us across. If you do not come back to me, I will despise you with every breath I draw in this life, but if our love is true, no matter what happens, we will one day meet on that bridge and be together for all eternity."

He vowed over and over to return, so that they could spend the rest of their lives together and one day cross the rainbow side by side.

But then the dream, so vivid, became a nightmare just as real. He was floating across the rainbow and its dazzling hues. The earth below was an endless sprawl of green, interspersed with rivulets of crystalline blue waters. Seraphic music wafted from the other side of the arch, and he held out his arms in gleeful anticipation of Lakoma coming to greet him as she had promised. Only Lakoma did not appear out of the dazzling white light awaiting at the other end. Instead, the glow became a black mist from which a grotesque monster materialized amid gales of taunting laughter to lunge at him and send him plummeting to a netherworld far below.

He awoke with a shriek of horror and bolted upright to stare wildly about the room. His body was wet with perspiration, and he gasped and heaved with terror; then relief flooded him as he realized it was just a dream.

Sinking back against the pillows, Ned felt the heavy rise and fall of his chest as his heartbeat struggled to return to normal. How much longer till the nightmare became real? he wondered miserably. How much longer could he cling to this life before going to the hell that surely awaited him?

The curtainss were tightly closed. Dr. Sawyer had told Elijah to see that Ned got as much sleep as possible, so Elijah kept the room dark, despite Ned's grumbling. He had, however, left a lantern turned down low, in case Ned wanted to use the chamber pot on his own. But Ned could not remember the last time he had been out of bed, possessing neither the strength nor the will.

When Steve had first left for Texas, Ned's hope that he would be able to find Raven had helped him fight the sickness ravaging his body. But as time passed, hope faded, and he felt himself growing weaker.

Vaguely, he felt thirsty and was about to reach for the bell that would bring Elijah when his eyelids began to feel heavy once more. If he went back to sleep, thirst would not matter. He could return to the happy times with Lakoma . . . before the nightmare took over.

And he could stand the horrible ending, because the good part made up for the bad.

Raven was aware that Lisbeth and Julius were watching as she and Steve went up the stairs. He had introduced her to them without explanation, and while they had asked no questions, she had a strange feeling that they knew who she was. She told Steve about it when they could not be overheard, but he assured her they couldn't possibly. "Ned said I was the first person he'd ever told, and I doubt he'd ever tell either of them till after he knew you were found. Like I said earlier, they've never been close."

As they walked down the hall, he suggested, "I'd better go in first and break it to him easy that you're here."

"But I don't want to stand in the hall alone. If anyone comes along and sees me, I won't know what to say to them."

"You won't be in the hall. There's a small parlor. You can wait there."

Raven thought parlors were on the main floor of a house, not everywhere. She knew she had much to learn.

They reached the end of the hall and the ornate double doors to Ned's wing of the house. Steve was about to go in when he heard a voice calling softly and turned to see Elijah coming from the direction of the servants' stairs. News traveled fast, and he had come as soon as he heard. "Praise the Lord! Master Ned wouldn't say where you went, but he kept telling me you'd come back. Then he just gave up. Seeing you is bound to make him feel better." His eyes fell on Raven, and because rumor was already rampant, he dared to venture, "Have you gone and took yourself a wife, Mister Steve?"

"No. This is Miss Raven," Steve said as she managed a shy smile. "How is Ned doing?"

Elijah kept his eyes on the young woman. She was a pretty thing, but she looked scared. He wondered why but was not about to ask. "Well, he's no better than when you left, and he might be a bit worse. I can't remember the last time he was on his feet. Doc Sawyer is still giving him that tonic he makes up from alum and blackberries, and when he gets to hurting real bad, I can give him a little opium.

"Every day he asks if there's any sign of you," he went on, "and I always remind him how he don't have to ask, 'cause he knows you'll come see him the minute you get back. He might be sleeping now. Doc Sawyer says that's good for him, 'cause he needs his rest, but I don't see how it can be, when he has them bad dreams and wakes up screaming. And just before he does, he always calls out a name I don't ever recollect hearing before. Sounds like he's saying *Lakoma*. I asked him once who it was, but he acted like he was embarrassed and told me to mind my own business, so I don't say nothing about it anymore."

Steve and Raven looked at each other. Raven could not help but be touched that Ned Ralston was dreaming about her mother even now.

"We'll call you if we need you, Elijah." Steve opened a door and led Raven inside.

She breathed deeply of the pleasant smell of the leather sofa and chairs positioned cozily before a fireplace. The walls were lined with books, and the floor was covered with a thick white rug.

Steve told her to wait where she was as he walked toward another door, but curiosity propelled her to follow.

Almost before he could notice she was behind him, the sound of moaning caught his attention. Raven heard it too and stood on tiptoe to peek over his shoulder into the shadowed room. The wretched sounds were coming from a large bed, where she could see someone thrashing about.

"The nightmares Elijah was talking about," Steve said. "He must be having one now."

Raven hung back as he walked over to the bed. She could tell it was positioned between windows, for a tiny bit of light filtered through the thick curtains.

Steve touched Ned's shoulder and shook him gently. "Wake up, Ned. It's me. I'm back."

Ned did not hear him. He was reaching out for Lakoma's hand. As she had promised, love had transcended everything in the end, and she was waiting with a forgiving heart to lead him into paradise for all eternity. But then, just as they were about to touch, and he could actually feel the warmth emanating from her flesh, her fingertips drew back into the pastel clouds. He called to her, but the sound of his voice was drowned amid shrieks of taunting laughter. Black claws reached out of the haze to seize him and send him plummeting toward hell.

"Lakoma, no, no, come back!" he screamed, arms

flailing out, groping, grasping in blind desperation as he lunged up from the pillows, trying to escape the darkness and reach the light.

His eyes flashed open.

Raven, captivated, had moved to stand beside the bed without realizing it. Ned look at her and whimpered, "Oh, God. This is heaven and you are real, Lakoma." She was as beautiful as he remembered. Her hair still shone like a blackbird's wing, but her eyes were wide with fright. Why was she scared of him? He reached out to her. "There's nothing to be afraid of, my darling. Just take my hand and lead me home."

Raven jumped back and Steve pushed her to one side as he tried to make him understand. "No, Ned, this isn't Lakoma. This is Raven, your daughter. I found her and brought her back. You aren't dreaming. This is real."

Ned stared at Raven, rubbed his eyes, and stared again. "I don't believe it."

"It's true, Ned." Steve patted his shoulder.

"I just don't believe it. You really found her." He began to cry. "Oh, thank God, thank God. Open the curtains. Let me see her in the light. Please. I've waited so long."

Raven was still clutching the little reticule that matched her dress, squeezing it so hard she realized her fingers were hurting. Steve saw her distress and moved from Ned's side to put his arm about her and help her to a nearby chair. "It will be all right," he soothed. "This is a big shock for both of you, and you need to relax a minute."

He opened the curtains, and the room was instantly flooded with sunlight.

Ned blinked against the glare, then propped himself on one elbow to drink in the sight of his own flesh and blood. His vigor was renewed by excitement, and suddenly he felt exhilarated, reborn. "Tell me everything. I want to know everything about you."

Raven looked to Steve in desperation. "Ned, not so fast," he said. "You need to take it easy."

"I can take it easy in my grave," Ned fired back impatiently. He struggled to sit up, and Steve helped prop him against the pillows. "Ring for Elijah. Tell him to bring us something to drink. Do you like tea, child?" he asked Raven anxiously. He could not tear his eyes away from her. Suddenly it was important to please her in every way.

"Tea would be fine," she managed to say in a small voice.

Dismissing Steve with a wave of his hand to do his bidding, Ned's gaze swept her hungrily. "Lord, you're the image of your mother. So lovely. How did Steve find you? And how is Seth? Oh, I've so many questions. Eighteen years of questions." He offered a smile that quickly faded when a cold shadow crossed her eyes. He reminded himself it was only natural she would harbor resentment over his not appearing in her life till now.

"Seth died over a year ago," she told him.

"I might have known. But who has been taking care of you since?"

She lifted her chin. "No one. I can take care of myself."

He looked to Steve, who nodded with twinkling eyes to confirm that she most certainly could—though he was not about to confide to Ned how she had gone about it.

"But you're here!" Ned exulted. "That's the important thing. And I will see to it you're taken care of for the rest of your life."

Raven was beginning to feel trapped. The man was sick, and she did not want to upset him, but dear God, she couldn't help having loathed him for as long as she could remember. "I don't want you to take care of me," she blurted out, "and the truth is, I only came because Steve made me. I don't mean to be disrespectful, but you have to understand that I don't want anything you have."

To her amazement, he nodded. "I had an idea you'd feel that way, just like I figured you wouldn't come willingly."

"Well, I'm here."

She had rapidly assessed him and decided he was a nice-looking man despite being pale and sickly. His dark hair was peppered with gray, and he had good, chiseled lines in his face. It made her feel strange to see how he had a dimple in his right cheek identical to hers.

She went on. "I think I should also make it clear that I don't think I can forgive you for hurting my mother."

"I'm not going to ask you to."

Steve was bewildered to hear that, wondering how Ned could say such a thing after he had gone to so much trouble to get her there. He had thought that was the whole point of his quest, so Ned could beg her forgiveness and set his soul to rest.

Just then Elijah arrived and was surprised to see how Ned was almost sitting up and actually had some color in his face.

"Tea and sugar cakes, please," Ned requested

heartily, then said to Steve, "You can run along now. I'd like to be alone with my daughter."

Steve looked uncertainly at Raven. He had to do as Ned asked, even though he doubted she was ready to be left by herself with him, but to his astonishment she indicated by a slight nod that it was all right.

When they were alone, Ned explained what he meant about not asking her forgiveness. "How can I, when I can't even forgive myself? I can only hope, once you let me tell you about everything that has been eating me alive all these years, that you will at least believe that I did love your mother. And God alone knows how I've suffered."

"She suffered too, because I know she never stopped loving you, even after what you did."

He felt a stab of pain to think of it. "T'would have been better if she'd hated me instead."

"On the surface she did, but I knew it was only an act."

"Then she told you all about me—us?"

"Oh, yes, everything. But only when she felt I was old enough to know."

"Then let me have my chance to tell you why things happened as they did, Raven. Hear me out, please." He searched her face for a sign of compassion, but she merely continued to stare at him impassively, as though determined not to show any emotion at all.

She braced herself. "Go ahead."

He left nothing out, even though he had to reveal himself as the weakling he had been, unable to stand up to his dominating father and manipulative mother. He also described how he had even managed to convince himself that Lakoma was better off without him. "But believe me," he said when he was done, "had I known she was going to have you, absolutely nothing would have kept me from going back to her."

Raven was tempted to suggest that perhaps he had just made up so many excuses through the years for what he had done that he had actually started to believe them himself, but a part of her began to wonder if he might just be telling the truth. Perhaps, she realized with a jolt, she was hoping he was.

"So that's the way it was," he went on, when she did not respond. "But I can't make you believe me. I can only pray that you do."

"My mother said the money you sent for us was your way of trying to buy freedom from your guilt."

"In a way, I suppose she was right. It was the only thing I could do, and I felt like I had to do something. By the time I found out about you, I was married and had the responsibility not only of a wife but of two small stepchildren. I couldn't just walk out on them and claim another woman as mine, who was married to another man, even if she had given birth to my child. What was done couldn't be undone. So I did what I could, though it wasn't altogether trying to ease my conscience. I truly did want to make sure the two of you were looked after."

Raven glanced about at the sumptuous furnishings and murmured, "I seem to recall it wasn't very much money."

"Seth wouldn't accept much. The first time I sent a large amount, and he wrote and said he wouldn't stand for it, that it was his job to support his family. He'd accept a little to help out, but he'd not let me take full care of his wife and the baby he loved as his own. After that, I sent a mere pittance of what I longed to give you both. I had no choice."

Raven could easily believe that. Seth had been a proud man.

Neither spoke as Elijah entered, carrying a tray with a silver tea service. There was also a plate of pink frosted cakes, which Raven could not resist sampling as he poured the tea. Ned waited till he had left before confiding, "You know, until now it really didn't matter to me whether I ever got out of this bed again or not. The only real happiness I've known since your mother was the racking horses, and this damned sickness has made me too weak even to enjoy them. So I just stopped caring what happened—till now. But having you here, seeing you, loving you on sight, I can feel in my bones that I'll be able to find the strength somehow to get out of this bed and show Halcyon to you myself. Maybe if you see it through my eyes, you'll change your mind about staying after I'm gone."

Raven felt the need to be honest, even if it hurt him. "I don't think that's going to happen."

"Maybe not, but I'm going to try my best." He smiled at her fondly. "Oh, what a treasure you are! You're the best of both your mother and me, and I'm going to cherish every moment we have together."

He closed his eyes. Raven did not speak, and before long she could tell that he was asleep.

She wondered what she should do now. Someone was going to have to show her where she was supposed to bed down, but for the moment she just wanted to sit and look at him and think about how hard it was going to be to keep on disliking a man who seemed to care so much about her. Maybe he was only trying to make up for everything before he died. There was nothing wrong with that. Some men never cared about the mistakes they had made in their lives; her father did. And despite everything, she knew she was going to have to give him a chance.

There was something else, too, even though she didn't like admitting it. She was going to have more time with Steve. Maybe not much. They wouldn't be together as they had been on the trail, but he'd be around. And that was something. Even though nothing lasting would ever come of it, she'd have her memories . . . and that was more happiness than she'd ever had before.

At first, Steve was relieved when he went downstairs and found that Lisbeth and Julius were nowhere around. But, as badly as he wanted to see about the horses, he wasn't about to leave Raven to answer the deluge of questions that was sure to come. And something told him Ned wasn't going to get around to explaining things any time soon. So he sat down on the porch and waited, and before long Lisbeth came out.

He started to rise, but she motioned for him to stay where he was and took the rocker beside him. "Who is she?" she asked.

As much as Steve had wanted Ned to be the one to tell it, he knew it couldn't wait any longer. "Maybe you'd better call Julius out here so I can tell you both at the same time."

She did so.

And he told them, in as few words as possible, and as he looked at them while he talked, he had the same feeling as Raven—that they already knew. "You don't seem surprised," he said when he had finished.

Julius had planned how he would react. "Actually,

we guessed as much. You see, our mother told us a long time ago that she suspected there had been another woman in Ned's past. So when you went away without saying why, and the servants started talking about how Ned was having nightmares and calling out a strange name, we started wondering what was going on. Now we know. He sent you to find his illegitimate daughter, and you did."

Steve nodded soberly. "That's about the way it is. I hope you won't make things difficult for her while she's here."

Julius exchanged a quick look with Lisbeth before asking, "You mean she's not planning to stay?"

"Only till Ned's gone. She wants no part of this world."

Lisbeth could keep still no longer. "I guess not. She's a half-breed, I can tell. That hair. Her coloring. She's part Indian, for sure."

"That's right. Her mother was a full-blooded Tonkawa."

"Oh, she'd never fit in here," Lisbeth said confidently. "It's best for everybody that she leave."

"Well, Ned has other ideas about that." He stood, anxious to get to the stables. He did not want to talk about it any longer, and he couldn't do anything more for Raven. She was on her own now. "Like I said, I hope you'll be nice to her while she's around. This is all strange to her."

Julius made his eyes go wide. "Why, we wouldn't dream of being anything but cordial to her. After all, if she's Ned's daughter, this is her home too, isn't it?"

Steve nodded and went on his way but was not reassured by Julius's words. There had been something in his tone of voice, and he'd not missed the gleam in Lisbeth's eyes.

He supposed it didn't matter if Raven was determined to leave. But it needled him to realize how much he was beginning to hope she wouldn't.

14

Steve leaned against the stall railing, his brow knitted with lines of concern. Starfire was definitely off his feed. His ribs were beginning to show, and he was hollow-eyed. Joshua, the only stable hand he trusted to help care for the expensive racking horses, had assured him that he'd given the stallion his oats and hay faithfully, and Steve believed him.

He ran his hand down Starfire's nose, but the horse tossed his head and backed away. "It's okay, boy. I know you miss your master." Ned was too weak to walk out to the stable, but Steve wondered if he might be able to make it to the porch. Starfire could be taken out on the lawn, and Ned could reach over and give him a pat and talk to him. Horses were funny. Most people didn't realize it, but they could grieve to death. Starfire had always been a one-man horse. When Ned died, it wouldn't surprise him if Starfire did too.

Steve had wanted to pay Ned a visit that morning to

see how things had gone with Raven but reminded himself his job was done. If Ned needed him, he would let him know, and Steve knew it was best to keep his distance from Raven if he was going to try to stop thinking about her.

"Well, well, the wanderer is back, and he hasn't even taken the time to say a private little hello to the one who missed him the most."

Steve groaned under his breath and did not turn around. "Good morning, Lisbeth."

"I said—" she stepped closer to dance her fingers down his arm—"that you haven't said a private hello."

He stepped away from her. "I didn't see any need. I still don't."

She laughed thinly, pretending not to care because she wasn't about to throw herself at him again. "Well, I suppose it doesn't matter. It's Raven I want to talk about anyway. I'm curious to know how you were able to find her."

"It wasn't hard," he lied, not about to go into detail.

"No doubt she was living with her family." She made a face. "Filthy Indians. I'm just glad you didn't bring any of them back with you. That's all we need—Indians swarming all over Halcyon. It's embarrassing enough to have people find out my stepfather's bastard half-breed daughter has suddenly turned up like a ghoul to demand her share of his fortune without turning the lawn into a reservation."

"She didn't 'turn up,' as you put it. Ned sent for her. And it's none of your business, but she didn't want to come. I had to persuade her."

"Well, I don't imagine you had to twist her arm very hard."

"As a matter of fact, I did, but that's not important. So why don't you stop worrying about it and get to know her? The two of you might become friends."

"That will never happen, believe—"

"Good morning."

They turned to see Raven standing in the doorway, framed by the morning sun.

Noticing how they were staring at her, and how a shroud of tension seemed to have fallen the second she spoke, she thought maybe she had interrupted something. "I can come back later. I just wanted to see the horses." She turned to go.

"No, wait." Steve was relieved. She wouldn't have stood there eager as a tail-wagging puppy if she had heard anything Lisbeth had said. "You aren't interrupting a thing. I'll be glad to show you around."

Raven come in, a bit hesitantly.

"This is Lisbeth's mare, Belle," he said.

"Oh, she's beautiful!" Raven exclaimed, stepping up on a railing and leaning over. "I remember your telling me she's due to foal. It doesn't look like it will be much longer." She stretched to touch her belly, then frowned. "She doesn't feel quite right, though."

She jumped down, opened the gate, and went inside.

Lisbeth protested. "What do you think you're doing? That's my horse. You've no business in there. My stepfather gave her to me, and she's very special, so watch what you're doing." She knew she sounded petulant and childish but she didn't care.

Raven was too busy examining the mare to pay any mind to Lisbeth. When it came to horses and her love for them, nothing stood in her way. "It may be breech," she said worriedly. "She's lumpy in the wrong places."

"Oh, what do you know?" Lisbeth snapped.

Steve did not intervene. He figured Raven had got herself into this situation, and it wasn't up to him to get her out. Besides, she seemed to know what she was doing.

"I know about horses," she informed Lisbeth with aplomb. "I know about foaling . . . giving birth."

"Really?" Lisbeth could not resist a malicious glance at Steve. "Well, maybe you can assist Selena Leroux when she has her baby. She's the daughter of one of the overseers, and her father is furious because she won't tell who's responsible for her disgraceful condition, but everyone has their suspicions."

"I know—about who she is and how she's having a baby, I mean," Raven added.

Lisbeth cocked her head in surprise. "Oh, do you now? And how is that?"

"Steve stopped and talked to her as we were coming in yesterday."

Lisbeth looked at him, eyes narrowing. "So you found time to say hello to Selena."

He flashed a grin. "Of course. She's my friend."

Raven was still preoccupied with examining the mare, and the barbs being exchanged by Lisbeth and Steve slipped past her. She rose, gave the mare a pat, and left the stall. "If she has trouble and you want me to help, let me know," she told Steve, not looking at him. Then, turning to the opposite stall, she cried, "Oh, is this Starfire?" and ran to stand on the next-to-top railing so she could lean way over and pat his head. "I can see why they named you that. You're red as fire, and that mark on your forehead really is shaped like a star. You're beautiful. Will you let me ride you sometime?"

As if he could understand what she said, Starfire

gave a mighty toss of his head to knock away her hand, then stamped backward before rearing up on his hind legs to paw the air in warning that she should not come any closer.

Steve grabbed Raven by her waist and pulled her down. "Your father would have my hide if I let you get anywhere near that horse and you were hurt. I told you how dangerous he is. He'll never let you ride him. Don't you dare try."

Lisbeth did not miss the way Steve's hands seemed to linger a few seconds longer than necessary as he helped Raven down. It dawned on her that there might be something going on between them. After all, they'd been unchaperoned for quite a while.

"He looks like he's starving," Raven said of Starfire, concerned as she saw his bony sides.

"He is. He's doing it to himself." Steve pointed at the bucket of oats, the hay-littered floor of the stall. "He's got food, he just misses Ned."

"Maybe he just needs to know someone else really cares what happens to him." She reached through the railing, dipped her hand into the oat bucket before Steve could stop her, and stepped up on the side of the stall again.

"Raven, don't."

He reached for her but paused to notice how Starfire had begun to twitch his ears and wriggle his nose as though he might be interested.

"Oh, get her away from there," Lisbeth said, exasperated.

But Steve allowed her to stay right where she was, because, to his amazement, Starfire started eating right out of her hand. "I don't believe it!"

Happily, Raven allowed him to eat all the oats,

then scooped up another handful, and another, till he finally stopped. "See?" she cried in triumph, getting down and dusting her hands on her skirt. "He just needs coaxing, that's all."

"I have coaxed. So has Joshua. We've practically got down on our knees."

"Oh, pooh, that's silly," Lisbeth scoffed. "If he gets hungry, he'll eat. Whoever heard of begging a horse to do anything?" She turned to go. "I'm going back to the house. It's dusty and hot in here. Smells bad, too."

Steve was glad to see her go, but Raven called, "Lisbeth, wait. I was hoping we could go for a ride together." She had made up her mind to do her best to try and make friends with Lisbeth and was sorely disappointed when she just kept on going.

Steve saw how her shoulders slumped, and his heart went out to her. "Give it time. Lisbeth is spoiled, but she's got her good side. You have to remember finding out about you after all these years has been quite a shock to everybody."

She murmured that she knew that, then contented herself with watching Steve as he went about making sure the horses were all properly shod. He didn't offer to make conversation and neither did she. She had lain awake most of the night before thinking that maybe Steve had been right: she didn't have anything to lose by staying till her father died. It would be an experience to remember for always. She had also decided it was something her mother would have wanted her to do, to try and make Ned's last days happy regardless of past resentments.

She had been pleasantly surprised to discover what a pleasant sort of fellow he seemed to be. Their first meeting had been brief, but she had found warmth in his lackluster eyes and she had no doubt he wanted to spend every possible moment he could with her. Probably he had it in mind to ask a million questions about her mother, rekindling his own memories as well as his apparently never-ending love.

Finally, Steve yielded to his curiosity. "How did it go yesterday? Was meeting your father as bad as you thought it would be?"

"It was awkward. But he seems like a kind man."

"How do you feel about him now?"

She reached for a piece of straw from the floor and began to chew on it absently. "I'm not sure."

"If your mother were alive, do you think she would believe him?"

The corners of her mouth lifted wistfully. "Oh, yes. And if he had suddenly appeared in our lives, I'm sure she'd have wanted to go away with him, which would have killed Seth."

"Well, I guess that's how it is when you love somebody."

They stood a moment, both feeling uncomfortable. Steve was the first to speak. "I've got some chores to do before I leave for Mobile to take the carriage back, so I'd better get busy. Do you want me to get Diablo for you? I can have Joshua ride with you since you don't know your way around yet."

"No, I'll wait." She hesitated, then had to know, "Why can't you send someone else to Mobile with the carriage?"

Not suspecting how her heart ached to think he was actually using the trip as an excuse to visit the whores at the waterfront again, he said, "Oh, I'd rather do it myself. I always enjoy a night in town."

She knew she had to get away lest he suspect her

feelings were hurt. She threw down the straw she'd been chewing and forced herself to say brightly, "Well, have a nice time. Thanks for showing me around."

She turned, only to cry in surprise to see Elijah pushing her father toward her as he sat in what looked like a chair with a big wheel on each side.

Steve saw them too and laughed. "What in the world is that?"

Ned was beaming proudly. "It was my grandfather's. He had it sent over from England. He wanted it so he could still get around the plantation in case he got old and decrepit and couldn't walk, only he didn't live that long. Neither did my father. So it's been stored ever since, but I remembered and had Elijah get it out and clean it up so I could show Raven around. I didn't realize how weak I've let myself get. I tried to walk a little and fell down, didn't I, Elijah?"

"You sure did, but you just keep trying and you'll be strong again." Elijah didn't really think so. Like everyone else, he was amazed that Ned had rallied so miraculously since Raven's arrival but worried that wouldn't last. He was still a sick man.

"Well, this is wonderful," Steve was saying.

Ned was paying no attention to anything except Raven, marveling again over how she looked just like her mother. He held out his hand to her. "Would you like to walk beside me and make sure Elijah doesn't let me go rolling off into the river?"

Shyly, she returned his hopeful smile. "Of course, but don't worry. If you did go in the river, which you won't, I'd pull you out." She took his hand.

As they started to leave, Steve said, "Wait a minute, Ned. You've got to see Starfire eat out of Raven's hand. It's unbelievable."

"No it isn't," Ned said, unimpressed. "She's got my blood, and he knows it. Who knows? Maybe one day he'll even let her ride him, when the time is right."

Steve stood and watched them till they were out of sight. Maybe things would work out after all—at least for Raven and Ned, he thought with envy.

15

Raven spent almost every waking moment with her father and was profoundly puzzled to discover she enjoyed his company. He was not, she had realized, the selfish, overbearing man she had envisioned all those years. With tears in his eyes, he told her over and over how he had suffered in finding out about her after it was too late to undo the tragic mistake he had made. He repeatedly described his punishment, telling her how miserable his life had been married to Edith.

"Lord knows, I tried to push all thoughts of you and your mother out of my mind," he said again one morning as she pushed him across the lush green lawn in the wheelchair. "I even tried to drown my misery in liquor, but it made me so sick I couldn't even do a good job of getting drunk. The only thing that gave me any kind of peace was Seth's letters. But there weren't that many. I could tell he only wrote to let me know he got the money I sent. I could also read between the lines that he would really have liked for me to get out of your lives entirely, but the fact was he needed the money."

Raven stopped the chair beneath the gently dancing fronds of a weeping willow tree. It was a beautiful spot overlooking the river. A few flatboats were lazily drifting by and, in the distance, one of the Ralston packets, bound for Montgomery. He liked for her to bring him here, every day saying how much he wished he were strong enough to walk and not need the chair, but despite his will his body was not cooperating.

She went around to sit on the ground in front of him, spreading her skirt on the grass. Madame Bonet had provided her with an elegant wardrobe, but after Raven let her know she liked simplicity, new gowns had arrived within a few days. She was wearing one of her favorites, a soft blue muslin with plain lines and light trimming.

Ned liked it as much as she did. "You're so much like your mother in everything you do, Raven. I remember how I tried to buy her a fancy dress the first day we went to the settlement, when I got the message about being needed here. I saw it in the window and thought it was so pretty, all lace and satin, with little pearls sewn right into the skirt. I wanted it for her so bad I didn't even care about reading the message in my hand, I was so busy trying to talk her into it. But she said no, she preferred simple things. I can see you do, too."

"Yes, but it's also nice to have a choice." She glanced toward the house, so grand and glorious. "I think she would have thought so, too. She would have liked it here," she added.

Ned clenched the arms of the wheelchair. "I wish I'd had the backbone to make it happen."

"But if your parents hadn't welcomed her, she wouldn't have been happy."

"I'd like to have given her the chance. She sure wasn't happy thinking I lied about how much I loved her."

Raven knew that was so, and there had been a time when she would have said as much and not cared how it hurt him. Now it was different, for she had come to believe him and knew how he had suffered.

"But at least I've gotten to know you," he said. "You're a living symbol of our love. I like to think your mother is looking down from heaven, happy to know you're going to have what should have been hers."

Raven plucked a blade of grass and began to twine it absently about her fingers, aware of how he yearned to hear her promise to stay. She was beginning to wonder if she dared, for as much as she wanted to be around Steve, she knew it would only mean heartache.

Ned was watching her keenly, trying to discern what was going through her mind. Gently, hesitantly, he said, "I'm sorry I can't offer you something to take with you if you decide not to stay."

"I haven't asked for anything."

"I know you haven't, but even if you did, I'm afraid I'd have to refuse, bad as I'd hate to. Oh, it would be so easy to have my lawyer rewrite my will and fix it so you could leave here and never want for anything again, but I've got to do everything I can to make you stay."

"I know that," she said quietly. "And I have to be

honest and say I'm tempted, because Halcyon is truly the most wonderful place I've ever seen in my whole life, but I'm just not sure I could ever fit in. And while Lisbeth and Julius try to be nice about it, I know they resent the thought of me taking what they've always thought would one day be theirs." She was not about to divulge how stupid Lisbeth made her feel, or how the way Julius looked at her sometimes made her terribly uncomfortable.

"And they'll get it all if you go," he said bluntly, sadly. "It would only be right. But that's not how I want it, because even though they've always treated me with respect, I know they don't really give a damn about me, thanks to their mother. I never knew just how much Edith hated me for running off like I did, but once we got married, she sure let me know it.

"At first," he went on, "when we still spoke to each other often enough to argue, she accused me of being in love with somebody else. I guess my silence was as good as an admission, so she hated me even more. It got so we didn't have anything to do with each other. She went her way, I went mine. All she cared about was my money, and she raised her children to be the same way."

"I'm sorry you've had such an unhappy life," Raven said, for she could see the misery etched in every line of his face.

"It will be better once I'm with Lakoma again, but I don't want her mad at me for not doing right by you. She's got enough to fuss at me about." He winked. "So you think about it, girl."

Raven's heart was warmed. He was such a charming man. She could understand why her mother had been taken with him. Seth had been kind, but such a serious, no-nonsense man, occupied with surviving in a world not given to making survival easy. There was seldom laughter in their home, and no one worried about whether or not they were happy. Food in their bellies, clothes on their backs, a roof over their heads: That was all they had ever worried about.

He broke into her reverie. "I've told Julius I want to have a party for you in four weeks' time."

Raven did not know what to say. She'd never been to a party in her life. She'd seen some at the fort, when she peeked through a window, wondering what it would be like to dress so fine and whirl around the floor in a man's arms while music played. But never had she dreamed of actually being a part of it. "Why would you want to do that?" she asked.

"Because I'm proud of you, that's why. And I want everybody to know it. I want them to know *you*"—he emphasized the word with a big grin—"so I've told Julius to plan a weekend celebration. I want a fancy ball one night, and the next day the menfolk can go hunting while the ladies have tea and get to know you. Then there'll be a big barbecue on the lawn, like my mother and father used to have when I was a boy. Edith never entertained outside. Said she hated bugs. But I love the outdoors, and I can tell you do too.

"I told him to invite all the bachelors around," he continued enthusiastically, "and who knows? If I can't talk you into staying to claim my fortune, maybe some young man can do it by claiming your heart."

Her protests fell on deaf ears. His mind was made up. She would have argued further, but he looked beyond her to grumble. "Here comes the old sooth-sayer. All he does is nag me to take that foul-tasting elixir he brews, which doesn't do me a bit of good.

When my kidneys finally quit working, nothing him or anybody else concocts is going to mean a hill of beans."

Raven saw Dr. Sawyer's buggy coming up the drive. When she had first met him, he was taken aback, like everyone else, to learn she was Ned's daughter. But he had been nice to her, and she liked him.

She got up and began to push her father toward the house, watching as Dr. Sawyer reined up his horse at the stables. Steve came out to talk to him. He was shirtless, and she feasted on the sight of his muscular chest, bronzed from the sun. He certainly had a magnificent body. Hot waves moved over her as she remembered what each and every inch of it looked like. She would never forget seeing him naked—and, shamelessly, she did not want to forget.

Elijah was waiting at the porch steps with another manservant to lift Ned from his chair and take him up to his rooms.

"Join me for lunch after the old fool has gone," Ned said.

"I'd love to. I'll go to the kitchen and ask Mariah to help me fix a nice tray."

Mariah was glad to see her. So were the other kitchen workers. They had been leery of her when she had first started going out there, wondering why she did it. Lisbeth never went; she left everything to do with meals to Mariah. But Raven had told them she loved to cook and wanted them to teach her everything they knew and she, in turn, would show them how to make some Indian dishes, so now they welcomed her.

She took her time slicing cold chicken for sandwiches, wanting to give Dr. Sawyer time to finish his examination. Finally, she took the tray and was walking through the back door when she bumped into Lisbeth, who was in the process of fussing at one of the laundry workers for doing an unsatisfactory job on one of her gowns.

Raven did not see her in time but managed to keep from dropping the tray as Lisbeth cried, "Oh, for heaven's sake. You could have spilled that all over me. What are you doing skulking about, anyway? Why don't you let a slave carry that for you? When are you going to learn it's ridiculous for you to do their work for them? Now take that back to the kitchen and have someone carry it for you."

Innocently, Raven said, "But that doesn't make sense when I've already got it. I'll do it next time," she conceded, starting by her.

"Do it now, please. I'm only trying to help you learn how you're supposed to act, and ladies aren't supposed to carry heavy trays."

Raven laughed. "But it isn't heavy, Lisbeth. Honest. I can hold it with one hand, see?" She held it up, thinking Lisbeth would be impressed, but saw her expression and knew she had failed again. It seemed she just couldn't please her no matter what she did.

"Stop that. Really, Raven, why do you have to be so stubborn? I'm only trying to help you, but you won't let me. You seem to enjoy acting like a little—"

"What's going on here?" Julius asked, coming into the hall.

Lisbeth felt like screaming. She could hear the muffled sounds of the laundry room workers, trying to keep from laughing over her perplexity with Raven. "Can't you see? She just won't let me teach her proper decorum."

He took the tray from Raven and set it on a table

nearby, then put a comforting arm around her as he glared at Lisbeth over her head. "She'll learn all she needs to know in good time," he said, adding the lie, "And just this morning you were saying how pleased you are that she's doing so well."

Lisbeth wanted to strangle him. What she had said was that she wished the earth would open up and swallow Raven whole.

"Now let's go to the parlor. I've just had a talk with Dr. Sawyer, and I want to share what he said with both of you."

Raven was seized with apprehension. "My father isn't worse, is he? He seems to be feeling better every day."

"Let's wait till we get to the parlor. I don't like to discuss family matters in front of the servants if it can be avoided."

Lisbeth snapped, "That's something else you need to remember, Raven. You chatter away with them as if they're your best friends, for heaven's sake."

Julius shot her another disapproving glance, but she ignored him.

With the parlor door closed and everyone seated, Julius recounted how Dr. Sawyer had warned that even though Ned seemed to be doing so well, the fact was he would not get any better and could go downhill fast and without warning. "He says we shouldn't get our hopes up."

Raven felt a lump come into her throat. She had never dreamed she would learn to care for her father so deeply in such a short period of time.

"What about the party?" Lisbeth was anxious to have it, sure that Raven would embarrass herself so terribly she would want to leave for good.

"Let's postpone it," Raven said immediately. "It might be too much of a strain."

"He won't hear of it. It means a lot to him," Julius said.

"I'm looking forward to it too," Lisbeth chimed in.

Julius knew the reason for Lisbeth's enthusiasm, but he had begun to have ideas of his own as to what to do about Raven. "Maybe you shouldn't take him out so much, Raven. Dr. Sawyer seemed to think he needs more rest. I realize you want to be with him as much as possible, but quite frankly, before you came, he slept a good bit of the day."

"I know. But he also didn't feel as good as he does now," Raven pointed out, matching his pleasant smile and demeanor. "So maybe it's just as important that he enjoy himself as it is for him to sleep."

Without Raven's noticing, Julius was able to signal to Lisbeth that he wanted her to leave them alone. She was only too glad to oblige, because it was too much of a strain to have to be nice all the time.

When his sister had gone, Julius moved to sit next to Raven and casually draped his arm across the back of the sofa. "You know," he began, "you spend so much time with Ned I never have a chance to be with you. I'd like to get to know you too, Raven."

For just an instant, she was overjoyed, but the emotion was short-lived when she felt his arm on her shoulders.

"Let Ned nap in the afternoons." He leaned closer. "There are some things I'd like to show you."

When he caressed her with his fingers, she bounded to her feet. "Maybe another time. He's probably awake and waiting for his lunch."

Julius stared after her as she rushed out. He was disappointed but undaunted. His time would come.

Raven retrieved the tray and took it up to her father's room, but Elijah met her in the parlor and told her Dr. Sawyer had given him some laudanum, and he would probably sleep for the rest of the afternoon.

"But he didn't say anything to me about being in pain," she worried aloud.

"Yes'm, I know he didn't, 'cause I heard him tell the doctor he didn't want you to fret."

Concerned and worried over how her father was obviously only pretending to feel better, Raven left the house and wandered across the road to the pasture. A ride would be nice, but Diablo was nowhere in sight. He liked to roam way off whenever he had the chance.

"Crazy mustang," she muttered under her breath. Remembering how Steve had made him throw her that day by whistling, she was glad he had. Otherwise she would have gone on despising her father and never gotten to know him. And, her heart reminded her, she would not have seen Steve again either. Now she could at least worship him from afar, and that was better than nothing, wasn't it?

She saw Steve then, riding toward the fields, and wondered if he was going to see about Selena and just how much time he actually spent with her. But it was none of her business, Raven reminded herself. She was foolish to keep brooding about a man who wasn't interested in her. If only she could find a way to stop.

Thinking she might find a horse in the stable she could ride since Diablo wasn't available, she went there and looked around, to see only Starfire and Belle. Scooping up a handful of oats from the bucket, she climbed up on the railing and leaned so Starfire could eat out of her hand. She did that every day, and he was starting to fill out a bit.

"I wish I could ride you," she said wistfully.

The more she thought about it, the more logical riding him seemed. If she succeeded, it would solve the problem. And since Starfire had let her feed him and didn't shy away from her anymore, perhaps it was time for her to try. Diablo had certainly been wild, and she had ridden him when no one else could and then gone on to train him to pretend to let someone ride till she whistled to make him throw them off. She was only chagrined to think she had neglected to teach him that this did not include her.

First she made sure no one else was around; then she saddled Starfire, attached reins to his bridle, and led him from his stall and out the back door of the stable into the training ring.

He stood perfectly still as she mounted him. She patted his neck. "Good boy. Now we'll take a turn or two around the ring so you can get to know me, and I can get to know you, and then we'll take off for the wide open spaces. How would you like that?"

She took a deep breath and held it.

He did not move.

She gave him a slight nudge with her heels, and that was all it took.

He gave one mighty kick, then reared up and came down on his forelegs to throw his hind end up at the same time. And despite all her experience riding and handling horses, Raven found herself sailing over his head.

She did, however, have her wits about her enough to remember what she had been taught by the Indians: She should try to go limber as she fell so that when she hit the ground the chances of anything breaking were lessened.

She landed on her bottom with a painful thud and sat there, wondering what she had done wrong, but only for an instant, because Starfire was acting strange, and she was getting scared. Slowly she got to her feet as he began to prance around her, and each time she took a step, he would move in that direction to block her. He began to toss his head and whinny, lifting his forelegs higher with each step. Panic ripped through her to know that if he decided to charge, she would be stomped to death beneath his powerful hooves.

"Don't, please," she said, holding up her hands in surrender. "It's all right. I understand. You don't want anybody riding you but my father. I'm not going to try again. Not today, anyway."

Starfire drew closer.

She decided she had to make a run for it. It was her only chance. If she could reach the fence, she could dive under it.

Steve came out of the stable just as she took off running. At once, he saw what was happening and threw himself against the fence, holding out his arms in readiness to grab her. "Jump, Raven. I've got you."

She leaped for him, and he swung her up and over just as Starfire came to a halt right behind her in a cloud of dust. He reared up, mighty forelegs striking at the air as he gave a loud whinny of fury. Then he began to gallop around the ring, shaking with the indignity of it all.

Steve exploded. "What are you trying to do, get yourself killed? I told you to stay away from that horse."

She had never seen him so mad, not even the fateful day he had found out she wasn't really a boy. His face was red, his mouth was twitching, and his hands, clenched into fists at his side, were shaking.

"It's nothing to get so upset about," she said, slapping at her skirt to try and brush away some of the dirt from her fall. Then, because he was still looking at her as if he could choke her, she flashed a smile to add, "Besides, I actually did stay on a few seconds while he thought about letting me ride him."

"You little fool." He grabbed her shoulders and gave her a shake. "How many times do you have to be told? He's a one-man horse! He won't even let me ride him, and there's never been a horse I couldn't break. He wasn't thinking about a damn thing except how he was going to try to kill you."

She jerked away from him, her own ire beginning to rise. "You aren't supposed to break him. That's not the way."

He snorted. "Well, I sure as hell didn't see you doing it your way."

"Well, you sure as hell will one day," she fired right back.

"God, you are stubborn." He took off his hat and slammed it to the ground, then picked it up and dusted it off and put it back on, looked at her again, and shook his head in disgust. "Don't you realize if I hadn't forgotten something and come back you might not have made it over the fence before that horse stomped down on you?"

"I was going to dive under it. And I would have made it," she said confidently. "Thanks for what you did, but I'd have managed on my own."

"Maybe. But I don't have time to argue with you. I'm on my way to Mobile."

She followed him as he went back in the stable. "Why are you going there?" She hated the thought.

"I need a break, and Belle is due to foal in a couple of days, and I don't dare leave her after tonight."

"Well, don't let me keep you," she said. She shouldn't have been been so snappy, but didn't care. She hurried away before she broke into tears to think of him on his way to some other woman's bed.

He stared after her till she was almost to the house, wondering why she was so cranky about his going to town. Maybe she was envious that he had freedom she no longer had. After all, she had been on her own for a long time.

He could also not help wondering what she would think if she knew the only reason he was going to Mobile was to get as far away from her as possible for a while. He would have a few beers. Maybe play some cards. Talk to some of his friends. But he wouldn't be paying a visit to Hedda or any other woman. Feeling as he did about Raven, no matter how hard he fought it, another woman just wouldn't do.

It was after midnight when Mariah woke Raven to tell her Jasper was at the back door, wanting to see her. "I hate to disturb you, but Master Julius won't help him, and he says to ask if you will."

"Help him do what?" Raven sat up and rubbed her eyes. She had not been asleep for very long and was groggy. Her father hadn't fallen asleep right after supper as he usually did, and she had sat reading to him till late.

"It's that mare of Miss Lisbeth's."

Now she was wide awake. "What about her?"

"Jasper said she's in trouble, and Mister Steve went to Mobile and won't be back till day, so he sent Elijah to Master Julius, but he told him he didn't know what to do and to leave him alone. Jasper don't dare let Master Ned know, or he'd try to help and he just ain't able."

"No, he isn't." Raven was already up and throwing on her clothes, bristling to think of Steve in the arms of some woman while Belle was foaling early and having problems, just as she had feared. But there was no time to think about that now. "Tell Jasper I'll be there as soon as I can."

Lisbeth could not sleep. It was hot, and there was not even the hint of a breeze coming through the doors. She got out of bed and walked out on the veranda, thinking it might be cooler.

At first, she thought she was imagining things. Then, gripping the railing and straining to see in the light of a half-moon, she was sure it was as she thought: Raven was running across the lawn in the direction of the stables.

So, she thought with smug satisfaction; she had been right. Raven and Steve were lovers, and she was on her way to meet him in his room. Now Lisbeth had seen them, and all she had to do was give them a little time and then she would walk right in and catch them in the act. She knew her way around up there now. She would not be stumbling and bumping into anything. They wouldn't know she was anywhere around till it was too late.

She was confident Ned would be so infuriated when she told him that he would banish them both. Halcyon would again be destined to belong solely to her and Julius. She would have her revenge on Steve for spurning her, and Julius would have to admit she was smarter than he was, because she had been the one to ultimately figure out a way to get rid of Raven.

She hugged herself with delight.

16

Raven knew that foaling was ordinarily a quick business and, if all went well, was usually over in about half an hour. The mare would break out into a sweat, appear uneasy, get up and down a few times, and then begin to strain. After a while, if no part of the foal appeared, it was a sure sign something was wrong.

"You say she's been like this for over an hour?" she asked Jasper.

"Maybe longer. I'm so scared I've lost track of time. It's gonna break Master Ned's heart if this horse dies."

She rolled up her sleeves. "We aren't going to let that happen." She sounded braver than she felt, because time was important when a mare was having problems. Even a short delay could mean her death as well as the foal's, so there wasn't a second to lose. It appeared Belle had been suffering for quite a while.

A quick examination confirmed her fears that the foal was in the wrong position. Normally, forelegs arrived first with the nose lying on them. In a breech, the hind legs would be first. Any other position meant danger if the foal couldn't be turned, which was what she was faced with having to try to do. "Joshua, run to the kitchen and bring back a bucket of lard. And hurry."

He took off.

While she waited, she attempted to soothe Belle by stroking her neck and talking to her in a gentle voice. Belle's eyes gleamed with fright, and she was sweating profusely as Raven rubbed her.

Josh returned, and as Raven slathered her hands and forearms with the creamy white lard, she tried to remember everything the army doctor had told her when she had helped him once with a hard foaling at the reservation. He said there was lots of room farther up inside the mare, and the foal had to be pushed back before trying to reach for a leg, which could be bent down. Or she might have to draw forward a twisted-back head.

"Get a good grip on her now," Raven urged. "I'm going to try to turn the foal."

Bracing herself, she tried not to hear Belle's painful grunts and prayed Joshua had a tight hold or she might get kicked in the face.

Time seemed to stand still as she manipulated her slick fingers, but finally, with a gasp of triumph, she fastened about a leg and began to tug gently. "I've got it. Praise God, I've got it."

Slowly, patiently, she succeeded in finding the other

foreleg and carefully maneuvered it into position. "You can let go," she said breathlessly, getting out of the way. "It's up to Belle now."

In seconds, the foal slipped into the world, and Raven was struck with wonder, as always, to witness the miracle of birth.

Joshua had tears in his eyes. "You done it, Missy Raven, you really done it! Praise the Lord. Belle's fine, and she's got herself a fine colt."

They laughed with joy as they watched him struggle to stand on wobbly legs and finally take his first uncertain steps.

Raven knew she was a mess. Her arms were covered in blood and lard and so was her dress. She was anxious to go take a bath, but she needed to tell Joshua to give Belle time to rest a bit and then try to get the colt to nurse. "If he doesn't seem to want to, a little honey smeared on her will help. I'll be back as soon as I can—"

A thin scream startled them both.

Lisbeth was standing in the doorway, her hands pressed against her cheeks in horror as she cried, "Oh, look at you! What have you done? You're covered in—" She could not say it and shook her head wildly from side to side as she squeezed her eyes shut.

"I just delivered Belle's colt," Raven told her proudly. "They're both fine."

"Thanks to Miss Raven," Joshua added. "If not for her, your mare would've died for sure. The colt too. He was turned wrong, but Miss Raven, she didn't bat an eye. She reached in and turned him around and—"

"Stop it." Lisbeth moved her hands to cover her

ears. "I don't want to hear about it. And you"—she glared at Raven in disgust—"should be ashamed. A lady would—oh, what's the use? You'll never be a lady. It's impossible. *You* are impossible."

Raven was stunned because she had thought Lisbeth would be happy everything turned out all right. "I had to help," she said. "Steve's not here, and Belle was in trouble."

"You should have let Joshua take care of it."

Joshua was quick to protest. "Oh, lordy, Miss Lisbeth, I couldn't have done what she did. I've seen Mister Steve turn foals, but I wouldn't dare try."

Lisbeth ignored him. Raven was making her stomach roll, because the sight of blood always made her sick. "You can't go back to the house till you've had a bath."

"But where can I take one?" Raven asked anxiously.

"There's a place out back where the overseers wash sometimes. They won't be up at this hour, so you can use it. I'll send a servant with fresh clothing and towels, but don't you dare leave here till you've cleaned yourself up. And don't let me hear you complain about cold water either. It would take too long to heat some up."

Joshua felt sorry for Raven. After Lisbeth left, he tried to make her feel better. "It's really a nice place. Probably better than a tub. Mister Steve built it. It's got walls around it, and a rope that runs up to buckets overhead. I'll go fill them up with water, and you just yank the cord when you need some. I'm sorry it won't be hot."

Raven didn't care. She was too lost in misery that she'd made Lisbeth mad at her again. She wished

Lisbeth would appreciate what she'd done but knew she never would. The truth was, Lisbeth did not like her, did not want her there, and nothing Raven did was ever going to change that.

Things would probably get worse if she decided to stay, and more and she was wondering if she should. By rights, Halcyon was her home. Her father wanted her to have it. So why should she turn her back on what was hers for—what? What awaited her if she struck out on her own again? No matter how resourceful she was, it would be a constant struggle to survive as a woman, for never again would she be content to pretend to be a boy.

She did not have the answers. Perhaps she never would. But for the time being, she resolved to take one day at a time and do the best she could and continue to try to make Lisbeth change her mind about her. Julius was a different situation, because she did not like his subtle advances and the way he had started looking at her.

And all the while, she thought dismally, she would be trying not to dwell on the other futility of her life, her longing for Steve.

A few moments later, Joshua brought her out of her fretting to tell her, "Everything's fine. The colt is nursing. I filled up the buckets. And somebody brought clean clothes for you. So I'll get on now and come back in a few hours to see how Belle and the little one are getting along."

Raven thanked him and found her way out the back door of the barn. There, just as Joshua had described, was the contraption Steve had made. She had seen it before without realizing what it was.

She went inside and closed the door behind her.

There was no lock but she wasn't concerned, since no one was up and stirring yet.

Peeling out of her filthy clothes, she tossed them in a corner, then glanced up to see there were three ropes, each connected to a bucket. She gave one a yank and squealed softly as the icy water cascaded over her.

She found a bar of soap and began to lather all over, scrubbing vigorously. She took her time, dreading the next frigid splash of water.

Focused on what she was doing, Raven did not hear anyone moving around inside the barn.

Steve beamed at the sight of the newborn colt suckling and patted Belle on her rump. "Good job, girl. He's a fine one. I'm sorry I wasn't around, but I had no idea you'd drop early." He saw the bucket of lard and looked around for Joshua, wondering why it had been needed.

But he was nowhere around. Then he heard the sound of water splashing from out back. The bathing stall he'd built was only for himself and the overseers, not the slaves, and Joshua knew it but probably figured he'd get by with it since Steve was gone. Steve didn't care if he wanted to clean himself up right away, but he was going to teach him a lesson. The shock of cold water was bad enough when a man was expecting it, but to throw a bucket on him when he wasn't would be even worse—which was what Steve had in mind.

The lantern over the stall was burning, providing light for bathing. Steve quietly pulled up the bench nearby, not noticing the bundle of clothing on the end of it.

He stepped up. The top of the wall came to his

chest, and he reached out to yank the cord controlling
the water bucket closest to him. At the same time he
looked down and choked on a gasp to see it wasn't
Joshua, it was Raven. But she did not see him,
because she had soap on her face and had squeezed
her eyes shut.

He loomed over her, unable to tear his gaze away
as he feasted on the sight of her nude. And as he continued to stare, heat moved over him to settle in his
loins. God, how he wanted her!

But he was not watching what he was doing, and
his hand brushed against a bucket, and that's all it
took for it to tip over and dump cold water all over
her.

She gasped, and for an instant she could only stand
there, the scream from being chilled to her bones
sticking in her throat. But then she swiped furiously
at her face and looked up. All she could make out
right then, water and soap still in her eyes, was the
blurred face of a man staring down at her. "I'll teach
you to spy on me," she cried.

She grabbed her towel, wrapping it around her at
the same time as she lunged at the door to send it
banging back against Steve. He did not have time to
react and was caught off guard. The bench tipped,
and he went sprawling to the ground.

Raven stared in the lantern's glow, water running
down her face. "Steve! I—" She swallowed in disbelief.
"I never took you for a . . . a peeper," she stammered.

"I never knew anyone I wanted to peep at," he
said, laughing, as he reached out to grab her ankle
and bring her toppling down on top of him. "Till
now," he added huskily, soberly.

Casting aside all restraint to the night winds blowing

gently over them, his hand moved to the back of her neck to bring her face close to his. Slowly, ever so slowly, he began to brush his lips over hers, hardly touching as he sought to savor the moment. He could feel the rapid beating of her pulse against his fingers as he gently continued to caress her throat, as she stared at him with—what? Terror? Desire? He did not know but intended to find out.

He rolled with her till they lay on their sides, facing each other. The towel caught and pulled away. She made no move to retrieve it and lay tight against him, naked, as he had dreamed of holding her.

His tongue traced the lines of her mouth, and then he was aware that her hands were no longer frightened claws, clutching his shoulders, but had yielded to a shy caress. He kissed her then, hard, bruising, for all the desire he had fought to suppress for so long suddenly erupted and he wanted her, deeply, desperately. His arms went about her, crisscrossing her back to imprison her ever tighter. She did not struggle. Her lips parted as his tongue assaulted them, and he could feel her entire body sighing against him in surrender.

They were on the ground, wet from the runoff from the shower. Lost in rapture, neither noticed or cared about the mud as they continued to cling together, bodies moving with the sweeping fervor of ever-heightening desire. Dizzily, Steve knew he did not want it to happen like this, not here, on the ground outside the barn, where at any moment someone could happen along, even at such an unlikely hour. With another woman, the ones in his past, it wouldn't have mattered. He'd done his pleasuring in all sorts of unlikely places: pool tables after hours in a bar, a back alley behind garbage cans, barn lofts, stalls, carriages, buckboards, even right out in the open if the mood struck and nobody was around. He hadn't cared. Neither had the woman. But this was different. This was Raven. And he'd not have their first time, perhaps their only time, sullied by likening it to an act of unbridled lust. It had to be more because *she* was more.

He tore himself away from her. "Not here. Upstairs. In my room." He stood and reached down for her.

Raven looked from his outstretched hand to his face. She could see his heated gaze, his flushed cheeks, the nerve twitching in his jaw. His shirt was unbuttoned to his waist, and she could see the thick mat of hair, trailing downward. He stood with legs slightly apart, and she fought to keep from staring at the swell between them. She was not sure exactly what she wanted, only that she wanted him, in all his glory, then and there. But above and beyond the drums of desire that were beating within, something told her that once her fingers closed about his, there would be no turning back. He would take her upstairs, to his bed, and once he did her heart was lost to him forever.

He saw her hesitation and dared to ask, "You weren't trifling with me again, were you, Raven? Are you going to scream and bring everyone running to make me look like a fool? I think not. I *hope* not. . . ."

He drew her into his arms again, and though she commanded herself to pull away, she could only yield to the longing.

"Miss Raven, are you here? Miss Lisbeth said you were. . . ."

Steve recognized Elijah's voice and this time was not glad to hear it.

They sprang apart. Steve stooped to retrieve her towel and thrust it at her, along with the bundle of clothing he had suddenly spotted. Giving her a push toward the shower stall, he whirled to disappear around the corner of the barn so they would not be caught together.

"Give me a minute, Elijah," she answered, hoping he did not notice how her voice trembled. Oh, Lord, what had she been thinking? Another few seconds, and Steve would have carried her inside and up the ladder to his bed, and then he would possess her body as well as her soul, for though he did not know it, he already possessed her heart.

After wiping away the dirt from rolling on the ground, she dressed quickly and left the stall to hurry into the barn where Elijah was waiting. Smoothing back her hair, hoping she had regained her composure, she said, "I'm all cleaned up. Maybe Miss Lisbeth will let me in the house now." She stopped short to see the stricken look on his face and was barely able to ask, "Elijah, something is wrong. What is it?"

"It's Master Ned. He's bad off, Miss Raven, real bad. I done sent for the doctor, but"—he made a choking sound as he swallowed around the knot in his throat—"he might not get here in time. I hate to tell you this, but I'm afraid your daddy is dying."

Steve came in the front door then, having circled around. He caught only the tail end of Elijah's wrenching words, but it was enough.

"Let's go." He held out his hand.

This time, she did not hesitate to take it.

17

Dr. Sawyer had come as quickly as he could, but he knew it was almost over. There just wasn't anything else he could do. The poison from Ned's ill-functioning kidneys was spreading through his whole body. His tissues were swelling with fluid and his skin was turning the color of mustard, while an ever-climbing fever took him in and out of consciousness.

Looking at Steve, he shook his head ever so slightly.

Steve understood and felt as though he were dying himself. Ned meant more to him than any other man he had ever known. When he went, he would take a piece of Steve's heart with him.

Raven had pulled a chair close to the bed and sat holding one of Ned's hands. It was so cold.

She was all knotted up inside with guilt over how she had despised him her whole life but now under-stood him and why things had happened as they did.

She could no longer hate him but could feel only pity for how he had suffered because of his mistakes.

She squeezed his hand and swallowed back a sob to feel him squeezing back, ever so slightly. A second later, he opened his eyes and said, "I wish I could be at your party, child. I wish I could be there to see people's faces when they see what a beauty you are. I'm so proud of you. But I'll be there in spirit, you can be sure of that."

"Don't talk about that now, please. You need to rest and save your strength. The party isn't important."

"Oh, yes, it is. . . ." He drew a breath that rattled all the way down into his chest.

Dr. Sawyer shot Steve a worried look. The noisy breathing was not a good sign. It meant the lungs were filling. Some called it a death rattle, for it usually meant the end was near.

Ned struggled to get the words out. "I want the whole county, the whole state, to know about you. I want them to know the only thing I was ever ashamed of in my past was not being man enough to claim the only woman I ever loved."

"Please." She begged him to be still, reaching to brush his hair back from his feverish brow.

Ned turned to Steve with rheumy eyes. "You're going to see to it, aren't you? You'll make sure things go on like I planned?"

"Don't worry." Steve was also having trouble speaking, his throat constricting.

Through the gray mist that was rapidly swirling around him, Ned searched for Raven again and was able at last to focus on her. "I'm not asking you to make any deathbed promises. That wouldn't be fair. But I will ask you again to think about staying and keeping what's yours. Lisbeth and Julius won't like it, but they'll grow up one day and see it was the right thing to do and fair to them too. They're spoiled and willful, but they've got some goodness in their souls somewhere. At least I like to think they do."

Raven appreciated the touch of Steve's hand on her shoulder just then, a reminder that he was there for her. Neither were thinking of the passionate moments of only a short while ago, too lost in the sorrow at hand.

Ned struggled onward to empty his heart. "That first day, I said I wouldn't ask you to forgive me. I'm not asking you to now. All I can hope is that you don't think too harshly of me. Try not to hate me. I swear I loved your mother . . . and I love you."

Raven's lips were trembling; without Steve's touch to lend her strength, she would not have been able to speak at all. "I've realized I never really hated you, and I do forgive you, and I love you too, Father. . . ."

Her voice broke on a sob, and she could hold back the tears no longer. Steve leaned forward put his arms about her, also anguished to the core.

Ned's eyes closed. He was drifting away, into the mist. But the mist was no longer gray. It had begun to take on multicolored hues.

And then he saw it: the rainbow of his dreams, the prismatic colors of the arch in the heavens—pink, lavender, yellow, and green, with a brilliant golden light radiating all around.

The arch came closer, and Ned could see it was no longer merely a rainbow but a bridge, a beautiful spanning bridge, with blue skies beyond and lights so dazzling that he blinked against their splendor. And out of the radiance came the familiar honey-colored hand reaching out to him. Only this time, when he held out his fingers to clasp it, it did not withdraw, and the haze did not become a fearsome creature of the netherworld.

"Lakoma!" he cried, as the clouds parted for her to step onto the rainbow bridge. "Oh, sweet Jesus, my beloved, it is you! Take my hand, darling. Don't let it go."

A dazzling light framed her as she spoke. "Never, my love. I will never let you go. We will be together for all eternity . . . as I promised. Come with me now. Forget yesterday. We have only endless tomorrows in the great world that awaits us."

His eyes opened to fix upon Raven, his face igniting in a smile of happiness and peace. "Lakoma," he said strongly, heartily. "Yes, I'm coming . . . now. . . ."

Raven felt his hand go limp.

Dr. Sawyer was waiting with a small mirror, which he held beneath Ned's nostrils for a few seconds to confirm he was no longer breathing; then he touched his fingertips against Ned's eyelids to draw them closed. Drawing the sheet up over his face, he said, "He's gone."

Raven sat motionless. She felt a sudden need to be alone with her grief. Dear God, it hurt so bad; she had come to love him so much.

Without a word, she got up and went to the door, just as Julius and Lisbeth appeared. They had been in earlier but had left to give Raven time alone with Ned.

Seeing Raven's expression, Lisbeth whispered, "Is he gone?"

Raven managed to murmur, "Yes. He's not suffering anymore." She hurried out.

With a broken sob, Lisbeth also left.

Steve would have liked to go after Raven and make sure she was all right, but he hung back to make sure Julius would be able to take over and make all the necessary arrangements.

Julius bit back his grief, for despite everything he had cared for Ned, though he never showed it, and now he found it difficult to maintain his composure but knew he had to do so.

He turned toward the sound of weeping that came from a shadowed corner of the room. In the dim light, he saw Elijah and Mariah, their arms about each other as they cried together. Gently, he said, "There'll be time for grieving later. Right now, we've got things to do."

He crossed the room to clasp Dr. Sawyer's hand.

"Thank you for everything you tried to do for him."

"My deepest sympathies to the family." Dr. Sawyer gave a slight bow and left.

Julius avoided looking at Ned's body as he began giving orders. "Elijah, tell the carpentry shop to stop what they're doing and make a casket. It should have been done long ago, but Ned wouldn't hear of it. Mariah, you and the other women prepare his body. You know what to do, how to dress him.

"Couriers need to go out to deliver notices of the funeral. It will be"—he pressed a finger to his chin to think—"in five days. That should allow people coming from Montgomery and Birmingham to make plans to be here. The weather seems stable, so that should be enough time."

He began to circle the room, thinking out loud.

"The grave will be next to Mother's, of course. I need to get busy writing the funeral letters. That's going to take awhile, and they need to go out as soon as possible." He paused to wipe his hand across his forehead and felt how he was perspiring. He was nervous, talking fast, and knew he was slowly losing control. He was also racked with misery. How he wished he had treated Ned better before it was too late!

Suddenly he wanted, *needed,* a drink. He started for the door.

"Julius."

He turned and looked at Steve blankly, as though trying to remember who he was and why he was there. "Yes?"

"I think you should know that one of Ned's last wishes was for the party for Raven go on as planned. People will assume it won't." He steeled himself for Julius to refuse. He could understand if he did, but for Ned's sake, since it had meant so much to him, he hoped he wouldn't.

"Why, of course." Julius looked at him as though he were surprised he could think it would be any other way. "We'll do exactly as Ned wanted, even though some people will be shocked since we're in mourning. But it will be done in good taste, and I'll make sure they all know it was Ned's wish. Don't worry." He nodded and smiled tightly. "I intend to take very good care of Raven."

Suddenly his tone made Steve wary. When Ned had taken his last breath, two things had happened: Raven had suddenly become a very wealthy woman, and Julius would soon discover what it was like to work for a living. But maybe he already knew and had decided that Raven was his key to a better future.

Steve went to look for her.

Something told him he might not like what Julius had in mind for her.

Raven wept against the great horse's neck, her arms about him, her tears dampening his silken mane.

She was standing in the far pasture, out of sight of the house. Starfire had distanced himself from the other horses. He was not grazing. He was not doing anything, just standing perfectly still, his nose to the summer breeze as though he could sense his master's soul as it passed by en route to the rainbow bridge that led to infinity.

Raven wondered if Starfire knew, somehow, that Ned was gone. When she had first approached him to put her arms around his neck, he had seemed to lean into her embrace, and she had been too consumed by grief to think he might harm her. All she was concerned with was the hope that he would somehow make her feel closer to her father.

She ran her fingers over his back and sides and could feel his leanness, despite how she had managed to get him to eat during the past weeks. Now she worried he would stop altogether and die unless he mustered the will to live.

She pressed her lips against his ear. "Ned let you know he only wanted to share your spirit, not take it away from you, didn't he? I wish I could do that too, because now you stand alone. You've still got your spirit, but no one to share it with, and that makes you sad, doesn't it, boy? I know how you feel, because I'm lonely too. Life was meant to be shared, I guess."

He twitched his ears as though he understood, gave a soft whinny, and tossed his head.

Slowly, in the uncanny way nature had blessed her with, Raven felt that Starfire was trying to tell her something. "Would you like for us to share our spirits? Is that what you're trying to tell me?"

He became still, but his eyes took on a strange sheen she had never seen before. Cautiously, she positioned herself at his side. She placed her left hand on his neck, her other on his back, but he remained perfectly motionless. He wore no bridle, no halter. She had nothing to cling to except hope.

She swung herself up.

He swished his tail, as though impatient.

She gave him a slight nudge with her knees.

He started forward, slowly at first, but then she dared to dig her heels into his flanks, and he took off like the wind, galloping across the verdant pasture.

With a triumphant, thrilling wave of joy, she knew he was not going to try to throw her off.

Workers in the fields bordering the pasture paused to stare. They recognized the galloping horse as Starfire and assumed the girl riding him was Raven, her long black shiny hair streaming behind her. They murmured among themselves, for well they knew the legend of how Starfire allowed no one on his back except Master Ralston.

Suddenly the haunting sound of pealing bells began to spread like a pall across the land.

A hush fell, moving from field to field. The slaves laid down their picking sacks, their rakes, and their hoes. Mule drivers dropped the reins. Kitchen workers stood rigidly, hands covered in dough or wrist deep in soapy water. Blacksmiths set aside their irons. Potters stilled their wheels. Masons stepped away from firing ovens.

All over Halcyon, time came to a momentary standstill as the message spread that the master's life had ended.

Raven rode Starfire onward, across the land her father had died begging her to claim, and felt closer to him than ever before. And suddenly she knew that for his sake, and also for her mother's, she had to try at least to make Halcyon her home.

It would not be easy. She didn't know the first thing about running a plantation of any size, much less one of such magnitude. But there would be people to help, the overseers . . . and Steve.

Thinking of him brought what had happened at the stables only a few hours ago rushing back. It frightened to know that she had been about to give herself up to the love that had been growing inside her for so very long. She had to keep her wits about her and be in control of her every emotion if she were to run Halcyon successfully as her father had. She needed total concentration.

But perhaps most of all she needed her heart, and something told her that if she surrendered her body to the desire that Steve alone could provoke, she would surrender her heart as well.

She would have to fight to keep that from happening.

It had taken Steve awhile to track her down. Mariah looked for her in her room, then all over the house, and told him she had no idea where Raven had gone. So he had got on his horse and ridden out and made inquiries, and a field hand finally said he had seen her going toward the far pasture.

She was making ready to mount Starfire when he

spotted her. His first instinct had been to gallop toward her and shout for her not to try it, but a strange feeling had come over him, as though something was holding him back.

And then she was up, and Starfire was not bucking but galloping, and he dared to believe the stallion would not throw her.

He was not about to intrude, watching till she and Starfire disappeared over a slight ridge.

And though there had been no rain or storms of late and the sapphire sky was cloudless, Steve could have sworn that for the briefest of moments it looked as though they had ridden beneath the arc of a rainbow.

18

Raven looked at the neat row of bottles, each positioned on a stump some thirty feet away. A double holster was strapped about her waist, an unlikely accessory to the yellow lace-trimmed gown she was wearing, but then nothing about her appearance was akin to that of a gunslinger.

"Look. She's fixin' to do it again," one field hand whispered to another, pausing in his weeding of the sweet potato patch. "I swear, you can't even see her hand move when she draws."

Six shots sounded in rapid succession, and all six bottles exploded in sequence.

"Lordy," the other worker said in awe. "Lightning don't even strike that fast. I never saw her move a'tall."

They leaned on their hoes to watch as Raven reloaded the pistol and the man she had chosen to assist her set up more bottles.

The sweet potato patch was situated in a remote area. Raven had chosen the area beside it in hopes the gunfire wouldn't be heard all the way to the house. She did not want to disturb anyone but had felt the need to practice her shooting, for she'd not had a chance since Steve had come into her life to change everything about it so drastically.

In the three weeks since the funeral, she had been busy trying to learn about the operations of Halcyon, which had not been easy. Julius apologized for not helping her, saying he'd never paid much attention. And she did not want to ask Steve anything, keeping the promise she had made to herself to avoid him. The only time she saw him was when she went to the stables, and she always made sure others were around.

But now she was satisfied that she was well on her way to knowing what she was doing. As soon as the lawyer, Mr. Deyermond, had read the will, she had called each overseer to her father's study, now *her* study, and had written down what their responsibilities were as she interviewed them. After carefully going over her notes, she had called them in again to let them know she had familiarized with what they were supposed to be doing and would learn even more as time passed, and they would not be able to slacken their duties without her knowing it. They had reacted with proper respect and acquiescence, and though she knew she would have to keep on her toes, she had dared to feel optimistic she was meeting the challenge and would succeed.

Except for Julius and Lisbeth, she was dismayed to remind herself.

She had been surprised that they had not seemed at all astonished to learn of Ned's provisions for them. It was as though they had expected it. And when they excused themselves as soon as Mr. Deyermond had finished the reading, leaving him to make her an offer on their behalf, the suspicions she'd had all along were intensified. They had to have known about her, *and* the will, for how else would they have known everything would then go to them if she chose to leave?

Mr. Deyermond had wasted no time in making an offer on their behalf, something Ned obviously had not foreseen. She would not be penniless if she left. Instead, Julius and Lisbeth agreed to give her such a large sum that she would not have to worry about money again.

But Raven had declined.

Mr. Deyermond had been quite taken aback. "But you'll have plenty of money, young lady. This is an extremely generous offer. If you turn it down now and later realize you're not happy here, they might not be so benevolent once they start to build their lives elsewhere. You wouldn't get anything."

She had tried to explain to him that the money didn't matter. That was not why she was staying. "It was my father's wish, and I want to honor it. And while I appreciate their offer, I would rather they felt that we're all family. There's room here for all three of us."

But it hadn't happened, not yet. Maybe it never would. Lisbeth was cold to her, even downright mean sometimes in her admonishments over Raven's *faux pas*, as she called them. Raven looked on them as social blunders and promised herself to try harder to learn the proper ways of doing things.

Julius was another matter. He was being nice,

almost too nice. Sometimes he made her feel uneasy the way he looked at her, as if he could see right through her clothes to her naked body. He smiled at her a lot too, a sickening kind of smile. And he touched her every chance he got, taking her arm, trying to hold her hand when they talked. She wished he would just treat her like he did Lisbeth. He certainly didn't touch or look at *her* as if he could eat her up.

As for Steve, he had declined to be at the reading, and when Mr. Deyermond had announced the amount of money Ned had left him, Julius and Lisbeth had exchanged incredulous glances. Obviously they hadn't been aware of that provision, or of the exact amount, anyway.

But as Mr. Deyermond had continued, explaining how the racking horses would go to him only if Raven so desired, she had shaken her head at such a notion, not knowing it was how Ned had hoped she would feel.

She could not help wondering and, yes, worrying if with so much money Steve would leave Halcyon. After all, he could afford to buy a small ranch and start breeding racking horses of his own. She hoped he didn't—even though it might be best if he did. Then a few days later Mariah had confided joyfully that Steve had told her he had no immediate plans to leave. Raven was secretly pleased. Even if she did not intend to keep anything from happening between them, she could not help wanting him near . . . just as she could not help loving him.

She fired six more rounds, and six more bottles shattered.

She supposed she had practiced enough but was in no hurry to go back to the house. The reception was being held that evening. She was not looking forward to it and wanted no part of the preparations. That was why she had quietly left the house with her guns and ammunition, determined to stay away till it was time to get dressed.

She started to reload but paused as she heard Julius call out. "So here you are." He rode up to her and dismounted with a frown. "I couldn't find you anywhere in the house and went to look for you. When I heard gunfire, I worried there might be trouble and got here as fast as I could. Whatever are you doing? And where did you get that gun?"

"It's mine."

He laughed. "Yours? *You* have a gun? Who gave it to you?"

"I bought it." She was not about to tell him where she got the money. To do so would mean confiding that she had worked as a scout, saving everything she made till she had enough money to buy it.

"Why on earth would you want a gun?" He looked from her to where the field hand was setting up more bottles. Bits of glass were everywhere. "Did you hit all those?" he asked incredulously.

"Stand back and I'll show you," she said proudly.

"No, no, it's all right, I believe you. May I see it?" She obliged. Julius turned the weapon over in his hand a few times and then gave it back. "I don't like guns."

"You mean you don't have one of your own?"

"Just a derringer I carry for protection when I'm in Mobile. It can be dangerous sometimes, especially on the waterfront."

"But a derringer is no protection." She knew the weapon well. "It only fires one shot. What if you miss? With mine, you've got five more chances. It's called a Colt revolver, and it was first used in the Mexican war."

"Well, I suppose guns are a necessary evil, but even when I was in military school I never liked handling them."

"You would if you got used to them. Did you shoot much?"

"Rifles. Only when I had to."

"Well, you need to learn how to use a pistol. Let me show you." She holstered the gun, then whipped it out so fast that he, like the slaves, never saw her draw as the six bottles exploded with lightning precision. "Now you try it," she said amiably, offering him the gun. "I'll watch and see what you need to work on."

He took a step backward. "I'd rather not. I'm satisfied with my derringer. It's all I need."

"No, it isn't. If you were jumped by more than one man, you would certainly need more than one shot, don't you agree?"

Julius gave her the adoring look he had practiced so many times in the mirror. Women, he found, liked for men to appear to adore them in any situation. "I only agree that you're too pretty to be concerned about such unpleasant subjects as guns and violence. Let's go back to the house. We've got time for lemonade before we have to get ready. You're going to have a wonderful time tonight, Raven."

She doubted that but didn't say so.

As they rode side by side, Julius thought about his decision to ask her to marry him. He was confident it was the answer to everyone's problems. Not only did he want her fiercely, but their marriage would ensure that he and Lisbeth would have Halcyon forever. The only hard part was convincing Lisbeth it was the right thing to do. But he would worry about that later.

Pleasantly, he talked about the schedule for the weekend. "Tonight will be formal, of course, but tomorrow will be casual. I'll take the men on a trip into the hunting preserve while the pigs are cooking for the barbecue later. You'll have a delightful day with the ladies. Lisbeth tells me Maudina Tremayne has a new quilting pattern she's anxious to show everyone."

He droned on. Raven's spirits sank ever deeper to imagine an afternoon talking about making blankets. If she became too bored, she feared her mischievous streak might surface and she'd describe how to make an Indian quilt but fashioned out of dried animal skins instead of spun cloth. That was sure to elicit a few gasps. Maybe even a few attacks of the vapors, as she had learned it was called when someone fell unconscious.

"What are you going to hunt?" she asked abruptly in the midst of his praises of over Maudina's sewing skills.

"Deer. Rabbit." They were almost to the house, and he slowed to see a carriage coming up the drive. "That's probably the Doerter family. They're always the first to arrive and the last to leave."

"Then we'd better hurry. I'm afraid I lost track of time."

He reached out and took her hand. "You've got plenty of time, because everyone will expect you to appear last and make a grand entrance. Besides, we need a chance to talk in private about us." He wanted to settle things between them now, so he could spread the word they had an understanding, lest the unmarried men among the guests have notions of their own.

"Us?" she echoed uneasily and pulled her hand back.

"Yes, us. You mean you haven't noticed what I've come to feel for you?" He laughed softly. "Perhaps I'm a better actor than I thought. Even Harold"—Harold was his manservant—"has noticed and teased me about it," he lied.

She prayed he didn't mean what she feared he did and pretended to think otherwise. "Of course. We've become friends, and I'm glad. I *want* to be your friend, Julius, and Lisbeth's too. I want us to live here together in peace and be happy, like a family should be. We can all share Halcyon, and—"

"And you and I can share a life together," he interjected quickly, as he kneed his horse closer to hers. "The fact is, I want to court you, Raven. Under normal circumstances, it wouldn't be proper while we're in mourning, but I'm sure everyone will understand our wanting to be married as soon as possible, circumstances being what they are. Besides, people around here would never dare criticize anything a Ralston does—only you won't be a Ralston once you marry me. You'll be Mrs. Julius Alexander White. Doesn't that have a nice sound to it?" Her grabbed her hand again and pressed it to his lips. "I can make the announcement tonight, if you like."

Again she yanked her hand back. She did not want to hurt his feelings, but she was not about to let him think she was even remotely interested. "No. I wouldn't like that at all. I'm sorry, Julius, but I can't accept your proposal."

He struggled to remain composed. He had expected her to be flattered, as any young woman in her right mind would be. It was no secret that the father of every unmarried girl in the county, maybe even the whole state, wanted nothing better than to see his daughter marry him. Added to that, Raven should be well aware she needed a husband now, more than ever. But he was not about to give up. "You don't mean that. You're just surprised, that's all. I can understand why, because no doubt you thought I'd resent your showing up here when I never even knew you existed, but I don't. I want to marry you, Raven, and once you get used to the idea, you'll see it's the only answer."

"To what?" she asked innocently.

"Why, to your situation, of course. You need a man to help you run this place."

"But you already told me Ned never taught you how. Besides, everything seems to be going smoothly. The overseers do their jobs. I know it will take awhile for me to come even close to being as efficient as I'd like to be, and I'll probably make a few mistakes along the way, but if everyone will be patient, I'll succeed. I really don't need a man to help me.

"Then you need one for something else," he said tightly, because he was losing his patience. He hadn't expected her to argue, for heaven's sake. He'd thought she would be flattered and leap at the chance. "You need a husband, children."

"But I don't love you," she pointed out.

"You'll learn to. Besides, people get married for other reasons besides love."

"They shouldn't. Marriage is for people who love each other and become one, sharing their spirits."

"That sounds like some Indian belief," he said with a snort, fast becoming annoyed. "You can't think like that anymore. You're in a white man's world now, Raven, and you have to forget the Indian part of you."

"That has nothing do with it. It's something I learned about horses. . . ." She was silent. He would not understand. She had explained her philosophy to Steve but was not certain even he had grasped her meaning. Perhaps she should keep it to herself in the future. "Never mind. But while I'm flattered you want to marry me, the truth is, I don't intend to ever marry anybody. Now if you'll excuse me, I think I really should start getting ready." And with a snap of the reins, she set Starfire into a gallop toward the house.

"Yes, you do that," Julius called after her angrily.

He reached for the flask of whiskey he always kept in his saddlebag and took a long, deep swallow as he watched her ride away. Then, wiping his mouth with the back of his hand, his mouth curved in a wicked grin.

She was wrong. She did need a man.

And he was just the one to show her why.

Lisbeth's eyes sparkled as she described to Julius how she had laid a bright red satin gown on Raven's bed. "She'll think I did it because I think it's what she should wear tonight. Then, when she realizes how she's made a spectacle of herself in such a garish color when the house is in mourning, I'll blame it on one of the servants. She won't have sense enough to know that even *they* would know better."

"I don't think she's that naive." Julius tossed down another drink.

"Of course she is. How could she know of propriety and social mores? She's nothing but a savage."

"That's not fair. I think she's really tried to be lady-like. I also think she's tried hard to take over for Ned.

Several nights she's been up till all hours going over his papers, familiarizing herself with how things are done. You know she does read and write. She's *educated,* Lisbeth, in case you haven't bothered to notice.

"And what's more," he reminded her testily, "she hasn't told us to leave. Mr. Deyermond says she has the right to do that, because there were no provisions in the will for us to keep on living here if she doesn't want us to, and it's bad enough that I'm going to have to labor like a common dockworker for the next eight years for meager wages without being forced out of here permanently, so he suggested that we both do our best to get along with her, which you don't seem to be doing."

He was out of breath when he finished, and Lisbeth drew hers sharply before exploding. "Are you actually suggesting that I do her bidding like a slave? You're such a fool, Julius, and so am I for believing you had any kind of plan at all for getting rid of her."

He took another long swallow of whiskey and braced himself for the outburst sure to come when it dawned on her what he had in mind. "Why do we have to get rid of her?"

"What's that supposed to mean?"

"There are other ways to ensure I control Halcyon— that *we* control Halcyon," he was quick to add.

Lisbeth narrowed her eyes suspiciously. "Tell me you aren't thinking about marrying her. Oh, I've seen how you look at her sometimes when you think nobody's watching, but I thought it was merely curiosity over being around someone so different from us. Surely you wouldn't consider something so absurd."

He smiled over the rim of his glass. "Well, you have to agree it would solve all our problems."

"You *are* considering it. Oh, dear God." Feeling as though she were about to faint, she sank to the nearest chair, pulled her lace hankie from the cuff of her sleeve and began to fan herself frantically. "Mother would turn over in her grave. You can't mean this, you just can't. There has to be another way."

"Well, I'm afraid there isn't. I've thought it over carefully and come to the conclusion that it would be extremely difficult, if not completely impossible, to drive her away now. She's no fool. She's had a taste of wealth and luxury and naturally prefers it to her past life of destitution. And knowing you as I do, I think I'm justified to worry that sooner or later you'll do something to really make her mad, and then a life of destitution will be *our* future. I can't bear the thought, so I'm not going to risk your causing it to happen. And best of all"—he paused to drain his glass—"once I marry her, I won't have to honor that stupid stipulation about working at the shipyard till I'm thirty."

"But think of the scandal," she argued in desperation. "Remember, she was alone with Steve Maddox all those nights when they were traveling back here, just the two of them."

"What are you getting at?" he prodded edgily.

"They had no chaperone. Don't you see? And Steve is a man, and he certainly can't be blamed if something happened between them. After all, you can't expect Raven to have any morals, raised as she was." She was not about to divulge how she had gone to the stable to try and catch them together the night Raven was actually delivering Belle's colt. He would say that proved her suspicions were wrong, but she was still not convinced.

Julius pursed his lips. He didn't like imagining Raven in bed with Steve or any other man, but he was not about to let that stand in his way. "You don't know anything about how she was raised. I haven't seen any evidence of anything between them, and I don't care about the past."

"You're making a mistake. I can only hope you realize it before it's too late."

"I'm doing what's best for both of us. You'll thank me one day." As she started to leave, he warned, "Don't you dare try to sabotage my plan, do you understand?"

Seething, Lisbeth managed to nod her head.

"Good. Now go make sure she hasn't put that red gown on, and if she has, you tell her it was a mistake."

Lisbeth hurried on her way but did not do as he asked. If Raven wore the gown, so be it. Maybe if Julius saw people laughing at her, he would realize that if he married her they would eventually laugh at him instead.

If not, then her work was cut out for her, because there was no way she would let him carry out his asinine scheme.

19

Raven stood before the gilt-edged mirror that covered one wall of her dressing alcove. She had looked a long time at the red satin gown she had found draped across her bed before deciding not to wear it. If Lisbeth had picked it out for her, it had to be a sign she was warming to her and trying to be friends and did not want to hurt her feelings. But the truth was, Raven despised red. Warriors used it as part of their warpaint, so, to her, the color meant conflict, something she was desperately striving to avoid with both Lisbeth *and* Julius. She would never have asked for anything red in her wardrobe, but the dress had been in Madame Bonet's first delivery.

So now she stared at her reflection and hoped Lisbeth would like what she had chosen to wear: a soft peach overlaid with white Brussels lace trimmed with satin ribbon and silk flowers. But the décolletage was designed a bit lower than she preferred, so she had draped a lace shawl about her shoulders and across her chest.

Raven thought she looked nice. Mariah had set her hair in ringlets with a heated curling rod, then pulled them up with a matching ribbon of peach silk.

She tried not to think how miserable she was in the tight corset Mariah had insisted she wear. "It don't matter if you have got a waist no bigger than my hand. Young ladies have to wear proper underthings," she had said, and now Raven was afraid that if she took a deep breath and let it out, the laces would pop.

Mariah had been standing to the side watching and now clapped her hands in delighted approval. "I swear, you are the prettiest woman who's ever lived in this house, Miss Raven. And if you don't believe me, you just go downstairs and look at them portraits in the hall and see for yourself how not a one of them even comes close to being as fine-looking as you."

Raven flushed to wonder whether Steve would think the same but told herself it didn't matter, all the while knowing that it did—very much, indeed.

Finally, it was time for her to make her entrance. She went to the top of the stairs and gazed down on the people gathered below. At the sight of her, gasps went up in unison, for, like Mariah, their reaction was that she was truly the most gorgeous woman ever to grace Halcyon.

Her hand trembled as she held the mahogany railing. She prayed she would not stumble and fall, because she was not used to the high-top leather shoes and missed the comfort of moccasins.

She caught sight of Lisbeth among the sea of faces and offered a smile of apology for not wearing the gown she had picked out. At Lisbeth's familiar look of scorn, Raven knew she had disappointed her again. But there was no more time to think about that, because just as she reached the bottom, Julius stepped forward to announce loudly, proudly, "I would like to present to you my stepsister, Miss Raven Ralston. Join me, won't you, in welcoming her not only to Halcyon but also to the great state of Alabama."

He led the applause, and when it died down he began to introduce her around. She knew she would not remember all the names right then but hoped she would by the end of the weekend. When she sensed some reluctance in a few of the polite nods and handshakes she was not surprised, because despite Ned's wish to let everyone know he was not ashamed of her, there was no getting around the fact that she was his illegitimate daughter and half Indian to boot.

However, there was certainly no hesitancy among the unmarried young men, who were most anxious to make her acquaintance. And even though the atmosphere was reserved and restrained due to the circumstances of mourning, she found herself being deluged by requests to call on her as soon as it was proper.

"Let me get you some punch," Raymond Williams offered when he saw her cup was empty. Then, glancing in annoyance at the other men hovering about, he leaned to whisper in her ear, "I know you must need some fresh air. Wait a moment, then slip outside and meet me on the terrace. It's a lovely night with a full moon."

She turned to decline, not about to sneak out to meet him or anyone else, and that was when she saw Steve. He was standing off to one side, leaning against a wall and holding a cup of punch. He raised it to her in a kind of salute.

Her heart turned over at the sight.

He was so handsome in a fawn-colored coat with matching trousers. His white shirt was ruffled and open at the throat. Had he been wearing a cravat earlier but cast it aside in discomfort? A few strands of his dark hair curled about his ears and collar, and she could see the dimple in his chin when he smiled at her, ever so slightly. God, how I love him, she thought, as she felt her heart skip a beat.

"Raven, I was asking about tomorrow evening."

She was forced back to the men circling around her.

Tom Haynes was speaking. "You know we men are going on the hunt tomorrow, but I was hoping maybe you and I could sit together for supper later."

"No, she'll be with me," Julius said, joining them.

Like the others, Raven noticed his speech had become slurred. Obviously when he disappeared every few minutes, he was slipping liquor into his cup of punch.

He lifted his glass and drained it; then, seeing how everyone was looking at him so oddly, he snapped, "Well, what's wrong? Is it such a surprise to find out I've already staked a claim on my stepsister? After all"—he hiccuped—"I met her long before any of you fawning pups." He glanced about in challenge.

Tom Haynes, however, was undaunted. "I don't hear Raven confirming that she's spoken for," he said.

"Tell them." Julius gave her a nudge, harder than he meant to because of his drunken state.

She stumbled back a step a step or two, and Barley Tremayne, who happened to be walking behind her at the time, grabbed her waist to steady her.

Lisbeth, nearby, saw his hands on Raven, and that was all it took for her to hurry over and say coolly, lest he have any idea of joining the group, "Barley, I want you to come with me to chat awhile with your parents."

Barley obediently held out his arm, but before walking away, Lisbeth leaned to whisper to Julius so no one else could hear, "I think you've had enough to drink tonight. Stop it before you make a spectacle of yourself." On several occasions in the past, he had become obnoxious with his overimbibing, and she hated to see him do so tonight. Worrying that Raven would do something embarrassing was bad enough.

But Julius was beyond reason. "Did you forget I'm celebrating?" He reached for Raven's hand, which she could not discreetly withhold without making a scene.

Tom exchanged amused glances with the other men. "Well, you can't be celebrating her promise to sit with you tomorrow evening, because she hasn't said a word."

"She will. She just hates to disappoint all of you. Isn't that right, Raven?"

Just then, Raymond returned with her cup of punch, disappointed that she'd not accepted his invitation to meet him outside. Glad for an excuse to escape Julius's grip, she reached for the cup.

"Tell them," Julius urged, frowning and starting to sway just a little. Lisbeth was right. He knew he'd had too much to drink but couldn't help it, because he was worried. Raven had sounded very firm in her refusal to marry him, and if he could not change her mind, the future looked grim. "Go on," he persisted when she didn't say anything. "Tell them I'm the one you want to be with. You know you do."

"Ignore him," Tom said. "We want to hear you talk, Raven. Tell us what it was like out west. I've always wished I could go there."

"Yes," Raymond joined in. "Do you miss it?"

"Oh, how could she?" someone else asked. "Look around. Ned Ralston sure named this place proper, because Halcyon means peaceful and quiet and the west is anything but. Isn't that right, Raven?"

Raven was not about to dwell on that aspect of her past, knowing that while on the surface everyone appeared to accept her, there were those who secretly looked down on her and, if not for the Ralston name and money, would never be in her company. To describe anything about her past life would only add to hidden feelings of resentment, so she spoke, instead, of life at an army post, making it appear that was all she had ever known, having had a stepfather who was a government agent. She felt hypocritical doing so, for the fact was she loved the west in all its rugged glory and had no shame for having lived there. But this was her home now, and she had to leave the past behind.

She was not sure exactly when she noticed Julius was no longer around. She hoped he had gone to his room to pass out, because she did not like the way he was acting.

As soon as she could discreetly do so, she excused herself, wanting respite from all the attention. Pretending to be going to the necessary room, she slipped unnoticed through the side doors that led to the terrace overlooking the rose gardens. Raymond Williams had been right, she was delighted to discover; it was a lovely evening. The sky was cloudless, a brilliant moon shone down to make the river seem to roll and undulate like liquid silver, and the breeze was perfumed by the sweetness of the roses just below her.

But all of it merely served to emphasize her loneliness, for something so enchanting should be shared. It was easy then, in her forlorn mood, for her mind to drift to thoughts of Steve and the sweetness of the nights they had shared on the trail. A smile touched her lips to remember the delicious meals of rabbits roasted on a spit, how they had laughed together while cooking. True, they'd had their sparring moments, but there was no denying the experience had been one she would never forget.

"There you are. I've been looking for you everywhere. I thought one of those idiots had squired you away, and I would have been very upset if they had."

She groaned. It was Julius. "You gave me a start. What are you doing here?"

"I told you, I've been looking for you. I think we should talk."

He started toward her, and she could smell the whiskey on his breath. "Well, I need to go back inside. It will have to wait until tomorrow. Besides, you have to be up early tomorrow to take the men on the hunt, and it's getting late."

She had started to walk by him but he stepped to block her way. "It won't keep till tomorrow. We've got to settle things now so the men will stop laughing at me."

"But they aren't." She was alarmed to realize he was even drunker than she'd thought. She also did not like how he was looking at her, his tongue flicking over his lips, his eyes glazed with heat.

"Yes, they are," he said with childlike petulance, "because they can see how you're spurning me."

"That's your fault. You shouldn't have said what you did. Now let me by, Julius. You're in no condition to reason."

"No. You have to listen." He tried to put his hands on her shoulders but she stepped back. "What is wrong with you, Raven?" he whined. "You should be pleased that I've shown everyone you're welcome here."

"I am. But that doesn't mean I have to marry you to show I'm grateful. Come inside with me," she coaxed. "A cup of coffee will make you feel better. You've had too much to drink to think clearly."

Petulance gave way to frustration. "I don't want any coffee, damn it, I want you. And you should be damn glad I do, because you haven't got sense enough to run this place on your own. You'll take Halcyon to ruination. And I'll not see you hand it over to one of those scalawags that were fawning all over you tonight.

"You think they're not laughing at you too?" He rushed on cruelly, not caring whether he hurt her. "Of course, they are. Word spreads in this county like poison ivy. They know you're Ned's love child, that you're half Indian, but they're willing to marry you for your money, only you don't have sense enough to see it, you little fool. Marry me, and I can protect you from them."

He took a step closer, and Raven held up her hands to fend him off, her own ire rising. "Now stop right there, Julius. Don't come any closer. You don't know what you're saying, and tomorrow you'll regret it, but I'll forget everything if you'll just please, leave me alone."

"Please," he mimicked. "You'll say please to me, all right, when I get you in my bed. You'll say 'Please stop' at first, because I won't be able to get enough of you, but when I teach you how good I can make you feel, you'll be saying 'Please, please, Julius, make love to me again.'"

She continued to back away. "This has gone far enough. You're drunk. Now stay away from me. I'm warning you."

He snatched away her shawl, and tantalized by the sight of the swell of her breasts in the moonlight, whispered hoarsely, "My God, woman, you make me crazy! I can't wait till we're married. Let's sneak up to my room right now, this very minute. Before this night is over, you'll find out why you need a man . . . why you need *me*."

"Julius, get away from me." She knew she was running out of room, because the edge of the terrace was mere inches away. "I don't need a man and never will and least of all a drunk like you."

"Come to me, damn it." He grabbed her.

She struggled against him, beating on his back with her fists, hoping to bring him to his senses, but when she felt him forcing his tongue inside her mouth and trying to maul her breasts she knew he had left her no choice.

With one swift sharp movement, she brought her arms up to break free of his embrace, simultaneously grabbing his arm as she pivoted about. Then, leaning back into him, she threw all her weight forward to push him off balance.

Finally, with a mighty heave, she sent him sailing up and over her head to land with a loud crash right in the middle of a rosebush and all its painful thorns.

Hearing Julius's screams of anguish, everyone rushed out to see what was happening.

Julius continued to howl, clothes tearing as he fought to free himself. "Somebody get me out of here," he yelled. "I'm being ripped to pieces!"

Lisbeth pushed through the crowd to see him and promptly wailed in horror, "Do something, someone. Help him."

But the men did not move. They could see how the thorns were tearing into Julius and didn't want the same thing to happen to them. Finally, Elijah appeared and jumped in to pull him free, fortunate to be wearing the white serving gloves he'd had on all evening.

Raven stood back from the others as she watched, sorry it had to happen but knowing Julius had brought it on himself.

"Get him to his room. He needs bandages," Lisbeth said, as he was being lifted back up to the terrace. "Oh, Julius, I knew you were drinking too much, but I never dreamed you'd be so drunk you'd fall off the terrace."

Some of the onlookers chuckled but not for long, as Julius angrily denied that was how it had happened. Spotting Raven, he pointed at her and roared, "It was her fault. She did it, she threw me down there. Lisbeth is right, she's nothing but a savage. If you all don't want to lose your scalps tonight, you'd better lock your doors."

Laughter replaced the chuckles as everyone realized Julius had been bested by Raven, no doubt after making drunken overtures. They felt he deserved it, but Raven thought they were laughing at her. Humiliated, she ran down the steps at the side of the terrace to disappear into the night.

Barley Tremayne saw and started after her, but

Lisbeth was right there to clamp a firm hand on his arm and warn in a voice unheard by anyone else, "If you take one step in her direction, Barley, I swear I will never speak to you again."

He had only to look into her stormy eyes to know she meant every word she spoke, so, reminding himself how much he would like to enjoy the generous dowry it was rumored her stepfather had left her, he sighed in surrender and he allowed her to lead him back into the house.

Steve tossed aside the cheroot he had been quietly smoking as he watched the frenzied scene on the terrace. He had slipped away for a walk in the garden but, hearing angry voices, had investigated. Seeing that Julius was giving Raven a hard time, he had been about to intervene but held back, wanting to let her handle it herself if possible. He was well aware she would be embarrassed to know anyone had been around. Now she had fled, obviously thinking people had been laughing at her when it was Julius who was the brunt of their ridicule.

He hurried to follow her.

20

Raven stood on the riverbank, recklessly wishing she could jump in and swim all the way back to Texas. Not that she had been particularly contented there either, but at least while passing for a boy she'd known a little peace. Here, since her father died, she felt as though she bore the weight of the world on her shoulders. There were people to help: bankers and bookkeepers in Mobile, her father's lawyer. They did what they could, but she had promised herself when she had made the decision to stay that she would not sit back like some pampered empty-headed belle and allow others to make all the decisions. She was certainly willing to work, down in the dirt with the field hands if need be. But it just seemed that every way she turned, tensions with Lisbeth and Julius were waiting like a spider's web to entrap her.

She stooped to pick up a rock and sent it sailing through the air to make a faint splash somewhere distant.

She supposed she should get back to the house and then wondered what difference it made. Everyone would be in bed. Nobody cared what happened to her. If she fell in the river and drowned, she'd probably not be missed till her body had time to float all the way to Mobile.

A tear rolled down her cheek, and she brushed at it furiously. There was nothing to cry about, she chided herself. After all, she had felt unwanted at the reservation after Seth died. She had been out of place there too; and even Thad Slawson had thought the only thing she could do was find a husband. No one had cared what happened to her. The only difference now was that she had money. But what good did money do her when she was either despised, ignored, or ridiculed as she tried to fit into a world that did not want her?

She picked up another rock and threw it so hard she could not hear when it finally hit the water. Being rich was not what was keeping her there.

It was Steve.

No matter how hard she tried, she could not put him out of her mind. It was foolish; she meant nothing to him. He had his women in Mobile whenever he wanted. And the few times they had been in each other's company since that reckless night in the barn, he had given no indication he remembered . . . while she could not forget.

She had wandered through the formal gardens and crossed the bridge over the lagoon. An opening in a hedge of fragrant gardenia bushes had led her to the sloping riverbank. It was so isolated and peaceful she could not bring herself to leave just yet. She longed to stay there till after the guests left Sunday afternoon but knew that would be impossible. Like it or not, she had to face them, which was going to be extremely difficult in the wake of what had happened.

But at least she would stay here for a while, she decided, so she sat down on the grass and took off her shoes, which were hurting her feet.

Steve had trailed after her, giving her time to calm down before letting his presence be known. A couple of times he had thought about turning back and leaving her alone, but when she headed toward the river, he stayed in pursuit. She might have just shown she could handle herself with one man, but rowdies on the river traveled in packs.

He stepped through the opening in the hedge and called softly, "If I join you, will you promise not to throw *me* over your shoulder?"

She recognized his voice before turning to see him framed by the moonlight. "What . . . what are you doing here?" she stammered, trying not to let her excitement show. Then the meaning of his words dawned and she was horrified. "Oh, no! Don't tell me you saw what happened on the terrace."

"I sure did." He dropped to sit beside her. "And I have to say it was an exciting end to an otherwise boring evening. I hate those things, anyway. Ned did too. He never gave many parties, and when he did it was just to reciprocate for invitations he received. But I went tonight, because I promised him—"

She interrupted. "And you're doing a lot of talking to take my mind off what I did, but there's no need. You heard how everyone was laughing. I know I made a fool of myself, even if I did seem to have no choice at the time, so nothing you say can make me feel any better. But thanks for trying," she added glumly.

"You're wrong. Julius is the one who acted like a fool, and he's the one they were laughing at, not you."

"I wish I could believe that."

"Trust me, you can. Everyone knows how Julius is when he has too much to drink."

"He said Lisbeth was right to call me a savage. That hurt."

"Well, nobody cares what she says either. They think she's a brat, which she is. I've only known them since they came home from school, but that's been long enough to see how things are. Everyone wanted to applaud you for what you did, because they figured Julius must have had it coming."

"I wish there'd been another way."

"Sometimes you do what you've got to do."

"I suppose."

The silence that fell made Raven uncomfortable. She thought about getting up and leaving but could not make herself do so. It was nice being with him, even if it was a kind of sweet torture.

Finally, she said, "You haven't told me what you were doing out there."

"Escaping the party . . . and keeping an eye on you," he added.

"Well, now you know a savage like me doesn't need anybody to look out for her."

"You're not a savage. And maybe I look at you every chance I get for other reasons." He had not come to seduce her; he had only wanted her to know there was no reason to be embarrassed about what had happened. But now, sitting here at her side, her scent was an aphrodisiac that was fast ripping away all vestiges of rational thought. Before he realized it, he took her hand to give it a gentle squeeze, pleasantly surprised that not only did she not draw away, she returned the pressure.

"Maybe I should go," she said shakily.

"Maybe I should be the one to go," he murmured.

Neither moved for what seemed an eternity. Then, as though by silent mutual consent, they moved slowly into each other's arms and fell gently backward to the ground.

He did not kiss her just then, wanting to feast upon her lovely face. With a fingertip, he tenderly traced her forehead and brow, then her nose, and on to her cheeks and jawline, finally moving along the perfect bow of her mouth. His thumb rubbed across the fullness of her lower lip as their gazes burned into each other, locked with unspoken promise of wonder yet to come.

He pressed her mouth open. Back and forth he licked, deliciously, hungrily, the tip of his tongue to hers, ultimately closing his mouth over hers in a deep, stirring kiss that seemed to go on forever.

Raven returned the kiss with fervor. She closed her eyes and cast all thoughts of right or wrong from her mind. She could deny neither him nor herself any longer. Beyond all doubt, she knew she wanted him. *She wanted this. . . .*

Moving his mouth to her neck, he delighted in the taste of her flesh as his hands began to roam over her as though with a will of their own. He felt a groan deep inside. It had been a long time since he'd had a woman. Too long. Lust was a screaming demon inside him, demanding to be fed, but despite how desperately he longed to quench the hunger for her that had been tearing at him for so very long, he would not be rushed. He wanted to savor every delectable moment.

His breath was hot, ragged, against her ear. "I want to see you naked again, Raven, only this time when I look at you, I want to know you're really mine, that you aren't just torturing me."

"I was torturing myself then too," she confessed shamelessly. "But no more."

She sat up and tried to unfasten her gown but he had to help her with it, and with the corset, and then she stripped away the rest of her clothing until she was completely exposed to him.

His gaze swept across the beauty of her, even more stunning than he remembered. Closing one hand over a soft breast, he felt her shudder. With thumb and forefinger, he plucked at her nipple, already a tight little bud. He flicked it with his tongue, watching her as he did so, and saw how she gave a little gasp of pleasure. He then opened his mouth wide to take as much of her as he could, sucking so eagerly, so hard, that she felt the muscles in her belly contract and roll with deep-seated ecstasy. Her hands laced across the back of his head to hold him in position, for she never wanted him to stop.

As he continued to devour her breasts in turn, he explored the rest of her: the incredibly tiny waist, her flat stomach, the swell of her hips. Reaching her upper thighs, he moved between, and a cry of abandonment broke in Raven's throat as his probing fingers darted downward to touch and gently enter the lips of her love. They closed over him, and he dared not linger for he could feel her quivering and wanted to prolong that ultimate shudder of delight.

He pulled away from her only long enough to strip off his own clothing, then rolled to his back, taking her with him so that she lay on top of him. Cupping her buttocks, he spread them ever so slightly to slip his hardness between her legs. He began to rub to and fro, and she could not help moaning with sweet torment to feel the friction of him against the nuclei of her sex. She began to meet his undulations, and soon he could stand no more.

The world surrounding danced with magical shadows, and mystical moonbeams glistened down on their naked, sweat-slickened bodies as he gently rolled her over and then rose above her. Positioning himself between her legs, he spread them and bent her knees up to her chest. Her eyes upon him were dazed with wonder, and she held out her arms, beckoning him yet closer. He lowered his head and kissed her again as he slid his hand down her eagerly waiting body to guide himself into her. He was trembling with anticipation but knew, if it were her first time, that it might cause some pain. He dared to ask, and when she confirmed that it was, he promised, "I'll be as gentle as I can."

"No," she surprised him by saying. "Take me as you will. I'm not afraid."

And he did so, driving into the fiery heart of her, urged on by the feel of her nails raking down his back as she met his every thrust.

As much as she wanted him, as frenzied the state was he had brought her to, Raven was agonized in her desire to want the splendor to last forever. Perhaps, she wildly imagined, they could, by the fusing of their bodies, actually become a part of each other for all time. Words of love, promises of a future together, were not important, not now. There would be time for tenderness later. The spell would be broken by any attempt to grasp reality; only the moment could be caught, held, bringing him unto her, into her, for the ultimate blending and melding of their spirits.

All her senses were poised like an arrow drawn back in the bow, ready to be propelled mightily toward the target. She felt as though she were being sucked into him, for each time he entered her, he seemed to drive himself farther and farther inside.

Steve could feel her pressing against him as pleasure flowed like a mighty river below them. Her head began to whip from side to side as she felt herself taking all he had to give. He thrust harder, and she clung to him, sobbing, fearing he would let her go. She never, ever, wanted him to leave her. She was sinking, drowning, dying and did not care. All that mattered or ever would matter was the sensation of him, diving deeper inside her . . . until he *became* her, and she him, and the two were one, pouring into each other as one entity, one soul.

And in that crystallized moment of fulfillment, both of them knew their world would never again be the same. . . .

Afterward, for a long time, they lay side by side on their backs staring up at the sky, neither speaking for fear of breaking the spell between them.

Finally, reluctantly, Raven said, "Maybe we should go. Someone might come."

"At this hour of the night? I think not. Besides"—he squeezed her hand, which he had been holding tightly—"I don't want you to go. I'm afraid when you do I'll wake up and find this was all just a dream, that it didn't really happen."

"I'm glad it did," she confessed with candor. "But

we can't let anyone know." She shuddered to think of Lisbeth's finding out. She would think her a whore and tell everyone, and that would never do, not if she wanted the respect of the overseers and everyone else.

"No one will know. We'll be careful. You can slip out of the house after everyone is asleep and come to my room. Nobody is ever around the stables after dark." He rolled on his side and propped on an elbow so he could look at her once more in the moonlight. "You don't know how much I've thought about you since that night. If Elijah hadn't come, I swear I would have carried you up that ladder no matter how you fought me."

She smiled, "I seem to remember I wasn't fighting at all. I wondered if you even thought about it. You never seemed to when I was around."

"Neither did you," he pointed out, and she had to agree. "Besides, it's been rough these past weeks. I knew I'd miss Ned, but I never realized how much till he died."

"And I didn't know how deeply I had come to care for him. He was everything you tried to tell me he was, and I thank God I had time to find that out."

"So am I. And I'm also glad you decided to stay"—he leaned to kiss the tip of her nose and grin—"for lots of reasons."

She snuggled against him, reveling in his warmth, his closeness, and wondered how many nights she had dreamed of being with him this way.

He held her for a moment, then felt pressed to say, "I couldn't help overhearing Julius say he'd asked you to marry him. I guess I don't have to tell you his motive."

"So he'd get everything right away, as my husband?

No, I didn't have to think very long about that either. But I'm hoping I can talk to him and smooth things over. I don't want him for an enemy."

"I'll be surprised if you ever have him for a friend. What about Lisbeth?"

She didn't want to go into all the details of how Lisbeth was constantly belittling her for so many things, like not being able to arrange flowers properly and forgetting the right silverware to use. Raven tried to please but was embarrassed to admit she never seemed able to, so she said glumly, "I probably should have taken their offer."

"What offer?" he asked sharply. When she told him, he shook his head in disgust. "I might have known they'd think of something like that. Ned figured they would but didn't know how to get around it and just hoped you'd turn them down."

"But I shouldn't have."

"Don't say that. From what I hear, you're doing a fine job. Lisbeth and Julius will grow up one day and accept things as they are. Lisbeth will get married and move away, and Julius will settle down in Mobile."

She laughed softly. "I don't imagine I have to worry about his wanting to marry me after tonight."

"No. But from the way I saw the men flocking around you at the reception, I don't imagine you'll have a shortage of proposals."

"All wanting to marry me so they can take over Halcyon, no doubt."

They were both still naked, and he began to run the flat of his hand down her breasts, across her belly, and back up again. "Not necessarily," he murmured. "I would think they'd have a few other things in mind."

"Such as?" she teased. Her fingers were beginning

a dance of their own, twining in the soft mat of hair on his chest.

"Such as this." He turned to claim her mouth again, his hand moving between her legs.

She pressed against him, ready, eager to let the magic happen again.

He raised his lips ever so slightly and told her, "Midnight will be our special hour. Tomorrow night. Every night. Come to me. I can't promise you anything except that while we're together I'll do everything I can to give you pleasure. We have to protect your virtue. You'll be dealing with businessmen: lawyers, bankers. It wouldn't do for it to be known that you're sleeping with your horse trainer"—he flashed a grin in the moonlight—"so it will be our secret."

"And no more trips to Mobile to visit the wharves?" she asked lightly, not sure she had the right but wanting to feel she was the only woman in his life for the present, at least.

Steve easily grasped her meaning. He knew how women were. Even when it was understood a future together was not in the offing, they did not like to share a man. Whores, of course, didn't care about anything except being paid, but he'd never had many of those anyway. Because even though he dared not give his heart, he did enjoy the closeness of a relationship.

Feeling as he did, it was easy for him to assure her that he wanted no other and confided, "I haven't wanted anyone since I met you."

"Oh, don't tease me." She managed to speak above the joyous roaring within her at the thought it might be true. "I saw you from the hotel window that night in Mobile, walking toward the waterfront. The maid said that's why the men went down there—for women."

"Well, there are other reasons. Gambling. Drinking."

He wasn't about to tell her he had intended to bed another but hadn't been able to. That might reveal she had more of a hold on his heart than he'd ever felt for any woman. He had to get over that and think solely of pleasure, nothing beyond. What was between them was good. What awaited them in the future might be even better, as they learned to please each other in countless ways. That was the way it had to be, because he knew that was the way Raven wanted it. He was not about to make a fool of himself by letting her think he sometimes wondered if there could be more.

"Enough talk." He nibbled at her ear, his fingers dropping between her thighs to bring her to fever pitch. "It ought to be midnight right about now, and that's our time, so let the magic begin, sweetheart. . . ."

He began to take her to soar among the stars once more. And Raven knew, beyond all doubt, that she enjoyed the flight all the more . . . because she loved him.

21

Lisbeth was so upset she had scarcely slept a wink all night. At the first light of dawn, she was up and padding quietly down the hall to see how Julius was feeling.

She was surprised to find his door ajar. She pushed it open and stepped into his parlor, only to be even more bewildered by the sight of all the trunks and valises standing about. Just then Harold came out of the bedroom, carrying a stack of neatly folded shirts.

"What is going on here?" she demanded, aghast. "Where is Julius, and why are you packing his things?"

"Because I'm moving out, that's why." Julius breezed into the room. "And keep your voice down. We've got guests, remember? I'm trying to get out of here before they wake up." He turned to Harold. "What you don't have packed you can bring to me later. I'm leaving right away." He was pulling on his coat.

Lisbeth was flabbergasted. "You're moving out? I don't understand. You can't do this."

"Oh, can't I? Just watch me." He winced with pain as he struggled into a sleeve. "You should see my wounds. I'm covered with bruises, and Harold was pulling thorns out of my backside for three hours. If I ever do come back, I swear I'll have those damned rosebushes ripped out by the roots. The thorns are sharp as a knife."

"But you still haven't told me why you're leaving. Where will you go?"

"To Mobile. To do what my dearly departed step-father stipulated that I must do if I don't want to live like a pauper the rest of my life: work at the shipyards. There are some rooms over the main office that Ned used when he stayed overnight. I'll move in there." He grimaced at the thought of such spartan accommodations, but it was the best he could do for the time being.

Lisbeth dropped to a sofa, her head swimming. "But why now? And what am I going to tell everybody?"

His teeth ground together to think of the humiliation he had suffered, in addition to the agony. "How can you even ask? Isn't it obvious? I refuse to be around our half-breed bastard stepsister any longer. As for what to tell people, they already know: She went on the warpath and tried to kill me."

"What did you do to her on the terrace, Julius?"

"What do you mean?"

'You did something to make her mad. I know she's uncivilized, but frankly I find it hard to believe she would just go completely crazy and throw you in the rose garden." There, she thought. She had voiced her growing suspicions, and it was not because she was taking up for Raven. She just knew how odious her brother could be.

He towered over her, hands on his hips, eyes flashing his disgust. "Oh, so now it's all my fault."

"I didn't say that. I just asked what started it. We both know you'd had too much to drink. Did you do something ungentlemanly?"

"No I just asked her to marry me."

Lisbeth gasped. "And she threw you in the rosebushes? Because you proposed to her?"

"Exactly. It made her mad, because she said she knew the only reason I wanted to marry her was to get my hands on Halcyon, and she swore that would never happen and said if it was the last thing she ever did she'd get rid of both of us. Then she went berserk and picked me up as if I were no more than a puppy, swung me round and round over her head till I was dizzy, and threw me. It was terrifying. You were right: she *is* a savage. I don't intend to let her get her hands on me again, you can be sure of that. And she can have Halcyon too. I'm not willing to get myself killed over it."

"But . . . but what am I going to do?" Lisbeth's hand fluttered to her throat. She felt faint.

"Well, since my plan didn't work, see if you can come up with something better. I give up."

"But what about today? You're supposed to lead the hunt. And then there's the barbecue this evening. You're dumping everything in my lap. It's not fair."

Julius took his hat that Harold was holding out to him. "Well, that's too bad, but it can't be helped. Get Steve to lead the hunt. As for my absence, just say I'm too sore from the, shall we say, fall that I suffered last night."

"Please don't leave me like this," she beseeched.

"Oh, wake up, Lisbeth," he said irritably. "It's time you realized nothing is going to make her leave now. Can you blame her? She's lived like an animal her whole life and now she's richer than her wildest dreams. So it's over. Ned got what he wanted. Now I'm going to get busy and work my tail off so I can get my inheritance one day, and if you're smart you'll corner Barley today and get him to propose to you so you can get out of here and take your dowry with you. Now good-bye," he said, with a tip of his hat, "and good luck."

He walked out. Lisbeth stared furiously after him, but not for long. She raced back to her room and rang for Mariah, who appeared a few moments later, out of breath and worried as to why her mistress would summon her so early. She, of course, had been up for hours to see that the kitchen workers got the mammoth breakfast prepared for the houseful of guests.

Lisbeth was getting dressed and barked an order. "Send someone to the stable to find Steve and tell him he's to meet me on the east veranda as quick as he can get there. Hurry. Tell him it's important; there's not a moment to spare."

Mariah did not know what to think. She had just seen Julius leaving, and now Lisbeth seemed to be on the verge of hysterics. "Lord, child, what's going on around here?"

"Please, there's no time. Just do as I ask. And if any of the guests inquire about Julius, tell them he's not feeling well and is spending the day in bed."

Mariah was even more baffled, because she knew that wasn't so, but she didn't argue and went to do as she was told.

Finally dressed, Lisbeth hurried to meet Steve, expecting him to be waiting. Instead, she found Joshua standing apologetically on the lawn to explain that Steve had been gone since dawn.

"Gone? Where?" Dear Lord, don't let him have taken off for Mobile, she prayed. Surely he wouldn't, not with all that was going on.

"To be with Selena."

She lifted a brow. "What for?"

Joshua wished he did not have to talk about such things, but he had to answer Miss Lisbeth or be in big trouble. "I think 'cause it's her time. She sent somebody to fetch him, and just a while ago one of the women told me old Sadie, the midwife, had gone to the Leroux cabin."

"Well, you get yourself over there right away and tell him I need him to lead the men's hunt today because Master Julius isn't well. Now go."

He took off running, and Lisbeth forced herself to sit down and try to get hold of herself. If any guests meandered out to the veranda, it wouldn't do for them to find her distraught.

After what seemed hours, Joshua came running back, out of breath, eyes wide with fear of her reaction when he relayed the message that Steve was not coming. "He said he was stayin' with Selena till the baby gets here, and he also said since she was havin' a hard time, it might take the better part of the day."

Exasperated, Lisbeth got up and ran into the house, muttering under her breath that if it was the last thing she ever did, she would get even with Raven for all the grief she had caused.

*   *   *

Raven, wearing a simple lime-colored cotton dress, her hair swept back from her face and tied with a matching ribbon, stood outside the door to her room for a few seconds to make sure no one was about. It was early, with yet another hour before breakfast, and the men's hunt was scheduled to begin immediately afterward. She knew eventually she would have to face everyone, but first she wanted to talk privately to Julius in hopes of making peace. There just had to be a way for them to put aside what had happened.

She'd not had much sleep and smiled to remember the reason. It had been nearly dawn when she and Steve had finally been able to tear themselves apart. Now she was counting the hours until she could be with him again.

All seemed quiet, so she walked to Julius's quarters and knocked softly. When there was no response, she knocked louder, and that was when Lisbeth came upstairs and saw her. Shoving her away, she opened the door and pushed her inside.

Raven was stunned but Lisbeth did not make her wonder for long. "He's gone, thanks to you. He says he can't stand to be around you another minute. Furthermore, he's so sore he can hardly move, so he couldn't have led the hunt today anyway. I hope you're satisfied. Now the whole day is ruined, because Steve can't lead it. He's busy."

So much was hitting Raven that it was hard for her to grasp it all at once, but one thing puzzled her above all else. Steve had been looking forward to the hunt, so it had to be something serious to keep him away. One of the horses might be sick; she would go find out as soon as she managed to get Lisbeth calmed down. "I never meant to hurt Julius. You can't know how sorry I am. Where is he? I'll go talk to him."

"He's on his way to Mobile. He's moved out."

"Oh, no!"

"Oh, yes! And he's not coming back, and I've got to think of a way to keep the men entertained now that the hunt has to be canceled. I can't just tell everyone to go home, I'd never live it down."

"You don't have to. I'll take care of it."

Lisbeth sneered. "And just what can you do? I should think you'd be ashamed to show your face."

"Well, I'm not," Raven said. "Maybe I had to act like less than a lady last night, but that's because Julius was less than a gentleman. He knows that, but we'll straighten it out later. Right now, I'll see that everything goes according to schedule, so you can stop worrying."

She started out the door, but Lisbeth blocked her. "Where do you think you're going?"

"To change into riding clothes, of course."

"Riding clothes?" Lisbeth echoed. It had not dawned on her what Raven had in mind.

Raven smiled. "Of course. You don't expect me to lead the hunt dressed like this, do you?" Pushing by her, she hurried down the hall, leaving Lisbeth to stare after her.

Madame Bonet had sent two riding habits, one in black and the other made of a dark blue cloth, which Raven chose to wear. The jacket was short, with a cambric collar that would be cooler. The sleeves were wide at the ends with turned-back cuffs. She liked the wide skirt, for no matter how shocking it would be she'd have to ride full saddle. She had yet to master balancing with both legs to one side and feared she would might fall when Starfire went into a gallop.

Tucking her hair up into the matching felt hat, she pushed the annoying plume to one side, picked up her gloves, and hurried out to the stables.

As she glanced about in search of Joshua, she saw that the men's horses were already saddled.

Joshua came out of a stall. "Why, good morning, Miss Raven. What are you doing here?"

"It looks as though I'm going to have to lead the hunt, since there isn't anybody else to do it. Which one of the horses is sick?"

"Why, there ain't one that I know of. Who told you there was?"

She didn't answer. "Then where is Steve?"

Reluctantly, he repeated what he had told Miss Lisbeth. Miss Raven seemed to get even more upset than Miss Lisbeth had to hear Selena was having her baby. "Is something wrong?"

"No, just get Starfire ready." There were other things to think about for the moment, she told herself. There would be ample time later to wonder why Steve felt the need to be with Selena.

A short while later, when the men going on the hunt had gathered, she tried not to notice their skeptical looks as she told them she would be leading them. "Don't worry, I won't get you lost. I've managed to learn my way around pretty well. And I assure you I can shoot with both gun and bow." She patted the rifle tied to one side of the saddle, her bow on the other.

Everyone hung back to ride behind her except for Barley, who was pleased for her company and fell in beside her to make polite conversation. He asked enough questions to confirm that she really did know what she was doing and grinned to think what a shock the skeptics behind them were in for.

He was right. When they reached the preserve, she brought down a deer with one silent shot of her bow, rather than scatter the rest of the herd with gunfire, so the others would have a chance also to bring down trophies. She went on to do the same thing twice more. Consequently, by the time the hunt ended, she had earned the respect and admiration of each and every man.

Further astonishing them, when they got back to the house, eager to hand over the carcasses to the slaves, Raven rolled up her sleeves to help.

Everyone stared agape, and only Barley had the nerve to say. "Raven, we don't normally help with this part. We leave it to the butchers from the kitchen. They know what they're doing. It's not"—he swallowed self-consciously to have to remind her—"women's work."

She continued carving the buck that hung from a rack above. "Maybe not, but when I was in the smokehouse the other day, I looked over the cuts of meat there and noticed how a lot is being wasted, because the butchers don't know how to get the most out of a carcass. I'm going to show them. It's a shame to waste food, especially when they're missing some of the tastiest parts."

Barley turned away, not wanting to watch and knowing she was not to be dissuaded. Hurrying after the others to change for the barbecue, he met Lisbeth, perched sidesaddle on Belle. "I thought you'd be quilting with my mother and the other ladies."

"I got bored, and Belle needed some exercise." Actually, she had wanted to escape because all anyone seemed to want to talk about was Raven. She wouldn't have minded had they wanted to sympathize over what a disgrace she was, but instead they praised her, using words like charming, refreshing, and lovely, and while Lisbeth had been mortified over Raven being so brazen as to go hunting with the men, they thought it was wonderful and envied her having the nerve to do so.

She glanced about irritably. "Well, where is she now? What else has she done to embarrass me?"

"She's back there." He nodded and kept on going, not wanting to be around when she saw what Raven was doing.

Lisbeth trotted Belle around to the back yard where, seeing Raven hacking away at a deer carcass, she screamed in horror and dropped the reins.

Everyone turned toward the sound, including Raven, who saw quicker than anyone else that Belle had been frightened by Lisbeth's shrill scream. Consequently, with no restraint once Lisbeth let the reins go, the mare was out of control and took off running.

Lisbeth screamed again, which only made Belle gallop faster. She tried to hold on to the saddle, but Raven could see she would not be able to do so, for there was no large grasping horn as the men's saddles provided.

All around, the workers began to shout to one another. The horse was running away, but no one knew what to do about it.

Only Raven had the presence of mind to act. Starfire was right where she'd left him, only a few yards away, so she dropped her knife and ran toward him. There was no time to mount properly, so she leaped up Indian fashion by reaching up to brace herself on his rump with her hands while hoisting herself up at the same time, legs spread wide to fall naturally across his back.

"Go!" she yelled, digging her heels into his flanks, not taking time to settle her feet into the stirrups.

Starfire did not have to be told twice and took off, his mane flying in the wind. In only a few minutes, he had overtaken the frightened mare and Raven could reach out to grab the harness and bring her to a stop.

Lisbeth's hat, tied beneath her chin by a ribbon, had fallen forward onto her face. With her mouth open in screeching panic, the plume had dipped inside, and she spat it out at the same time as she yanked the ribbons free and threw it all to the ground in fury.

"Are you all right?" Raven asked gingerly, noticing Lisbeth had lost a shoe somewhere on the brief but wild ride.

If her stepsister expected gratitude, Lisbeth knew she was going to be greatly disappointed, because it was all Raven's fault and she intended to tell her so. "How dare you?" she challenged when she could find her voice. "How dare you do such a thing? Maybe I did scream and set Belle off, but anyone else would do the same to witness such a spectacle. You are supposed to be learning how to act like a lady. Not a . . . a butcher," she said in disgust.

Raven groaned to realize she had unintentionally made another blunder. Barley had tried to warn her, but she hadn't listened. Feebly, she attempted to justify what she had done. "I was just trying to show how a lot of good meat is being wasted, because they don't know how to cut up a deer in order to get the best parts. The Indians know how to make use of every bit, and—"

"And nobody cares," Lisbeth said, eyes wide with wonder that she could be so stupid. "We aren't Indians. We don't have to grovel for our food like the Indians."

"But to waste—"

"That's not important. Don't you see? We can afford to waste food, but be that as it may it is not your place to do such a thing. Can't you see that? Can't you try to forget your barbarian ways and at least pretend to be a lady for as long as we have guests?"

"If I've offended you or anyone else, I'm sorry, but I really don't see where I did anything so terribly wrong. Where is the harm in my teaching the butchers something new?"

"Oh, forget it. Just forget it." Lisbeth snatched Belle's reins from her and turned the mare around. "All I want is to try and get through the next few hours and get these people out of here before you do something really horrid, though I can't imagine what it would be. You've certainly outdone yourself so far."

Raven fell in beside her. She knew it was probably not the time but decided since Lisbeth was already upset she might as well make her suggestion. "Would you like me to teach you how to ride like I do? You would have better control over Belle if she ever tries to run away with you again. We could start tomorrow if you'd like."

Lisbeth slowed to stare at her incredulously. "Wait a minute. Did I hear you right? Did I actually hear you offer to give me riding lessons?"

"Yes, because—"

"Because you think I want to ride like you do, spraddle-legged like a man?" Lisbeth gave a sniff of disgust. "I'd sooner never ride a horse again."

"But you don't understand. I'd like for you to give me lessons too."

Lisbeth was suddenly suspicious. "Why?"

"Because I'd like to learn to ride sidesaddle. So we

can learn something from each other. And I'd also like to teach you how to use a gun. A woman needs to be able to defend herself."

Lisbeth was thankful they were almost to the house and people were running to meet them, because she was afraid she would scream again if Raven did not shut up. "You are beyond help," she said scathingly. "A woman doesn't need to defend herself, you little ninny. That's a man's job. And if she conducts herself like a lady, she won't need defending anyway. Now go away and leave me alone. You've embarrassed me enough for one day."

"I'm not going away, Lisbeth."

Something in Raven's tone made her slow. "What do you mean?"

Raven decided the time had come to speak her piece. "It means that I'm here to stay, and even though I might embarrass you again and again till I learn your ways, I am not leaving. Halcyon is big enough for all of us to enjoy, and in a few days I'm going to Mobile and find Julius and try my best to make him see that. I know he has to work at the shipyard to earn his inheritance, but he can come home on weekends. It would be nice if you'd go with me," she added.

Just then Barley ran up to help Lisbeth down. "Wasn't Raven wonderful?" he cried, loud enough for others to hear. "She saved your life!"

Under her breath, Lisbeth growled, "Shut your mouth, Barley. Don't say another word. I mean it."

He stared after her, bewildered, as she stalked toward the house, then doggedly followed.

*   *   *

Raven managed to get through the evening, but the atmosphere was tense. No one asked about Julius or dared mention the incident of the night before. Nor was anything said about Raven's hunting exploits or the fact that she had saved Lisbeth on a runaway horse.

The ladies spoke of flowers and babies and new recipes. The men discussed the price of cotton and corn and politics. None of the bachelors hovered around her as they had at the reception, but everyone was pleasant.

All Raven wanted was for the evening to end and everyone to leave, because she was counting the minutes till she could be in Steve's arms, where she knew she would find solace. But even as she longed for the hour of midnight, she could not help being plagued with wonder over why he had felt the need to be with Selena when she had her baby.

At last it was time. She crept out of the house and ran to the stable. The ladder was in place, and she scrambled up to his waiting arms.

"I thought you'd never get here," he said, before kissing her till they were both breathless. Reluctantly, he let her go to pull the ladder up, then led her to his room.

She glanced around in the mellow glow of the lantern. It was sparse but clean, and suddenly she felt a bit self-conscious. She had never been in a man's bedroom before.

He broke the awkward spell to commend her. "I haven't been back long, but Joshua was telling me how you led the hunt and brought back more deer than any of the men, and also how you saved Lisbeth when Belle ran away. You were wonderful, Raven.

But I already knew that." He brushed his lips across her forehead.

"I wish you could have been here." She was not about to ask him where he was, hoping he would offer to tell her.

And he did.

"I wanted to be. Especially after I heard Julius left like he did. But Selena needed me. She was in labor, and her father was drunk and raising hell. She sent for me because she was scared he might hurt her or the baby. When I got there, he was carrying on so bad I had to hit him and knock him out. She was nowhere near delivering, and I didn't want her to be around when he woke up, so I got a wagon and took her to one of the empty slave cottages. Her mother was scared of what Masson would do if she went with us, so I got Sadie, the midwife, to help."

Raven said thinly, "She must have had a difficult time, since you were with her so long."

"Well, there was nobody else. Just me and Sadie."

"And she had the baby all right?"

He smiled. "A girl. Pretty as her mother. Strong, too. She even squeezed my finger while I was holding her. I've never held a baby before," he added, thinking how nice it had been.

Raven told herself she had no right to be jealous, but it bothered her to think of Steve sharing such an intimate time with Selena.

Steve turned to the moment at hand, twining his fingers in her hair and drawing her close. "I missed you."

She leaned into his kiss.

He told himself to go slowly, to savor every second, but the intoxication of having her in his arms again drained him of all restraint. Her kisses were as eager as his own, making the fire in his loins burn even stronger, and it was all he could do to keep from ripping her clothes off then and there.

He began to fumble with the buttons of her gown with anxious fingers as his tongue plunged into her mouth, probing, seeking, bringing her to meet his passion in kind. She helped him undress her, and when she was naked, he pulled her down with him on the bed.

His touch was gentle as he felt of her all over, his lips finally closing about one nipple while his fingers gently squeezed the other. She arched against him as the heat in her belly spread to consume her body. She was still dazzled to realize how he could ignite desire the first instant he touched her, and suddenly she could not get close enough to him. She was shaking with wanting him, and, as she felt his hardness against her bare flesh, she reached boldly to unleash him from his trousers.

He sprang forth, and she caressed the length of him. He shuddered with pleasure. "I don't think I can wait," he groaned.

"I don't think I want you to." She guided him into her.

He entered quick and hard, but she did not care, for she was more than ready for him, eagerly meeting his every thrust till they crested together in rapture sublime.

Afterward, they lay with arms and legs entwined about and slept the peaceful slumber of contented lovers. It was only when the rooster crowed loudly just outside that Raven woke and knew it was time to leave.

She dressed quickly, all the while gazing adoringly

at him. His eyes were closed. He did not move, did not know when she brushed her lips across his before leaving.

And neither did he hear her whisper, "I do love you so."

Steve reached for Raven but she was not there, and he woke and thought for a moment that maybe it had all been a dream, that the wonder and the splendor had not happened after all. But as the morning sun streamed across his face, the grogginess left him and he knew that it had been very real . . . and wonderful.

The only shadow cast upon his joy in remembering it all was worry over how, despite all resolve, he was afraid he was falling in love.

22

Mariah set the breakfast tray beside Lisbeth's bed, took a few sniffs, and asked, "Is that smoke I smell?" She looked at the grate and saw a small pile of still smoldering ashes in the fireplace grate. Her eyes widened. "You haven't been trying to start a fire, have you? It's summertime, child, and terrible hot. If you're cold, you must be comin' down with a fever." She reached to touch her forehead.

Lisbeth slapped her hand away. "I don't have a fever. I was burning trash, not that it's any of your business. Now leave me alone."

Mariah was almost to the door but suddenly couldn't hold back any longer. "Miss Lisbeth, you just ain't acting right lately. Ever since Master Julius moved into Mobile, you don't leave this room and you eat like a bird."

Lisbeth twisted the hem of the satin sheet covering

her, wishing it were Raven's neck. "I don't want to see her. I refuse to be around her. I hate her."

Mariah did not have to guess who she was talking about. "Now child, that's no way to feel. She's your stepsister."

"She's nothing to me. She drove Julius away. People laugh at us. Oh, why did she ever have to come here?" She beat on the mattress with her fists.

As Mariah glimpsed the corner of an envelope in the fireplace that was not yet burned, it occurred to her what might have Lisbeth so upset. "Was it them letters that been coming here since the party? Have folks been saying unkind things about Miss Raven?"

"Yes," Lisbeth lied, "And I burned the letters because I can't stand looking at them." The truth was the letters had all been addressed to Raven, only Lisbeth had gotten to them first. Mariah wouldn't have known they were for Raven, because she couldn't read. But the letters had not been critical at all; instead they were filled with sickening accolades for Raven and promises of invitations to socialize once her period of mourning had ended. Each writer said how nice it was that Ned had insisted the reception be held as planned after he died so they could have the opportunity to meet Raven without a long wait.

Mariah made a *tsk*ing sound. "Well, I sure am sorry. She tries so hard."

"Tries hard to make me miserable, you mean." Lisbeth sniffed. "I don't like how you take up for her, Mariah. I want you to stop it."

"I don't mean no disrespect. Lord knows, I love you like you're my own, but it makes me sad to see you so unhappy. And Miss Raven *is* trying. She works awful hard. Just like this morning. I'm always the first one to the house, but when I got here she was already up and working. She's even called in the overseers again to make sure things are being done like they should."

Lisbeth thought she would love to eavesdrop on one of those meetings to witness just how stupid Raven was. The overseers probably burst out laughing the second they walked out the door. "Has she met with all of them yet?" she asked, an idea growing in her mind.

"She's got one more. The reason I know is I just took her a fresh pot of coffee, and she said Mr. Leroux hadn't showed up yet and she wished he'd hurry up, 'cause she was waiting to talk to him before going to Mobile."

Lisbeth was already out of bed and walking toward her dressing alcove.

"Why don't you go with her?" Mariah suggested. "It's a nice day, and it would do you good to get out. And you haven't seen Julius in a while."

"Pigs will fly before I go anywhere with that little twit. If I want to see my brother, I'll walk before riding in the same carriage with her."

With a sigh, Mariah left her.

Raven paced restlessly around the study. The coffee was cold, but it didn't matter, because she was so annoyed with Masson Leroux she wouldn't have offered him any had it been hot and fresh. He was nearly an hour late, and thirty minutes ago she'd sent another message to remind him of that fact. The other overseers had been on time for their meetings, but Masson was the one she most wanted to see. She was going to warn him that his heavy drinking had to stop or he would find himself out of a job.

She tried not to think that her motive had anything to do with the way Steve was having to spend so much time making sure Masson was not bothering Selena and her new baby. But the truth was it annoyed her, because in all the weeks she had been sleeping with him, not many nights passed that Selena didn't send for him, frightened because her father was drunk and lurking in the woods near her cabin.

Sometimes Steve chased him off. On other occasions, he couldn't find him. Raven said she should just fire Masson and that would solve everything, but Steve said it would only cause Selena added stress if her father took her mother, whom she adored, and went away. Besides, Steve had pointed out, Masson's drinking apparently didn't keep him from doing his job, and he was hoping that sooner or later things would smooth over and Masson would calm down.

One night, Raven frowned to recall, she had bluntly asked Steve why the father of Selena's baby didn't come forward to accept his responsibility. "If my father were still alive, you can believe he'd tell him how he'll regret it one day if he doesn't. There's nothing worse than a man abandoning a woman and his child."

Steve had denied knowing anything, but he had said it so that Raven wondered whether he was lying and why. She liked to think the two of them were so close there'd be no secrets between them. But after that, she had not mentioned Selena or the situation again.

Now she had made up her mind to do something about it unbeknownst to Steve.

At last Masson arrived. "A few of the workers were late getting started this morning," he said by way of excuse. "They gripe about it being so hot. If they felt a lash on their worthless backs once in a while, they'd know better, but since you're just like your daddy and let 'em get away with it, they'll stay shiftless."

"There will never be whippings at Halcyon," she said firmly, icily. She was not yet ready to inform him or anyone else that sometime in the future there would be no slaves there anyway. She hadn't had time yet to figure out how to free them and still keep them and pay them decent wages. But if there was a way she would find it.

He sat down, even though she had not invited him to. "Well, what did you want to see me about? I got to get back in the field before they all decide to find a shade tree and lay down for a nap."

Raven did not like him. Even if she did not know what she did about him, she would still not like him. He was arrogant, and she suspected he was cruel to the slaves. He was also the only overseer who seemed to resent her.

"The fact is, Mr. Leroux," she began, continuing to stand so she could look down at him, "I asked you here today to talk about your drinking. You're doing too much of it, and you've been causing trouble. If it doesn't stop right away, I'll have to dismiss you."

He bounded to his feet. "You can't do that. I've been here nearly ten years and always done a good job. Your daddy would tell you that if he was alive. Who's been poisoning you against me? It's him, ain't it?" His eyes narrowed. "Maddox. He's the one. He's told you about me drinking."

"It doesn't matter who told me. The fact is you

have been getting drunk almost nightly and threatening your daughter."

"Yeah, I sure have. She's a whore. She got herself in trouble and shamed me and her momma and the whole family. I may not have much, but one thing I've always had is my good name, and she ruined it. It makes me so mad that maybe I do drink too much. But I do my job. Anybody will tell you that. So you got no call to run me off."

"I said I'd give you another chance."

"But it *was* him, wasn't it?" he persisted. "Well, instead of blaming me for everything, how come you don't tell him to marry her and give her baby a name, and then I won't have to be ashamed? He's the one. I know it as good as I'm standing here. He's the one responsible, and he's lying if he says he ain't."

Raven reeled as though he had slapped her. It all came flooding back. The day she arrived, Masson had asked Steve why he didn't marry Selena, but Steve said it was only Masson's way of telling him to stay out of his business. Now she started wondering all over again. After all, Masson had to have good reason to name Steve as the father so boldly . . . didn't he?

She sank into the chair behind the desk, afraid her wobbling knees would not support her any longer as her mind began to whirl. Even if Steve did not love Selena, she and her baby were his responsibility. Thinking about it brought painful memories rushing back, memories of how she had loathed her father for abandoning her mother. But that was when she had believed he had known her mother was pregnant. Now she knew different. He would never have let anything keep him from going back to her had he known. If

Steve was the father of Selena's baby, he obviously did know it, and for him not to marry her was unforgivable.

Raven did not want to believe Steve would shirk his duty. Because she loved him, she would give him the benefit of the doubt until there was real proof. "Did your daughter tell you that Steve Maddox fathered her child?" she asked, looking Masson straight in the eyes.

"No, but she don't have to. Why else would he hang around her like he does? And why was he there when she had her little bastard? And look at this"—he pointed to a bruise that had almost faded away, leaving only a shadow on his jaw—"he hit me and knocked me out, because I raised hell about him being so brazen as to show up when the baby was coming. Why would a man act like that if it weren't his baby?"

Raven did not know but made up her mind that, until she could be sure Steve was the father, she would not allow herself to believe it. "I sympathize with you, but you're going to have to cope with this in another way. One more drinking bout and you're through here."

He got up and stalked to the door, grumbling. "He just gets to go on like he has been, and the best I can hope for is he don't give her another baby to have to raise by herself, lowlife that he is. Your daddy took up for him, so I reckon it's only natural you would too, but he'll get what's coming to him one day, you'll see." He slammed the door after him.

Lisbeth had been quietly sitting, unnoticed, on the porch just outside the open window of the study. She had hoped to witness Raven's incompetence but what she had learned was far more valuable, because now she was convinced, beyond all doubt, that Raven and Steve were involved with each other. It made sense.

Why else would Raven care about Masson Leroux's drinking? Everyone knew he was at odds with Steve over his daughter's shameful predicament, and Lisbeth had even heard some of the servants gossiping about how Selena sent for Steve, no matter what the hour, whenever her father was having one of his drunken tirades. Raven did not like the interruptions, and that was behind her warning Masson to quit his drinking. She certainly couldn't go to Selena and demand that she stop sending for Steve.

Hearing Masson leave, Lisbeth stole a quick peek through the window. Raven was sitting with her head in her hands, shoulders slumped. She was obviously upset.

Many things were becoming clear, Lisbeth was delighted to think—like how Steve was the reason Raven had turned down the offer she and Julius had made her after the will was read. He was her incentive for staying. She probably hoped he would marry her after a decent mourning period, but Lisbeth didn't care about all that. Now she knew Raven's weakness for Steve, she knew how to get rid of her. All she had to do was drive a wedge between the two of them, making Raven so mad she would be glad to take their offer of money and hightail it back to Texas. After all, she would have no cause to stay once she realized Steve had mercly been using her.

Lisbeth knew exactly how she was going to make it all happen.

Joshua reined up the horses in front of the office of the Ralston Shipping Company. It was a three-story brick building with a plain facade and had been built several blocks away from the main loading docks. It was midafternoon, no one seemed to be around, and he was worried. He did not like being there with Miss Raven and turned in his seat to tell her so. "I wish you had brought along one of the overseers. It's not safe down here, even during the day. I've heard about all kinds of things happening." He got down to help her from the carriage.

She held out a gloved hand to him. "We'll be fine. It's no one's business where I go, Joshua. Besides, if I'm going to run Halcyon, I can't be constantly asking some man to hold my hand, now, can I?" She had not told Steve for fear he would have insisted on coming with her. And maybe she would have welcomed him if not for hearing Masson's accusations, but now she wanted to be alone to decide if there was any truth to them. She hoped not. Because she was not sure what she would do if there was.

"Where is everyone today?" she asked, glancing about. "I can't believe it's always this deserted here."

Joshua told her he had seen a big ship coming in at the other end of the wharf. "Folks always go to watch. That's why we shoulda brought somebody with us."

"There is nothing to be afraid of. I have a gun, and I know how to use it." She patted her blue felt bag. It was small, but it went with the yellow cotton traveling outfit she was wearing, and she had managed to stuff her six-shooter inside it.

Guiltily, she wondered if she should be wearing the black garb of mourning that Mariah had told her some women wore—materials of serge, alpaca, or merino, with collars and cuffs of folded crepe and no other trim. But Lisbeth had said that was nonsense. "Only widows do that. As long as we conduct ourselves properly and wear conservative colors, no one will think ill of us."

Raven had accepted this logic. After all, what did she know of the white man's custom of mourning? If Lisbeth said it was all right, who was she to argue?

Joshua was still grumbling. "Well, I just hope you don't need it."

She left him and entered the building, pushing open a glass front door. She was relieved to see a clerk sitting behind a desk on the other side of the counter, who jumped to his feet to ask what he could do for her. Introducing herself and explaining that she wanted to see Julius, the clerk became flustered. He was well aware of her importance and hated to be the one to tell her that Mr. White was at the saloon at the end of the street. He was not about to add that was also where Mr. White spent most of his time.

"Well, I suppose I'll have to go down there."

With no enthusiasm, the clerk said, "You don't have to do that. I'll go get him for you."

She knew if Julius found out she was there, he might leave and go somewhere else to avoid her. "No, thank you," she said. "I have my carriage and driver outside."

The clerk did not argue. He hadn't wanted to go anyway but felt he had to be polite.

Joshua complained all the way, but Raven ignored him. When they reached the saloon, she saw it was a small rundown building surrounded by large wooden shipping containers that had apparently been discarded. Junk and trash was piled all around. She wondered why Julius would frequent such a disreputable-looking place. There had to be better saloons somewhere on the wharf, but remembering the paltry allowance the will had provided him, she knew he probably couldn't afford those places.

She also worried to think he was not working as he was supposed to. If the estate's administrators ever found out, he would lose everything, but she had no intention of telling them. She wanted to help Julius, not hurt him, and if he'd let her, she'd gladly supplement his income so he wouldn't have to live above the office.

After telling Joshua to stay where he was, she went inside the saloon, wincing at the sour odor. She paused to allow her eyes to get used to the dim light and was finally able to make out a bar, wooden tables, and chairs. She also realized that the laughter and chattering she'd heard from outside had ceased as everyone turned to look at her.

She felt terribly self-conscious but was not about to turn back. Clearing her throat, she announced, "I'm looking for Mr. Julius White. Has anyone seen him?"

An explosion of guffaws ripped the stillness, and some of the men began taunting her.

"You Julius's wife? He didn't tell us he had one."

"Naw, he sure didn't."

"Pretty, too."

"Yeah, with a fine filly like that, how come he's in the back room honeyed up with Lucy?"

"Aw, he ain't doin' nothin' but beggin' Lucy for a drink. He ain't got the money to pay for what she sells."

"You got money, sugar? You here to pay what he owes?"

They leaned against the bar or sprawled in their chairs, unkempt men raking her with hungry, insolent gazes. But she was not afraid and went farther into the room. "No, I am not his wife, and I am not here to pay his bill, but I would appreciate it if someone would tell him his stepsister is here to see him."

"Stepsister?" A man hooted. Raven saw right away that he was wearing a gun strapped beneath his pot-belly as he got up from his chair and came toward her. He looked her up and down and sneered. "You ain't no relative. You're a high-class whore, that's what you are. We know who Julius is, he's a rich boy that's too stingy to spend his money. He owes all of us too, including me. So I reckon if he's too tight to pay his debts with money, it's all right for me to take it out in trade with you!"

Some of the others urged him on, yelling, "Get her, Big Dan, get her!"

On the way there from the company office, Raven would not have been surprised if bandits had jumped out at her carriage from an alley. That was the kind of trouble she had anticipated. But the last thing she had expected was anyone so bold as to attack her in a public saloon.

"Stay away from me," she warned. "I don't want any trouble." She was not scared, for the instinct for survival quickly took over. Gone was the ladylike demeanor she had struggled so hard to acquire the past weeks and months. She opened her purse, fingers itching to close about the six-shooter before things really got out of hand.

But then her arms were grabbed and wrenched behind her and her purse fell to the floor. The man called Big Dan lunged at the same time, bellowing, "Threaten me, will you? I'll teach you what trouble is, you little spitfire."

A foul-smelling rag was stuffed in her mouth to stifle her screams. Held tightly by the man behind her, Big Dan began to grope her, squeezing her breasts, snatching and feeling her buttocks. His friends cheered him on as Raven struggled to no avail.

"What the—" Julius, hearing the commotion, burst through a door at the back of the room. He had been visiting Lucy, the prostitute, but only to beg for a loan as the men had said. Seeing what was happening and recognizing Raven, he roared, "Damn you, Big Dan, that's my stepsister! Let her go!"

The man holding her was startled by Julius's outcry and loosened his grip just long enough for Raven to make her move. The warriors had instilled in her the need to be ready for any opportunity to defend when in danger. So without having to think about it, she knew to bring her knee up into Big Dan's crotch and swing backward to slam her foot into the man behind her in the same vulnerable place. Both grabbed themselves in anguished shrieks and crumpled to the floor.

A shot rang out. Raven leaped up to the nearest table to see Julius was cornered. He had fired his one-shot derringer and missed, which only served to anger his intended victim, who had drawn his own gun, which was capable of firing several rounds. "I'll blow you to pieces, you bastard," the man yelled.

In a flash, Raven bent to whip out the knife strapped to her ankle and in a streak of silver sent it whizzing across the room to pin the gunman's sleeve to the wall where he stood. His gun fell to the floor with a clatter as everyone gasped.

Raven stooped to snatch a holstered gun from the man standing closest to her and fired toward the ceiling. "Just stay right where you are, all of you, and nobody gets hurt." She motioned to Julius. "Let's get out of here."

He could only stare at her in wonder, unable to move.

"I said let's go," she ordered sharply, "before I have to kill somebody."

As soon as they were back in his private office, he opened a desk drawer and took out a bottle of whiskey. There was not much inside, only a good swallow. He had hoped Lucy would see fit to loan him a bottle of her home brew till he drew his next allowance, but she hadn't. This was all he had, but he figured he'd never need it more than he did at that minute. After draining it, he sent it crashing against the wall behind Raven and demanded, "Now tell me what in the hell you thought you were doing?"

"Saving your life." She was surprised he was so upset. "But that's over now. I came to ask you to come home."

"Never. Go away and leave me alone."

"Not till you hear me out." She sat down, carefully pulling together the tattered front of her jacket. She made a mental note to take it off before she got back to Halcyon so no one would see it and want to know what happened. And she would make Joshua promise not to tell about any of it.

"There's no need for things to be like this," she continued. "I know you have to work here because of the will, but you can come home on weekends. And you don't have to exist on that paltry allowance you were given. I'll see that you have more money. I just don't want you going in places like that, Julius. You could get killed. And I do want you to come home."

"Get this straight," he said through clenched teeth.

"I don't intend ever to go back to Halcyon as long as you are there, and I never want to see your face around here again. This is my company, or it will be one day. And you have humiliated me. The very idea"—he banged his fist on the desk for emphasis, making her jump—"of you going into that saloon and acting like a—" He couldn't say it. He was too mad to go on.

"A savage?" She spoke in quiet hurt. "I suppose it did appear that way, didn't it? But when I was attacked I had no choice." She stood. It was no use. He hated her and always would. Nothing she could do would ever change that.

Julius leaped up. Her words had stung to the core, for in his eyes, she had denigrated his manhood. "You're saying I couldn't save us, aren't you?" He rushed around the desk to follow after her. "Is that what you're saying, that I'm a weakling? That I don't know how to handle a gun? That I can't take care of you?"

Sadly, she told him, "Julius, I hate to say it, but you can't even take care of yourself."

Then she left, quietly closing the door on his anger.

23

The instant she stepped off the ladder into the loft, Steve imprisoned her by gently tunneling his hands through her hair, holding her face close to his. Raven was helpless against the concentrated assault of his mouth, but nothing could have made her resist, for she wanted his kiss, this moment, with an urgency that would not be denied.

She reveled in the slow glide of his tongue upon hers, lingering as he relished the sweet taste of her mouth. She clung to him as desperately as a drowning man and felt as though she were indeed drowning, in a sea of endless desire, swept by infinite tides of fulfillment.

Steve had been waiting for her, eager to take her in his arms and guide her quickly into the safety of his room. He was shirtless, and she thrilled to run her hands over his broad chest, boldly sliding her fingers downward to caress the swell there, proof of his desire.

When they were both breathless from the kiss, he gently scolded, "You're one stubborn filly, Raven. Joshua told me he took you to Mobile today. I should have gone with you. It's not safe for a woman to travel alone around the waterfront. You need someone with you who's armed."

She touched the tip of his nose and smiled. "But *I* was armed. And I don't need a man to take care of me, remember?"

A shadow crossed his face. How well he knew she did not need him except for anything but the moment at hand, a reality that was needling him more and more as his feelings for her grew and deepened. "Yes, I remember," he said, fighting to keep the bitterness from his voice as he drew her to him almost roughly.

Helpless, she was once more caught up in the heat of their encounter, even though her heart cried out in silent anguish to tell him he was wrong; she needed him in so many ways, most of all to share her whole life, not just a part of it. But she dared not speak, knowing she could not beg for more than he was willing to give.

She helped him undress her and then lay back on the bed, unable to tear her eyes from him as he peeled his breeches down over hard, powerful thighs. Neither did she glance shyly away at the sight of his naked body, for she found it beautiful. Warmth coursing through her veins, she yielded to temptation and reached out to stroke the steely length of him.

With a soft moan, he fell beside her. Feasting on her perfection, he said, "You are magnificent." Slowly, he outlined each of her breasts with a fingertip, marveling at their shape, delighting to feel how she shuddered at his touch. Her nipples begged to be tasted, and he dipped his head to devour them.

A shiver ran through her as she closed her eyes and arched her neck, thrusting her breasts toward him in offering. She drank in the scent of his skin, and burrowed her face in his thick hair, luxuriating in its softness, still damp from his bath, as she traced the ridge of his brow and the line of his firm jaw downward to caress the corners of his mouth upon her breast.

Her hands began to explore farther, wandering over the firm, tight flesh of his shoulders, thrilling at the ripple of muscles beneath her caress. On down his back she moved, feeling his silent gasp as she touched his hips, the hard molded buttocks that trembled in response to the teasing squeeze of her touch. Finally, she reached and gently massaged beneath his shaft.

He could not hold back a ragged gasp as he retreated from her breasts to cover her mouth with his in a burning, bruising kiss. His hands began their own frenzied exploration of her body, diving to her thighs and between. He did not have to feel her moisture to know she was ready, but he wanted the glory to last as long as possible. He touched the nub of her desire, and she tore from his kiss to cry out in frenzy, "I want you now!"

He laughed softly, deep in his throat. "No, my sweet. Not yet. I want this to last as long as possible."

Her hand closed about him then. She felt him quiver and was delighted to give him such pleasure.

With a soft growl, he raised up to roll her over on her stomach and began brushing his hot, moist lips over her back and hips. His tongue flicked and fluttered, burning her skin, evoking squeals of shock and joy as he licked her all the way to her ankles. Her toes curled, and pleasure became one long, slow moan that seemed to reach all the way from the very core of her womanhood deep between her legs.

He skimmed all over, up and down her body, and just when she thought she could surely stand no more, he rolled her on her back again and, without warning, spread her thighs and dove between to devour her there.

Raven felt the supreme ecstasy peaking and twisted her face to the pillow to burrow and muffle the frantic screams of rapture she could not hold back. Even when she had soared to the highest zenith of passion fulfilled, he mercilessly did not relent in his assault but continued to make her soar wildly to a distant realm of enjoyment from which she prayed never to return.

She was panting, when he drew his face away, and smiled dreamily at him as he positioned himself between her. Slowly, by inches, he slid into her. As always, he was gentle, afraid of hurting her for he was so large. But wickedly, wantonly, she reached to cup his buttocks and pull him toward her in a hard thrust.

"My God, Raven, what have you done to me!" he said tightly, hoarsely, his breath hot and moist against her neck as he began to push in and out of her.

Her mouth was against his shoulder, her nails frantically digging into his moving hips. He rode her as if she were a wild stallion, high-spirited and determined to throw him, but he held tight and the race to the sun began.

He raised up, stiffening his arms, wanting to see her lovely face, wet with perspiration and gleaming like liquid gold in the lantern's mellow light. He continued to roll his hips upon her, driving himself deep with each thrust. He was also sweating, brow dripping, jaws clenched, every muscle in his body rigid and fighting to hold back, for he refused to allow the magic to end.

"Again," he commanded her. "Come again, my sweet, with me." And he began to roll himself about in her, making the fire in the tunnel of her passion burn ever brighter with each searing brush against her flesh.

She closed her eyes and gave herself over to the boiling rage within. It grew harder, stronger, spreading from head to toes and back again, rippling over her gently at first, then building as though the heat of the sun had opened her up to sear her, and she clamped her legs about him tightly and squeezed with all her might. She felt the throb deep inside as his hot release filled her. And she knew, if only for one fleeting instant, that they were one, and she reveled in the knowledge and wished, with tears stinging her tightly closed eyes, that it could always be so.

For a long time neither moved, and then Steve rolled to the side to lie on his back. She snuggled against him, her head on his shoulder, one arm across his broad chest. He cradled her to him, and after a time he fell asleep.

But Raven could not sleep for thinking how much she loved him and dared not let him know. He had once told her he never wanted to take a wife. To admit her feelings might ruin everything.

Everything?

What was *everything*? Stolen hours of passion after she sneaked out of the house in the middle of the night, ever afraid someone would see her? Forever guarding against a tender look shared, fearing her cheeks would flame with the heat of an accidental touch, lest anyone notice and wonder and, God forbid, spread gossip that the mistress of Halcyon was having a torrid affair with her horse trainer? It would brand her a hussy, a whore.

This existence was what she clung to as *everything*?

If so, was it truly better than nothing at all?

But what if Masson Leroux had been telling the truth and Steve was actually the father of Selena's baby? Could he secretly be sleeping with her also, dividing his insatiable passion?

She bit back a sob to think how devastated she would be if she found that to be true, because he was the one and only reason she tried so hard to make Halcyon her home. It was so frustrating she often wished she had never decided to stay, but her love for Steve had made her want to keep trying, despite all obstacles.

Now she knew she had to leave his side before she started to cry. She slipped out of bed, dressed quickly, and then, as always, kissed him lightly and silently mouthed her avowal of love.

He made a soft murmuring sound and stirred. She hesitated, hoping he would not awaken. If so, he would want her to stay till just before the first gray and rose shadows of dawn. He would probably even want to make love to her again, and she would yield eagerly, as always, but that was not what she wanted now. She had to be alone to nurse her misery and convince herself to continue to be grateful for a part of him, for she could not bear the thought of having none.

As she let herself out, quietly climbing down the ladder, she could not know that Steve was again caught in the throes of his own misery as he wrestled within himself while sleeping, tormented with fear over how he was starting to care for her too much.

*   *   *

Lisbeth crouched in a corner of the stable, waiting for Raven to come down the ladder. It was late, but she was too mad to care. Neither was she sleepy. Her anger was all she needed to fuel her energy and keep her awake.

She had been watching from the veranda when Raven left the house, but by the time she could get downstairs and trail after her, Raven was already in the stable and had crawled up to the loft.

So Lisbeth had settled down to wait and find out if Selena would send for Steve during the night. After all, it was only logical to expect Masson to be so angry over Raven's ultimatum that he would throw caution to the wind and really get rip-roaring drunk. Lisbeth needed to know if that happened, needed to know if he might be anywhere around Selena's cabin.

Because Lisbeth intended to pay Selena a visit this night and did not want anyone to see her when she did.

She was alerted by the sound of wood creaking. Peeking out from behind a bale of hay, she saw Raven climbing down the ladder and felt a rush of fury to think how coldly Steve had spurned *her* but could warmly welcome another.

She made sure Raven was back inside the house before skirting around to where she had earlier left a small lantern hidden in the bushes. Lighting it, she hurried down the well-worn path leading to the rows of whitewashed slave cabins a half mile or so away.

She had managed to find out, without arousing suspicion, that Selena was staying in the last cabin on the end, beside a creek feeding from the river. It was a squat, square structure, one of the earlier ones built by Ned's grandfather.

The door was open and soft candlelight fell on Selena, as she sat in a chair next to the bed, nursing her baby.

Lisbeth could not help but be moved by the tender scene, and for an instant she hesitated. Deep down, she hated what she was about to do but saw no other way.

"Who's there?" Selena called out as the lantern Lisbeth carried flooded the room with light. Then, seeing who it was, alarm yielded to surprise. "Miss Lisbeth. What are you doing here this time of night?"

Stepping inside, Lisbeth glanced about at the meager furnishings: a wood-frame bed with pine straw poking through holes in the sagging mattress, another chair that looked as though it was about to collapse, a three-legged table propped against a wall, and a tiny box being used as a crib for the baby. The floor was dirt. She had never been inside any of the cabins and never realized how dismal they were.

Selena could tell by her expression what she was thinking and said brightly, "Miss Raven says when picking season is over, she's going to put the men to work on the cabins. There'll be glass windows and good doors. Plank floors. She says she might even build new ones. I think Master Ned always wanted to but never got around to it."

"I wanted to see your baby." Lisbeth stepped closer and held up the lantern. She couldn't see any real resemblance to Steve in the infant but told herself that didn't mean anything.

Instinctively, Selena gathered the child closer. "Why?" she asked nervously, adding, "Her name is Amanda."

"I just wondered what Steve Maddox's daughter looked like."

Chills raced up and down Selena's spine. "She isn't his. Who told you such a lie?"

"Your father."

"Well, it's not so. He thinks that because Steve is my friend. That's all it is, I swear it."

"Then who is the real father?"

Selena lifted her chin. "That's nobody's business but mine." Only Steve knew it was Luther Bendale who had gotten her pregnant. She knew she'd made a terrible mistake, but nothing could undo it, and it had been best to bury her secret with Luther.

The baby had fallen asleep, and Selena got up and tucked her into the box cradle. "I can't understand your coming here to ask me something like that anyway. Why do you care? And what are you doing talking to my pa about me? I'm not bothering anybody. I earn my keep. Pa said I've got to start back in the fields tomorrow, and I'm not arguing. I know I've got it to do. But I don't need to be kept up talking about foolish things when I need my rest, so if you'd leave I'd appreciate it."

"Why did you send for Steve to be with you when you were giving birth? Didn't he sit beside you and hold your hand just like an expectant father?"

Selena was getting mad and fighting tears. "You've no right to say things like that when you don't know what you're talking about. I sent for Steve because my pa was making trouble and I was afraid he'd hurt me or my baby. Steve brought me here and stayed to make sure Pa didn't bother me. And I've told Pa over and over, Steve isn't responsible. Pa shouldn't have told you he was."

"Actually, he didn't tell *me,* he told Raven."

Selena's eyes went wide. "Why would Pa do that?"

Lisbeth did not mince words. "Because she's tired of you interrupting her lovemaking with Steve when you send for him to come chase your father off when he's drunk."

Selena's mouth fell open, and for a few seconds she could not speak. "Why . . . why, I don't know what you mean."

Lisbeth managed a tight smile. "It's simple. Raven and Steve are sleeping together. And your father gets drunk and bothers you, and you send for Steve. Raven is in bed with him, and he has to get up and leave her, and she's tired of it. But she couldn't tell you that, of course, so she called in your father this morning to chastise him for his drinking. She told him if it didn't stop she'd have to let him go."

"Oh, no." Selena sank to the bed. "That means my whole family would have to move. And I couldn't go with them; Pa wouldn't let me move back in with them now if I wanted to, which I don't. I'd be afraid he'd hurt me or the baby. He can be terribly mean when he's drunk."

Lisbeth sat down next to her and feigned sympathy. "I can understand your concern, but there's an answer to all of this. All you have to do is agree to my little plan."

Selena felt apprehension creep through her. "What are you talking about?"

"It's really quite simple. All you have to do is go to Raven and tell her that Steve really is your baby's father, and—"

"No," Selena cried, aghast. "I'd never do that. Why would I? It's not so."

"But he's sleeping with Raven."

"What difference does that make? He's my friend,

not my lover. I don't care who he sleeps with, do you? Maybe you wish it was you instead," she dared to suggest. "Maybe that's what this is all about. You want to get rid of her so's you can have him all to yourself."

Lisbeth held back her anger. "Don't be ridiculous. I'm not interested in Steve Maddox, for heaven's sake. As soon as it's proper, Barley Tremayne will officially court me, but that's none of your concern. The only thing you need to worry about is how you're going to be able to keep you and your baby from starving after Raven runs you out of here."

"Why would she want to do that?" Selena felt like her frightened heart was going to jump right out of her chest. Lisbeth was scaring her to death.

"Eventually, that's what she'll do because she won't be able to bear the thought that you've had a baby by Steve, and she'll worry that sooner or later the two of you will start sleeping together again. Heaven knows, she's probably thinking you are right now anyway— that he crawls out of bed with her and into bed with you. She won't want you around, Selena. That's understandable. You're a woman. You should realize she'd be jealous."

"She doesn't have any cause to be."

"But she thinks she does. Now listen carefully." Lisbeth slipped an arm around her and noticed how Selena cringed at her touch. "Steve is the only reason Raven is still here. She's half Indian, you know, and not really happy living around civilization. She's not used to wealth and luxury and doesn't care about it anyway. She'd go back to her old way of life if she didn't fancy herself to be in love with Steve. If not for him, she'd leave, and then my brother would move back home. And I could stay. You could stay. Everyone would be happy." She gave her a squeeze. "Cooperate with me, Selena, and together we'll get rid of her. If you refuse, you can be sure that sooner or later she'll get rid of *you.* And it might be too late for you to say anything then. She might be so much in love with him nothing could change her mind."

Serena frowned to think about it, then asked timorously, "Do you really think if I tell her Steve is Amanda's father, she'll be so angry she'll actually go?"

"Yes, I do, because I saw how upset she got this morning when your father told her he drinks because he's angry over Steve not doing right by you. When she hears from your own mouth that it's so, she'll be so upset she won't be able to bear being around him again. Now is the time to do it, while she's homesick for her people. Not later, when she's dug in her heels and made herself feel at home."

Selena shook her head. "I'm not sure it will work."

"Of course it will. It will crush her completely to hear it from you; she'll have to believe it. She already thinks everyone laughs at her. She has no friends. She knows my brother and I can't stand her. Once she finds out about you and Steve, she'll be so humiliated she won't dare stay."

"What if she's so mad at Steve she decides to run *him* off instead? Have you thought about that? You might be needlessly hurting her—*and* Steve," Selena added, awash with pity to think of how that would destroy him. They were good friends. He had told her how much Halcyon meant to him and how he would like to stay on after Ned died, if possible. He had not let on he was involved with Raven, but he was a private person, so she had no way of knowing if he really cared about Raven or not. That was not the issue as far as Selena was concerned. She just didn't like doing anything that might hurt him.

Lisbeth was quick to dash her hopes. "I did think about that, and it won't happen, because you are also going to tell her that when you found out about them sleeping together, you went all to pieces, and Steve told you there was no need for you to be upset, because she didn't mean anything to him. He was only using her to keep his job and it's you he loves. You'll explain that the two of you had planned to get married before she came along, but he's afraid she'll fire him if you do. But for the sake of your baby, you're begging her to stay away from him, so your baby can have a name and not have to live in shame anymore. Take the baby with you to see her. That will needle her even more.

"And afterward," Lisbeth said with a shrug to indicate it was all quite simple, "Raven will be so brokenhearted and mad she'll leave without saying a word to him. Her pride won't let her."

"But if she does tell him—"

"She won't."

Selena persisted, "But if she does?"

"That's the chance you have to take for the sake of your baby." Lisbeth's patience snapped.

Selena felt the blood drain from her face. "What are you saying?"

"That I will stop at nothing"—she lowered her voice to an ominous whisper—"to get rid of her. I'll pay somebody if I have to. So if you don't do as I ask, if you refuse to help me, I promise you that when I have succeeded I'll personally chase you out of here." But though she made herself sound fierce and determined, Lisbeth doubted she could ever go that far to drive Raven away. If she failed now, she would try to marry Barley as soon as possible and move away as Julius had done—but Selena did not know that.

Selena looked at her sleeping baby and gave a ragged sigh of surrender. "Then God forgive me, I have no choice."

Lisbeth bounded to her feet in triumph. "You won't regret this. I promise. And when my brother and I are in control of Halcyon again, we'll rebuild all these cottages and you'll have the nicest one."

She took the lantern and hurried out, unable to bear the look of desolation on Selena's face any longer.

And as she moved through the night, making her way back to the house, Lisbeth found herself whispering her own prayer that God would somehow forgive her for what she had done.

Selena had fallen across the bed and cried until there were no tears left. Then, drained and exhausted, she lay on her back and stared up at the ceiling, hating herself for what she had to do. And when she heard the stumbling, scraping sounds on the porch, which meant her father was drunk again and coming to rail at her, she did not bound to her feet as she usually did, to snatch up her baby and flee out the back door to find a neighbor to go get Steve. Instead, she continued to lie there.

"Well, well, you're all ready for him, ain't you?" Masson slurred as he swayed to and fro in the doorway. "Yep. All ready for Maddox to fix you up with another bastard to bring shame on our family."

Suddenly, Selena could stand no more. Sitting up, she looked at him with so much fury that he reeled back a few steps. "Maybe I did bring you shame, but you shame me by how you act, Pa. I hope you're satisfied, because now I've got no choice but to go to Miss Raven and lie and say Steve is Amanda's father, even though God knows he isn't."

Masson blinked his eyes furiously, trying to figure out what she was talking about.

Selena lost all control, the frustration spilling out of her as she confided in her misery what Lisbeth was making her do. "And I hope you're satisfied," she repeated, chest heaving with her tears and pain.

Masson hiccuped. He didn't see what she was so upset about. "You ain't got to do it, you know."

"Oh, yes, I do, because she says if I don't she'll pay somebody to get rid of her. And if she has to do that, then Miss Lisbeth'll be the one to run me off. Oh, this is awful. I don't know if I can do it." She covered her face with her hands and fell back on the bed in a fresh wave of tears.

Masson hiccuped and reeled again and reached with one hand for the doorframe to steady himself, gripping his jug of whiskey tight with the other. He had not heeded Raven's warning but had drunk too much again and come to Selena's cabin intending to raise all the hell he wanted, because no little half-breed bastard of Ned Ralston's was going to tell him what to do. If she ran him off, fine, he'd find work elsewhere, but he would show her he wasn't afraid of her. Not one bit.

But now, after what he had just heard, his lips twisted in a crooked smile to think he didn't have to worry about it anymore. He would be the one to help Lisbeth. Selena would never be able to muster the nerve, so it was up to him. Lisbeth wouldn't have to pay him either. He just wanted to make sure she was so beholden to him that his future at Halcyon would be secure for the rest of his life.

And he knew just how to do that. He would get rid of the little upstart himself.

But first he needed to sober up and think of how he was going to do it.

24

Lisbeth was hardly listening to anything Barley was saying as they sat on the terrace facing the river. It was unbearably hot, and she fanned herself furiously, wishing for a breeze. He was not visiting as part of his courtship, since the house was still mourning, but instead, as a neighbor, dropping by to inquire about her welfare.

Looking coolly comfortable despite the heat in his white suit and blue silk shirt, Barley droned on. "Father says we're going to have an unusually good cotton crop this year. We've had just the right amount of rain. I'll be going to New Orleans next week to see if the prices are even better there. Mother is going with me. By the way, she sent her respects to both you and Raven. She really liked Raven. She says she has so much mettle."

He had her attention then. "Mettle?" Lisbeth gave an unladylike snort, fanning herself even harder as she drenched him with a scathing glare. "That's a strange way to describe rude and uncivilized behavior."

"Oh, come on, Lisbeth. Don't be so hard on her. Maybe she does come from an entirely different background than we do, but you have to admit she tries. As for what happened with Julius, you know he was pretty drunk. Everybody could see that, just like everybody knows he gets obnoxious when he is. He was probably disrespectful and she had no choice except to throw him in the rosebushes." He couldn't help laughing to remember how ridiculous Julius had looked.

Lisbeth threw down her fan. "That's enough, Barley. I'll not have you criticizing my brother or laughing at him. Nor will I stand for your taking up for Raven. She's done nothing but make my life miserable and embarrass this household since she showed up, purely to get her greedy hands on Ned's fortune. She ran Julius off; he couldn't abide her any longer. And now I'm starting to wonder how much more I can take."

Barley took a sip of the lemonade Mariah had brought him earlier and did not say anything, knowing there was no reasoning with Lisbeth when she was upset. He also did not want to encourage her impulsive remark about how much more she could endure, for he well knew her only alternative was marriage. Since he was the one officially showing interest in courting her when the time became proper after her mourning period ended, she naturally would look to him to propose. And he wasn't sure how he felt about that anymore, not since he had begun to see, more and more, a very unpleasant side to her nature.

"Maybe I'm fretting for nothing," Lisbeth said,

more to herself than to him. "Maybe all my problems will soon be over."

Something in her tone alarmed him. "What is that supposed to mean?"

"That maybe she'll be leaving."

He laughed again. "Oh, I rather doubt that will happen. From what I hear, she's doing a marvelous job of running things. My father says the other planters are very impressed at how she's gained the respect of her overseers in such a short time. And from the numbers of cotton bales coming out of Halcyon, it would appear the slaves like her and want to produce for her. I've ridden in your fields. The spirit among the workers is the best I've seen since Ned took sick. No"—he shook his head firmly—"she has no reason to leave."

At that, Lisbeth leaped to her feet. "How can you say such things? How can you continue to defend her when you know how miserable she's made me? I think you'd better leave, Barley, right now. And I don't want you to come back until you're ready to be on my side."

"Now, Lisbeth, there's no need for you to behave like this, and there's no need for anybody to choose sides." He was up in a flash to try and take her in his arms but gave a startled cry as her hand cracked across his face.

"I asked you to go. Right now!"

He rubbed a hand across his smarting cheek. "All right, I'll go. But don't expect me to come back."

"Oh, you'll be back because you want to marry me, if only for my dowry. But you'd better change your attitude."

He had started to walk away but turned to look at

her in pity. "I'm afraid, my dear, that, unpleasant as you are to be around lately, there's not a large enough dowry in the world to make me want to live with you for the rest of my life."

She ran to the edge of the terrace as he walked to the hitching post where he had left his horse. "You can't talk to me that way! And don't you dare ever set foot on Halcyon again, do you hear me, Barley Tremayne? You are no gentleman, and I'm going to see that your parents hear about this."

He did not look back.

Lisbeth was blinking back tears, determined not to cry, even though she felt as though she were dying inside. Oh, what was wrong lately? Why did the whole world seem to be crashing down around her? And how could she have done something so awful as to slap Barley?

Raven! she muttered under her breath. It was all Raven's fault. If she had never come to Halcyon, none of this would be happening, would it?

But a tiny voice inside whispered that maybe things could have been different if she had tried a little harder to accept things as they were, tried to accept Raven.

"No!" she said out loud, and suddenly feeling the need to get away from the house, she ran down the steps and across the lawn to the stables without even changing to her riding habit.

"Saddle Belle," she ordered Joshua.

He could tell she was upset and hated saying anything but knew he had to warn her. "I don't think that's a good idea if you're going riding by yourself."

Crossing her arms over her chest and tapping her foot, Lisbeth challenged him. "And why is that, Joshua?"

"One of the stableboys saw some rowdies down by the river a little while ago. You know them tramps are up to no good. All they do is drift up and down the river looking for something to steal. Ordinarily, Mister Steve would go chase 'em off, but he left early this morning to go help John Hulse with a horse he's having trouble breaking. And there ain't no need in even asking one of the overseers to run 'em away, 'cause they ain't about to leave the fields with picking season at its peak. You'd best not to go out riding by yourself."

"I'm not worried in the least. Now go and saddle Belle," she said firmly.

A few minutes later, he led the mare out and tried once more to dissuade her. "If you insist on going, why don't you ask Miss Raven to go with you? She knows how to use a gun. My, my"—he shook his head and grinned to think of the day he had seen Raven practicing—"she sure can shoot. You wouldn't have nothing to worry about with her along."

"Oh, I imagine she can handle a gun, Joshua. As well as a spear, a tomahawk, a hatchet, or any other primitive weapon the rest of those savages used where she came from. But I don't need her along, and I certainly don't *want* her along. I'm not afraid." She tucked her toe in his cupped hands and allowed him to boost her up into the sidesaddle. "Rowdies would never dare bother me. They know who I am."

"Yes, ma'am, but they might not care."

She tossed him a glance of disgust and rode out.

The day, despite the insufferable heat, was beautiful. There were no clouds in the brilliant blue sky; the river, a deep, dark green, rolled lazily toward the coast. Lisbeth was glad she had decided to go for a ride so she could be alone to think how wonderful it was going to be when she and Julius were at last rid of Raven.

And why, she wondered, annoyed, did everyone like her anyway? Everything she did was positively barbaric. Like the way she dove right in to deliver Belle's colt, not carrying about how messy it was. That was certainly unladylike—even if she had probably saved the colt's life, Lisbeth grudgingly conceded. Then there was the time Raven had not hesitated to save her from breaking her neck when Belle had run away with her. Lisbeth had cursed her instead of being grateful. But the fact was, no one else had gone to her rescue.

As for Julius, Lisbeth well knew how repugnant he could be when he was in his cups, and as much as she hated to admit it, he probably had made a complete ass of himself to provoke Raven enough to throw him into the rosebushes.

Lisbeth allowed Belle to set her own pace, not really caring which of the trails they took as she yielded to the strange emotions sweeping over her. She had to admit Raven had never really acted greedy. If money was all she was after, she would have accepted the offer she and Julius had made and taken off. Instead, despite being ostracized and humiliated at every turn, she had stayed and worked hard. Apparently she had done a good job, too, because there had been no complaints from anyone.

Something else Lisbeth was forced to acknowledge was that Raven had not appeared out of the blue to claim her inheritance. If Ned hadn't wanted to ease his conscience before dying, no one would ever have known she existed.

And a prickling of her own conscience began as Lisbeth thought how, if Steve were the only reason Raven wanted to stay, she had to care for him deeply.

"What is wrong with me?" Lisbeth asked herself, appalled. She reined Belle to a stop, confused over why she was suddenly having second thoughts. It was only right that Raven go back to her primitive way of life. She knew she didn't belong here.

But might she not feel she did belong if she had been welcomed, if she had not been made to believe people laughed at her?

But she was a whore, Lisbeth reminded herself angrily, then quickly admitted that no, that was not so. Just because she and Steve were lovers did not make her a whore. Lisbeth didn't consider herself to be one for offering herself to him. She did not, in fact, consider it altogether immoral. After all, she was a woman with natural instincts and desires too, and what woman wouldn't want to sleep with Steve Maddox?

Then, too, the scene with Barley bothered her deeply. She pretended on the surface not to care for him, but actually she did. A lot. He had begun to call upon her often during the time Steve was gone, and of all her potential suitors, he was the only one she could imagine marrying. There had been stolen kisses, too, and Barley had made her experience emotions that made her think she might not want to take a lover after she was married after all.

And now she had done something so stupid as to slap him, and he would probably never call on her again.

"Oh, why do things have to be so awful?" She spoke aloud, shaken by her misery.

A gleeful voice rang out in the stillness. "Hey, little lady. Things don't have to be awful. I'd say they're lookin' better all the time."

With a bone-chilling lurch of terror, Lisbeth saw them, but it was too late to escape. There were three of them, bedraggled men, leaping out of the bushes to drag her from her horse. She tried to beat them off with her leather riding crop but was no match for them, and they threw her to the ground.

"Yeah," one of them snarled as he licked his lips in anticipation and began to unbuckle his trousers. "Things are goin' to get real good."

"She'll be real mad when she finds out I went and told you," Joshua said as Raven swung up on Starfire. "And she might not run up on them rowdies, but they can be real mean, and I was worried for her."

"You did the right thing," Raven assured him, reining the stallion about. She had come as fast as she could after he had run to the house in a frenzy over Lisbeth going off by herself. She had followed him back to the stable, taking time only to harness Starfire, leaving off his saddle to ride bareback.

Workers in the fields along the main riding path told her they had seen Lisbeth pass by. She seemed to be heading for the deep woods beyond the gardens, which was not cleared except for equestrian trails. It was dense, isolated, and certainly no place for a woman alone with river rowdies sighted, especially one as defenseless as Lisbeth.

Mariah had told her about Lisbeth having a quarrel with Barley, but Raven felt it was none of her business and had thought no more about it. Now she worried that Lisbeth would be brooding and not pay attention to where she was going.

She would have liked to give Starfire his head, to allow him to go full speed. Instead, she held him to a walk so she could be alert for any sound or sign that Lisbeth might be in distress.

Then she heard it—a shrill scream that was quickly muffled—not far away. To the right, toward the riverbank.

Raven knew not to go charging in on horseback, even though she felt the impulse to do so. But the scream had to mean Lisbeth or some other woman was in danger, and if guns were involved, shooting might start if the culprits heard anyone coming.

Dismounting, she moved stealthily through the bushes toward the direction of the sound. With her hunter's instinct, she knew how to avoid doing anything that might make a noise.

Finally, she peered through the leaves to see a nightmare unfurling. Three men had dragged Lisbeth to a clearing where they had made camp, there to guzzle whiskey till darkness, when they would creep about looking for something to steal. Lisbeth was being held down on the ground. One of the men had a hand over her mouth, and she was moaning in terror. She was about to be ravished, and the horror of it was that from where Raven crouched, she could not risk a shot without hitting her.

There was no time to wait. The man positioned between Lisbeth's legs was about to assault her. Unbuckling her holster, Raven dropped it noiselessly at her feet, then straightened and shouted, "Let her go!"

The men all turned at once. One of them whipped out a gun and aimed it at her. "Who the hell are you?"

"Never mind who I am. Let her go. She's my sister."

The one hovering over Lisbeth flicked his eyes at Raven and immediately decided she was much more fetching. She was filled out, not puny. And if she put up a fight, it would only make it better. He didn't like to take his pleasure on a crying, whimpering woman. "Is that so?" He snickered. "Well, we might just do that if you're willing to take her place."

Stunned, the man holding Lisbeth lifted his hand from her mouth. She raised her head, amazed that Raven had walked right into the clearing. She had to be out of her mind.

But Raven knew what she was doing and responded with a taunt. "If any of you rowdies think you're man enough, come ahead."

That did it.

Lisbeth was forgotten as they charged toward Raven. The one with his pants down tried to yank them up and stumbled but kept on going, determined to make the dark-haired beauty pay for her insolence.

Raven saw Lisbeth struggle to her knees, but she was still too terrified to make a run for it.

They drew closer, and Raven's hands began to open and close, fingers aching to plunge downward and grab her guns, but she could not make a move until Lisbeth was out of the way, and she was directly behind the approaching men. Raven knew if she didn't act quick, they would be on her, and it would be too late.

It was now or never. "Lisbeth, duck!" she screamed, dropping for her guns. She came up firing—one shot, two, three.

She clipped the first man right where she intended, in his upper right shoulder. The second man was also on target, directly in the leg. The third man she wanted to be special, for he was the one who had been about to take Lisbeth first. She shot off his ear to give him something to explain for the rest of his worthless life.

After making sure Lisbeth had crawled to safety, Raven fired off three more rounds to hit each man's holstered gun and shatter it. "Now get out of here," she told them. "And if you ever step foot on Halcyon ground again, you'll be buried in it."

The one with a shoulder wound helped the one with the leg wound hobble toward the woods. The man with only one ear left was having trouble with his pants. He would run a few steps, stumble, grab at his pants, then scramble a little farther before falling again. Finally he disappeared into the bushes with the other two.

Raven ran to help Lisbeth stand. "Are you all right?"

"I . . . I think so," Lisbeth said, then whispered, awed, "You were going to take my place, Raven. You were going to let them take you instead of me."

"Oh, not if I could help it," Raven said lightly. "I just had to get their attention so I could go for my guns. I had had to drop them on the ground so they wouldn't see I was armed and start shooting, and then I couldn't fire because you were in the way. But it's over now. Let's get you back to the house so Mariah can see to those bruises and scratches on your face."

Belle was grazing lazily on the riverbank. Raven helped Lisbeth mount. Then she whistled for Starfire, who came running toward her, as she had quickly trained him to do, instead of heading in the opposite direction as Diablo would have done.

They rode along in silence. Raven reasoned there was nothing to be said other than *I told you so,* which would only increase the tension between them. Finally, as they left the woods and the house came into view, Lisbeth asked thinly, apologetically, "Aren't you going to tell me what a fool I am?"

"Foolish, not a fool," Raven said softly. "There's a difference."

Suddenly Lisbeth had to know. "Are you able to shoot like that because you're part Indian?"

Raven almost laughed but didn't. She knew what it was like to feel ridiculed. "No. Being an Indian doesn't have anything to do with it. I was just fortunate that my stepfather—who was white—wanted me to be able to take care of myself and saw that I learned how. I'm glad he did."

"So am I." She hesitated, feeling awkward, then added, "And I surely do thank you."

"I'm just glad I got there in time." Raven's heart was pounding with excitement to think she had finally done something right in Lisbeth's eyes.

A thousand emotions were churning within Lisbeth right then. Among them was shame. But she could not talk about that. It was something she had to sort out for herself, later, when she could be alone.

A few more moments of silence passed, and then Lisbeth asked shyly, "Do you think I could ever learn to shoot like you do?"

Raven could not believe she had heard right. "What did you say?"

"I said"—Lisbeth swallowed hard—"would you teach me to shoot like you do? And maybe ride a horse too? These sidesaddles are kind of clumsy at times."

"Why . . ." Raven stammered, not knowing what to say. Then she laughed and nodded. "Sure. I'd like that a lot." She described how she would teach her first how to handle a gun, then how to shoot. And when Lisbeth got really good at it, she'd show her how to draw fast too. "I can also teach you to throw a knife," she added enthusiastically.

With all the sincerity she possessed, Lisbeth said, "I want to learn everything you can teach me, because I never want anything like that to happen to me again." She shuddered to envision what it would have been like to be raped by those men.

Raven held out her hand. "I'm glad, Lisbeth. And I hope this means we're on our way to being friends."

Lisbeth was at a loss for words. Only a short while ago, she had wanted nothing more than to have Raven out of her life forever. Now Raven was extending her hand, and she was actually taking it. What was wrong with her, for heaven's sake? Well, she knew the answer to that. Thanks to Raven, she had been spared the worst nightmare a woman could endure.

So how could she continue to hate her and want her out of her life? If not for Raven, Lisbeth knew her own life would never have been the same.

Then she remembered her scheme and knew she had to stop Selena before she went through with it. "There's something I have to do," she said, reining Belle toward the cotton fields.

"But your face—"

"I'm fine, really. I'll see you at supper."

Raven watched her ride away, pleased to think it was the first time she could look forward to the evening meal. She only wished Julius could be there too. Perhaps she should try to reason with him again. It would help the situation if Lisbeth would go with her. Raven dared to hope that after today she'd agree.

After supper, while Lisbeth was in a good mood, she would take her into the study and show her all the books and ledgers, so she would have an understanding of all the plantation's business. Raven wanted her to know that she had no intentions, no matter what the will decreed, of taking Halcyon over. If possible, she would like for the three of them to run it together.

Raven slowed.

The three of them. Not *four*.

Sadly, she knew she could never include Steve though she desperately longed to, because eventually he would drift out of her life. And while the moon-mad nights of passion were exquisite, she knew one day the memories would hurt, for they would be all that remained of the deepest love she would ever know for any man. But till that time came, for as long as she could believe he cared, if only a little, she would savor every moment.

Leaving Starfire with Joshua, she returned to the house, wanting to finish up her work in the study and tidy up so everything would be in order for Lisbeth. But just as she started up the front steps, Mariah came out to meet her. Raven could tell right away she was upset.

"It's that Selena Leroux and her baby," she said. "She's sittin' on the back porch waitin' to see you. I told her you weren't here, and she said she was gonna get a whippin' from her pa for sneaking out of the field anyway, so she'd just wait till you got back."

Raven felt a little chill of foreboding and told

herself she was being silly. "All right. Bring her to the study."

"Don't know what she's doin' comin' here anyway, white trash like that," Mariah grumbled as she went inside. "She won't tell nobody who gave her that baby 'cause she probably don't even know herself."

Raven went to the study and sat down behind the desk, wishing her knees would stop knocking together as she tried to think of why Selena might want to see her.

There was a hesitant knock on the door. After drawing a deep breath that seemed to be pulled from the very pit of her soul, Raven called out to her to enter.

In one of the cotton fields, Masson Leroux shaded his eyes with his hands against the relentless sun and watched Lisbeth ride by. She seemed to be looking for someone, glancing right and left among the thick rows of green leaves, dotted with popcorn blossoms of white. The slaves, dragging their shoulder sacks behind them, scarcely glanced at her as they toiled in the heat.

Masson figured she had to be looking for Selena; otherwise the prissy little snot wouldn't be out on such a hot day. Her kind stayed inside sipping ice-cold lemonade, fanned by a pickaninny with a big palm leaf. They didn't get out in the sun with the flies buzzing all around.

He wished he could tell her she could forget about her little scheme and not worry about Ned Ralston's bastard anymore, because he was going to take care of everything.

But he would wait.

It would be a lot more fun to tell her when it was all over and done with. When Raven was feeding the catfish in the bottom of the Alabama River.

25

Selena was trembling from head to toe as she held her baby. She was sitting in a chair opposite the desk. Her mouth was dry, and there was a big knot in her throat as she wondered if she would be able to speak the horrid lie.

Raven could see she was nervous but would not let herself think anything other than that it had to do with Masson. "Is this about your father, Selena? Is he still making trouble for you? I spoke to him yesterday about his drinking. I'm afraid I had to warn him that if it keeps up, I'll have no choice but to ask him to leave Halcyon."

Selena stared at her, thinking how pretty she was, how nice she seemed, kind and caring. If she were in love with Steve, it was even sadder what Lisbeth was making her do, because she sensed that Raven would be good for him; as lonely as he was, he needed somebody, even though he didn't realize it. But she had never stuck her nose in Steve's business—till now.

When Selena still did not speak, continuing to look at her with a strangely mournful expression, Raven prodded gently. "Please. Tell me why you're here. You don't have to be afraid."

Selena bit her lip to try and hold back the tears. Raven certainly wasn't acting like she was mad at her for sending for Steve all those nights, like Lisbeth had said. But she wouldn't dare let on about it anyway, would she?

"Selena, I want to help you, but I do have other things to do." Raven did not want to appear unsympathetic to whatever had her so upset, but she had not said a word in nearly five minutes.

Selena said, "I—" and stopped. She could not do such a thing to Steve. And then her baby stirred in her arms, and she looked down and saw how her mouth twitched with a smile as she slept. Babies smiled in their sleep, she had heard, because the angels were talking to them. Selena never knew she could love anything so much until she held her in her arms for the first time. She was hers, a tiny little person dependent on her for everything. And the life Selena had given her was still in her hands and would be for a long, long time to come.

Raven prompted again. "Selena, please. Why have you come here? What is it you want to tell me?"

Selena bowed to kiss her baby's cheek as she closed her eyes and prayed to God to forgive her for what she was about to do. Then she looked at Raven, took a deep breath, and said, "Steve Maddox is the father of my baby."

Raven swayed and gripped the edge of the desk.

"He was going to marry me till you came along."

Raven's anguished whisper was barely audible. "Oh, God."

Selena lifted her chin. Her brain was screaming at her to go on, get the lie out; she was doing it for her baby, and her baby had no one but her, and if she didn't, sooner or later Raven would run her off, or else Lisbeth would get rid of Raven and then Lisbeth would banish her. This was the only way. "We've been secret sweethearts for a long time." She began the recitation she had lain awake till nearly dawn memorizing. "I knew Steve wasn't the marrying kind, but I loved him so much I just kept sleeping with him, hoping he would change his mind and want to settle down. When he found out about the baby, he still didn't want to marry me, but as it got closer to time for her to be born, he started talking about it. Then, right before he left to go look for you, he said he'd do it."

Raven had leaned back in the leather chair. Her eyes were closed, her hands squeezed together in her lap. Every nerve in her body was screaming it could not be so, but with every word Selena spoke she knew it had to be.

"When he came back," Selena continued, "I saw right away he was different. He started talking about how he wasn't sure he wanted to get married after all. He said he'd look out for me and the baby, but he just wasn't ready to settle down. I thought once Amanda was born, he'd love her so much he'd change his mind, but he didn't, and finally he told me it was because of you."

Raven's eyes flew open. "Because of me?" she echoed thinly.

"That's right." Selena was able to put anger into

her voice, now falling into the role of a woman wronged. "He said he didn't want to leave here, even though he could afford to since Master Ned was leaving him some money. This is his home, he said, and he was afraid you'd kick him out. So he bedded you, and—"

"No. Stop it." Raven covered her ears with her hands. "This isn't true."

"Oh, yes, it is." Selena slammed her hand down on the desk, and Raven uncovered her ears as she rushed on to finish her lie. "He said as long as he beds you, he can stay on here and run the stables and do anything he damn well pleases, but if he marries me we'd have to leave."

Tears filled Raven's eyes and ran down her cheeks, but she made no attempt to hold them back or wipe them away. She was beyond awareness of anything except this hurtful moment when her life suddenly had no more meaning. "Why are you telling me this?" she asked.

"So you'll give him back to me. My baby needs a name, so she won't have to grow up marked a bastard. She needs a father to look out for her in other ways besides dropping money off once in a while. But as long as Steve thinks he's got to"—Selena paused to give the sneer she'd practiced in the cracked mirror on the cabin wall "—*service* you, she's never going to have that."

Raven felt a great roaring within and felt she was going to be sick to her stomach. Images flashed before her of Steve making love to her, whispering endearing words as he held her. So tender. So caring. Oh, she'd not been fool enough to think he loved her as she loved him, but she had never felt he was using her to keep his job. Every single second he held her, she had felt cherished and wanted for herself, not like she was merely being *serviced,* as though he were being paid like men paid the whores at the waterfront. "Dear God, no," she whispered again.

Selena pushed on. There would be time to hate and loathe herself later. Right now, she had to make her performance convincing—for her baby's sake. "Are you saying you won't give him up?" Selena made her eyes wide, and it was not hard to make tears appear. "Lord, what kind of woman are you? I know Steve is a handsome man, and well I know"—she gave a little snicker—"how good he can make a woman feel. I can see why you wouldn't want to give him up. But rich as you are, you can buy the best stud money can buy."

Another roll of nausea struck. "Please stop," Raven whimpered.

"No, I won't stop till you agree to give him up. And it's not fair to run him off after we get married, either. He's the best horse trainer in these parts. From what he says about them racking horses, they're plenty expensive and need the best care. Now, I don't have no hard feelings, and I won't fret about him being around you after we're married. I won't even care if he services you once in a while, if that's what it takes for us to stay on here, but at least give him up long enough so's he'll marry me."

Raven shook her head, not in refusal of Selena's plea but in rejection that any of it could really be happening.

But Selena saw it as rejection and begged even harder. "You got to, Miss Raven. You got to for my baby's sake. Don't tell him I came to you like this; he'd hate me, and it'd be Amanda who'd suffer. Just tell him that you don't want him that way no more, but you want him to stay on and work for you. Tell him he ought to find somebody and get married and settle down. He'll turn around and marry me then. I know he will. Do it for my baby. Please." Her voice cracked.

Finally, Raven managed to speak. "I never knew, Selena, about any of this."

"I know you didn't." Selena dabbed at her eyes with the hem of the baby's blanket. "And you seem like a good woman. Everybody speaks kind of you. That's why I made up my mind to come talk to you woman to woman, hoping you'd understand. I mean, if you were in my shoes and you had a baby and another woman was keeping the father from marrying you and giving it a name, wouldn't you do the same thing?

"I know my pa has his faults," she rushed on, "but when he's not drinking, he's a good man, and once Steve and me are married and he don't have to be ashamed of me anymore, he'll straighten up. So you see?" She faked brightness when inside she was sick to the core. "Everything will work out good for everybody. Unless"—she made her eyes narrow as though with suspicion—"you're in love with him too. Then I guess it's hopeless, because you'd never give him up to me if I had *ten* babies by him. But I warn you. I'm sleeping with him now, and I'll keep on, and I won't care how many babies I have, and you can run me off if you want to, but so help me I'll tell, and—" She could not go on and began to sob wildly to think she was capable of telling such outlandish lies.

"You're sleeping with him even now?" Raven said in wonder, then asked herself why it should matter.

Steve had abandoned Selena, but in a different way than her father had abandoned her. Her father had not known her mother was pregnant. Steve had known about his child, had even been there when she was born. He had shirked his responsibilities by choice, damn him, because he was so determined to look out for his own interests. Nothing he could do would surprise her.

"Sometimes," Selena acknowledged. "I know it's soon after the baby, but—"

"Please. I don't want to hear any more." Raven pushed back from the desk, started to get up, then realized her trembling legs would not support her and sank back down. "Go," she whispered. "Get out, please."

"Promise me you won't tell Steve." Suddenly, that meant more to Selena than anything else. "Promise me you won't tell him I was here."

"No. No, I won't."

Selena got slowly to her feet. "And you'll think about what I said?"

Raven waved her away, then folded her arms on the desk and bowed her head.

Selena hurriedly left the house and ran down the path to the sweet potato patch where one of the slaves was waiting with a buckboard wagon to take her to Mobile. She would stay there for a while with a married girlfriend whose husband was away at sea, because a lot of time was going to have to pass before she could look Steve in the face. Until then, everyone would think she was merely hiding from her father.

And when she returned, she could only hope that Lisbeth had been right, that Raven would leave without telling Steve what she had done.

Once more, Selena prayed it would turn out that way . . . and prayed to be forgiven for the horrendous thing she had done.

Lisbeth winced as Mariah dabbed her face with witch hazel liniment. "Ouch, that hurts."

"Not half as bad as what them men were gonna do to you. You didn't have no business ridin' off by yourself like that. You'd just best be glad Miss Raven was here to take off after you." Mariah had been terrified when Lisbeth had told her what happened.

"Believe me, I am," Lisbeth assured, then took the first step toward penitence for how she had treated Raven. "I've changed my mind about her, Mariah. And she's right. Halcyon is big enough for all of us, and I'm going to Mobile and tell Julius that tomorrow and try to get him to come home."

Mariah broke into a big grin. "Praise the Lord. I'm so glad. Now we can have some peace around here."

"She's going to teach me how to shoot a gun. And how to ride like she does. I wish I'd never acted like I did, but it was a shock, having her show up like that."

"Of course it was, but it's gonna work out just fine. And I do hope Master Julius will come on home. It'd be nice for you all to be a family."

"Yes, but he may take some convincing. He was pretty upset when he left."

"And pretty upset when Miss Raven went to see him, from what I hear."

"When was that?" She noticed Mariah smiling as though she knew a secret.

Mariah thought a minute. "Well, I suppose it's all right to tell it now, but don't you let Miss Raven know I did, 'cause she made Joshua swear he wouldn't say a word, but the truth is, he was so excited after it was all over he just had to tell somebody. 'Course, at the time, he said he was so scared that if he didn't already have gray hair, it would've turned gray for sure.

"He was supposed to stay in the carriage like Miss Raven told him to, but he got down and went to peek in the saloon window, so's he could see what was going on, and he said when the bullets started flyin' he nearly passed out."

"Bullets? Saloon? Whatever are you talking about?"

"You promise not to tell I told?" Mariah wanted reassurance.

"Yes, yes, go on."

She listened as Mariah detailed everything and finally burst into giggles to imagine it. Before, she might have been as upset as Julius, but now, understanding Raven as she did and knowing she meant well, and also aware she had probably risked her life to help Julius, Lisbeth found herself admiring her all the more. She would tell Julius that as soon as she saw him, too.

"She sure is somethin'," Mariah said. "I'm just glad nothing bad happened before you decided to make peace with her."

Lisbeth winced again, but not from the liniment. Something bad had not happened—*yet*. But it very well could if she was not able to find Selena and stop her from carrying out the plan. But she had not been in the fields, and one of the workers told her she had not reported back to work after lunch. Lisbeth had gone all the way to her cabin, but there was no sign of her there either. So she had come back to the house to have her wounds cleansed before going in search of her again.

Mariah finished. "Now all you got to do is change your dress before supper, and you'll be good as new."

"I'm going to do that now." She was already on her way. "But there's something I have to do before supper, so let's eat an hour later than usual. You'll need to tell Raven."

"I can't tell her nothing." Mariah fussed as she began to repack her medicine bucket. "She's done locked herself in the study and must be workin' real hard on something, 'cause I knocked to see if she wanted some lemonade and she told me to go away. Sounded funny. Like she was tired. Guess she was, having to put up with that white trash Selena Leroux."

But Lisbeth did not hear her, because she was all the way down the hall and skipping up the steps. In her room, she yanked off the torn dress and quickly put on a fresh one. She wasted no time. In minutes she was back outside to mount Belle and ride for the slave cabins.

The Negroes looked at her curiously as she passed by. They were outside, gathered around communal cooking pots, preparing their own suppers. Lisbeth could smell catfish frying in the cauldrons of bubbling lard and hear the sizzle of hush puppies. An old man sat on a porch picking a banjo while children skipped barefooted and sang to his tune.

Lisbeth looked around and thought about Selena describing Raven's plans for making the cabins nicer and decided she was right. And she would help her. It was time for a change in so many ways, time to turn her whole life around. As soon as she took care of Selena, she was going to send a courier to the

Tremayne plantation with a message of apology for Barley. She would invite him to call and tell him how sorry she was for everything. Mariah was right. Everything was going to work out just fine.

She felt a stab of apprehension as she drew close to Selena's cabin. There was no sign of her, and she should have been outside, like the others, preparing her evening meal. But perhaps since she was alone, she ate with her neighbors, who were busy in front of their own shack.

"Have you seen Selena Leroux?" she asked them as she reined Belle in.

"She's gone," a plump woman said, without looking up from the batch of cornbread she was stirring in a big wooden bowl.

Lisbeth tensed. "Gone where?"

"Don't rightly know. She told my man she was going away for a while. Wouldn't tell him where. We reckon she's hidin' from her pappy."

Lisbeth felt a rush of relief. Selena wasn't hiding out from her father, she was hiding out from *her,* because she had decided not to go through with the plan after all and was afraid to tell her so. But that was fine, and Lisbeth could not wait to tell her so. "Well, if you hear from her, tell her I said she doesn't have to hide anymore, all right? She'll understand."

The woman stared after her, wondering why she was happy, but kept on stirring the cornbread.

When Lisbeth got back to the house and passed the dining room, she saw that Mariah had only set one place. "What's this?" she asked Nolie, another kitchen worker. "Why is there only one setting? What about Miss Raven?"

"Mariah said Miss Raven don't want no supper,"

Nolie told her. "Somethin' about havin' a lot of work to do and not feelin' real good. I think Mariah said she's already gone to bed."

"Well, that's too bad," Lisbeth said. Then she realized that she was free for the evening. In the back of her mind she had wished she didn't have to wait before trying to make things right with Barley but felt she should be with Raven so they could sort of celebrate their new relationship.

Now she didn't have to.

As she hurried from the dining room, Nolie called, bewildered, "Where are you going, Miss Lisbeth? It's almost suppertime."

Lisbeth did not take time to answer. It was still early, and she had plenty of time to have Joshua drive her carriage over to see Barley.

She wasn't going to wait any longer to tell him how wonderful everything was going to be—for all of them.

Raven stood at the window of her room watching as Lisbeth skipped happily across the lawn. She did not know where Lisbeth was going, nor did she care—about her, about anything. Not anymore. Not since her heart had been ripped from her chest and torn into a thousand pieces.

She was wearing her army scout uniform and was ready to leave. All she was waiting for was darkness, so she could slip into the stable without anybody seeing her and get Diablo. She was not taking anything with her except a little bit of money from the wall safe in the study, and only because she needed that to sustain her till she got where she was going and found work.

Where *was* she going? she asked herself with a

deep shudder. Where was there to go that she might find peace?

Then she told herself that for the time being she could not care about that either. She had only one burning thought: to get as far away from Halcyon as possible . . . to get away from Steve.

It had never even occurred to her to confront him, to tell him what a lowlife scoundrel he was and how she loathed him and would hate him till he died. To do so would be to bare her soul, to let him know how much she loved him. She did not want to do that for the sake of her pride, which, sadly, was all she had left to salvage out of the ruins of her life. So she would ride away and be long gone before morning. If he did try to follow her, he would never find her. She would use every shred of Indian cunning she possessed to ensure she left no trail, no trace.

He and everyone else would think she just was not happy in her new life and had returned to her own world. He would marry Selena and give their baby a name and a home and sooner or later forget all about her. Bitterly she wondered if he ever thought of her anyway, unless she was naked in his arms and giving him his pleasure.

But she had received pleasure too, she was pained to remind herself. Her memories were nothing but warm and grand and would be with her for a long time to come, maybe forever.

She looked around her at the room she had come to love with its lace tepee over the bed and could not help smiling to remember that first night in Mobile when she had not known what a canopy was. Oh, there were such good times to think about as she had learned the ways of her father's world.

And there was also her father to remember. Despite the agony of how Steve had used her, crushed her, she would forever be grateful for having had the time to get to know and love her father. That was something even the pain and humiliation could never overshadow.

Yes, Raven promised herself, she would have many glorious things to remember, for she had also come to love Halcyon and all its people. It was a shame that she was leaving just as it appeared she and Lisbeth would, at last, be close.

She was also saddened to think that the slaves would not be freed by her hand and their cabins would not be repaired and made nicer. But that could not be helped, for as much as she wished it, Raven knew it was impossible for her to stay now that Steve had made her the ultimate fool.

Lisbeth disappeared inside the stables. She looked so happy. Raven hoped she would eventually find someone else to teach her how to ride and shoot. Perhaps she would, now that she had come to a new awareness of herself. And maybe some of it would affect Julius as well. They could turn their whole lives around.

Raven left the window, knowing she was only torturing herself to think of what might have been, and willed the hours to pass quickly so she could be on her way.

Masson Leroux leaned against the trunk of a great live oak tree. Lacy shawls of Spanish moss concealed him as he stood watching the house . . . watching Raven as she moved back and forth in front of her window.

He knew he might have to stay there all night. And maybe the next one and the one after that. But he would do it if that was what it took to catch her by herself after dark. She went for rides sometimes. He knew that. He'd seen her when he was out hunting. But now he was hunting for *her*. And he would be right behind her when she did go out—with his rifle loaded and ready.

26

Steve lay on his back and stared up at the ceiling of his room. It was hours till midnight, and he was miserable from wanting to be with Raven now. More and more, it irked him that they had to be so secretive. He could understand not letting anyone know they were sleeping together, but he saw no harm in spending time together in other ways: riding, picnicking, anything to enjoy each other's company. Otherwise, how could he make Raven see they might have a future together?

He bolted upright at the thought, then laughed out loud and shook himself as though he had just awakened from a long, long sleep—months of sleep, in fact. He had just acknowledged what he had known all along but been afraid to admit—he *did* want a future with Raven. More than that, he wanted a future with her as his *wife*.

He loved her, by God.

And he was sick and tired of waiting in his room every night for her to sneak up the ladder as if she were ashamed, as if *he* were ashamed, because he wasn't.

These days she stole into his thoughts every day. Memories of their time together on the trail flooded him with a sweet warmth, but everything about Raven was a joy to behold. Maybe he had promised himself never to fall in love, never marry and settle down with one woman. But that was before Raven. She had changed all that, had changed him. God, it was a wonderful feeling! He just couldn't wait to tell her, couldn't wait to find out if she might feel the same way about him.

He reached for his shirt and dragged his boots over, smiling to think how surprised she was going to be when Mariah told her she had a caller and then came downstairs to find out it was him, waiting to tell her he was there to state his intentions to court her proper. He could just see the look on her face.

He hesitated as he yanked on a boot. What if he was making a fool of himself?

After all, Raven had never given any sign that she cared for him beyond the raging passion that always left both of them spent with wonder. But neither had he ever given her reason to think she meant anything more to him.

So all he could do was go to her and pour out his heart, and if it turned out she didn't give a damn about him except for what they shared in bed, so be it. He had to know.

Because if she didn't, he felt a pang of despair to acknowledge, it was probably best that he start giving some thought to moving on, for a future of stolen passion was not what he wanted out of life.

* * *

Masson cursed softly as a tree limb slapped him in the face.

Despite a waxing moon, there were a lot of clouds in the sky, and it was hard to see where he was going as he tried to follow after Raven. Why was she riding parallel to the main road, instead of on it? She plowed the mustang right into the brambles and weeds.

He also wondered why she was wearing an army uniform. He wouldn't have even known it was her if he hadn't seen her come out of the house, creeping along like she didn't want anybody to see her.

He wished he hadn't had so much to drink. It was hard to think clearly with the buzzing in his head, but he had to try. It made no difference where she was going or why. Neither did it matter how she was dressed. This was a fine chance to get rid of her once and for all, and he was going to take it—even if he did feel like the world was spinning all around him.

And he had to try and keep after her, because he wanted to make sure they were a long way from the house before he killed her. It was still early evening, and already two wagons and a carriage had come along. Each time, though he could barely make Raven out in the distance, he saw her rein to a stop and get real still, so she wouldn't be noticed.

He lifted his canteen of whiskey to his mouth and drank, trying to figure what to do. If he kept plodding along behind, sooner or later she might spot him and that wouldn't do; she'd know he was up to something. He just wondered where the hell she was going, sneaking like she was. If she kept on, she'd wind up in Mobile—

He nearly choked on the whiskey he was swallowing. That was it: She was going to Mobile.

About half an hour's ride north, the Alabama River ran into the Mobile River, and she was going to have to cross the plank bridge. By the time she got there it would be late enough that nobody would be around, and he could waylay her if he got ahead of her. To do that, he had only to ride out on the road like he was going somewhere himself. Just keep on going, pretend he didn't know she was anywhere around, and it would be an easy ambush. He could shoot her as she crossed the bridge, then run out and throw her body into the river. So simple.

He kneed his horse into the road.

Raven slowed. She had heard first the wagons and carriages, but now only a horse and rider approached. She was keeping back, so that no one would see her and tell Steve if he were to try and come after her before morning. She doubted that he would. Probably when she did not appear in his room by half past midnight, he would run to Selena and slake his passion with her instead. "Damn you, Steve Maddox," she whispered through a veil of tears, "and damn me for loving you."

The rider passed by. She recognized Masson Leroux and wondered vaguely where he was going but didn't really care. One thing was for certain: he wouldn't be interrupting Steve and Selena. She burned with fury to imagine them together.

After a few moments, she swiped at her eyes and continued on. She knew she would reach the swamps soon and would have to get back on the road. Probably she should have waited till dawn anyway, but Steve would stand a better chance of finding her then, because he'd probably go looking for her after spending the night with Selena, to find out why she hadn't shown up at midnight. He wouldn't want her mad with him about anything, for heaven's sake. So he would look for her and realize Diablo was gone and wonder why she wasn't riding Starfire and decide to try and find her.

No. She shook her head wearily to think. She could not risk waiting till morning, but neither could she stay in the brambles and stumble into the swamps. She would just have to take a chance on the road. Surely no one would recognize her, even though they might wonder why an army soldier, particularly one with long black hair, was riding through Mobile County on a mustang.

She had no choice if she wanted to distance herself as much as possible by morning.

"Joshua, you'd better hurry up those horses," Lisbeth called cheerily from where she sat in the carriage. "We need to get on home. I didn't mean to stay so long at the Tremaynes."

"Well, you did," he grumbled, popping the reins and snapping the buggy whip over the horses' rumps. "I'm surprised you didn't stay for supper."

"They asked me to, but I knew we had to be getting back." She crossed her arms and hugged herself with delight. Everything had gone so well. Barley had been alarmed when he first saw her, no doubt thinking she was making good her threat to tell his parents about the scene between them earlier, but after a few minutes of her lighthearted prattling to his mother, he decided she had come for a different reason, and the second she managed to be alone with him, she told him. She had apologized and begged his forgiveness, and, she blushed to recall, she had come right out and told him she was sweet on him and hoped he would be the one to court her when the time was right. He had smiled and hugged her and they had sneaked a kiss, and now everything was going to be wonderful.

She had even told him what had happened in the woods with the rowdies, and he got so upset she knew he must really care for her. And when she told him about Raven, he was impressed and awed, and even more so when she praised Raven and explained she was now resolved to having peace between them.

Suddenly she sat up to strain to see in the moonlight. "Wasn't that Masson Leroux we just passed?" she asked Joshua.

"Yes'm. Sure looked like him."

"I wonder where he's going. You'd think it being planting season he'd be too tired to be out gadding about."

She closed her eyes, dreaming about the happiness to come, then bolted upright to hear Joshua say, "Well, I'll be. Wonder who that is." And she saw a soldier with long hair riding by on a horse that looked just like Raven's mustang. But it couldn't be. She had no idea who it was and didn't care anyway, because she was anxious to return to her blissful musing.

"What do you mean, she's not in her room? Where else would she be?"

Mariah wrung her hands. Mr. Steve seemed awfully concerned, and she was starting to think maybe she should be too. "I just don't know. I've looked all over the house, and I can't find her. Did you try the stables?"

"I just *came* from the stables," he reminded her irritably, and then apologized, not wanting to take out his frustration on her. "I'm sorry. It's just that I worry about her. She thinks she can take care of herself, but she still doesn't have any business taking off like she does sometimes."

"Oh, you don't have to worry about her," Mariah said proudly. "Why, from what Miss Lisbeth told me, there's three river rowdies nursing wounds tonight that can sure tell you that for a fact."

"What?" He had not heard, had not talked to anyone after returning late from the Hulse place, because they had asked him to stay for supper after he had helped them all day. He had come home, taken a bath, and gone straight to his room to wait for Raven. "What are you talking about?"

"Miss Lisbeth got attacked by three rowdies when she was out ridin' today, but Miss Raven, she got there in time to save her, and she shot all three. Didn't kill 'em. Probably could have, but Miss Lisbeth said she thought she just wanted to scare 'em so they could spread the word it's dangerous to come to Halcyon when you haven't got no business here."

"And did Lisbeth get mad? Did they have a fight? Raven is awfully sensitive about Lisbeth. You know how mad she got when Raven saved her when her horse ran away. Maybe her feelings are hurt again."

"No, sir, I don't think that could be so." Mariah was glad to give him even more good news. "She and Miss Lisbeth are gonna get along fine from now on. Miss Lisbeth told me so herself."

"What's that? What did Miss Lisbeth tell you?" Lisbeth asked with a smile as she stepped into the foyer and saw them. She walked on in, untying her bonnet. "Hello, Steve." She acknowledged him with a nod.

He blinked in surprise. Suddenly she seemed mature, polite, genial, for God's sake. What was going on? "Mariah was telling me you've made peace with Raven," he said dubiously.

"That I have. Things are going to be different around here. In a lot of ways," she added, hoping he would understand she meant that for the two of them as well. He had offered friendship before. She hoped he would again.

"Would you happen to know where she is?"

"She's not here?" Lisbeth looked at Mariah. "Nolie told me she had already gone to bed, that she wasn't feeling well. That's why I went over to the Tremaynes to apologize to Barley, because I found myself all alone this evening."

Steve was astonished to think of Lisbeth apologizing to anybody, but there was no time to wonder about that now. "What's this about her not feeling well?"

"That's what she said," Mariah confirmed. "She was in the study, and I knocked on the door and told her what you said, Miss Lisbeth, about how you wanted supper to be a little late, and she said it didn't matter, 'cause she wasn't hungry and was goin' to bed anyhow. I didn't see her go upstairs, but a little while later I passed by the study and saw the door was open and she was gone."

"I don't understand," Lisbeth said.

"I don't either, and I don't like it." Steve began to pace up and down.

Lisbeth saw he seemed genuinely concerned, and

now she was glad for another reason she had stopped Selena in time. Maybe he really cared about Raven. Maybe the two of them were in love. If so, it would be wonderful. Maybe they could even have a double wedding in the spring. The mourning period would almost be over, and people wouldn't think too much about them all wanting to be married in the prettiest time of the year. "I'm sure it's nothing to be concerned about," she said in an attempt to soothe him. "Maybe she went for a ride in the moonlight. It's a lovely night."

Mariah forgot her place and sat down on the satin divan in her frustration. "I know she was tired. She's been working awful hard lately. She might've gone off somewhere and laid down and fallen asleep."

Steve was wondering where to start looking, and Lisbeth was thinking about wedding plans. Neither was particularly paying any attention to Mariah.

"And I know she was too tired to fool with that white trash Selena too, but she made me bring her in the house anyhow."

Steve was quick to chide, "Now Mariah, you've got no call to talk about Selena that way."

"Oh, God!"

They looked at Lisbeth. Her face had gone pale, and she sat clutching her throat and swaying to and fro as she moaned over and over, "God, no . . . God, no. . . ."

Steve ran to drop to his knees in front of her and grab her hands. He was afraid she was about to faint. "Lisbeth, what's wrong? Tell me. Whatever it is, tell me, please."

"I . . . I . . ." she shook her head from side to side. "I can't. Don't make me."

"Whatever it is," he repeated sternly, icy fingers of apprehension beginning to claw at his spine, "you must tell me."

"You'll hate me," she whispered hoarsely. "Oh, Lord, if it's what I think it is, I hate myself."

"I won't hate you, I promise," he insisted. Anything to get her to talk before she went into a stupor or passed out.

Mariah had got up and backed away, frightened herself and not knowing why.

Lisbeth moaned, "Selena did it because I made her. That has to be why she was here . . . why Raven left. But that was before she saved my life. And I would've stopped her anyway. I know I would have. That's why I went for a ride by myself, because I was so miserable. I didn't realize it till I chased Barley off. I'm not really a bad person, Steve. You have to believe me. I've just been confused."

"Yes, yes, I know." He dropped her hands and clutched her shoulders and gave her a little shake. "We can talk about all that later, Lisbeth. Right now you've got to tell me where Raven is. She could be in danger out there by herself somewhere."

She raised her head to meet his eyes and saw the fear there and knew in an instant that for him to be so upset he had to be in love with Raven. "Sweet Jesus, what have I done?" She dropped her gaze, unable to look at him any longer. Keeping her head down, she talked fast and furiously, for there might still be time to find Raven and stop her. "God forgive me, Steve, but I thought I hated her and wanted to get rid of her, and when I followed her to the barn and saw her go upstairs to your room, I knew you were sleeping together. That's when I thought of what to do. I went to Selena and told her to tell Raven you were the baby's father, and—"

"Damn it, Lisbeth, you didn't." He shook her so hard her head bobbed to and fro; then, realizing he might hurt her, he let her go and bolted to his feet and started for the door.

"Wait, hear me out."

He turned with a groan, wondering if there was more to the nightmare.

"After Raven saved my life and I realized how wrong I'd been, I went to find Selena to tell her not to do it, but I couldn't. One of the slaves told me she had gone away, to hide from her father, she thought. I was relieved, thinking she'd actually left to keep from telling me she wouldn't do it, because she didn't want to. She cried about it. Oh, I feel so awful."

"You should," he said tightly.

"But I thought it was all right, that there was nothing to worry about."

Mariah informed her crisply, "Well, there was, and there is, 'cause Selena was here, all right, and I didn't see Miss Raven after that, so Selena is bound to have told her, and that's what got her all upset."

"I've got to go after her. Wait." He whirled on Lisbeth again. "You say you were over at the Tremaynes?"

Lisbeth nodded.

"Raven would head for Mobile. She wouldn't know another direction to go. From there she'd find her way easily to Texas. Did you see her on the road?"

"Oh, if I had, I would've told you, Steve. But I didn't."

"Well, if you didn't see her, she must have left earlier and already got by the road to the Tremaynes. Damn!" He doubled his hands into fists and smashed them together. "If she got that far, I won't be able to find her." He turned to go, knowing he had to try.

Lisbeth wished she hadn't stayed so long at Barley's. Maybe she would have met her on the road. "I'm sorry. We only passed two people: Masson Leroux and then, a little bit later, a soldier riding a horse that looked like Diablo. But it couldn't have been. I mean, why would . . ."

Her voice trailed off to wonder whether it might actually have been Raven at the same instant that it struck Steve: *a soldier on a horse that looked like Diablo.*

It could only be her.

He tore out the door. There was still time to find her if she was still on the road. Once she got to Mobile, she would lose herself in the crowds. And at daylight, she would head west, making her own trail, and he'd never be able to track her.

Joshua was brushing Starfire down when Steve rushed into the stable. "Lordy, you look like the devil is chasin' you."

"He might as well be. Help me get Starfire saddled. Quick." He grabbed a blanket from the stall railing and threw it on the stallion's back.

Joshua blinked in surprise. "Mr. Steve, have you gone plumb loco? You can't ride this horse. Nobody can, 'ceptin' Miss Raven. And she must've gone for a ride herself. But you know, just because she bested them rowdies today don't mean she should go off by herself at night. You can't never tell what might happen."

"If you're not going to help me, get out of my way." Steve ran to the tack room and got a saddle and hurried back to strap it on Starfire.

"He's gonna kill you," Joshua warned, hurrying after him as he led the horse out of the stall and toward the door.

"No, he's not," Steve said firmly, surely. He patted Starfire's neck and whispered in his ear as he adjusted the bridle. "Because if you do we may just lose Raven forever, and I don't think you want that anymore than I do. She once told me about sharing spirits, and if you'll understand that I've got no intention of breaking yours, I can find her in time. Because you're the only horse around here fast enough to do that."

Starfire miraculously seemed to understand and gave a soft whinny and tossed his head as though impatient to get started.

Steve swung up in the saddle and held his breath.

With his right foreleg, Starfire pawed the ground.

Steve knew then the great horse understood, and tears welled in his eyes. "All right, let's go!" he cried.

They thundered out of the barn, with Starfire in full gallop by the time they reached the gate. The stallion did not take time to wait for anyone to open it. With a mighty leap, he cleared it, glory rippling through Steve to feel the stallion's power beneath him.

On they charged, down the road and through the silvered night. Starfire, given his head, never stumbled, never slowed.

Raven had a good start. Steve had no idea just how much, only that there was not a second to spare. And as Starfire's hooves struck the road, Steve's heart constricted to wish he had told her sooner how much he loved her.

*   *   *

Masson Leroux found the perfect spot. A brick pillar stood to one side of the bridge, there by accident when the builders had started construction in the wrong place. When they had corrected it, they left the pillar, so now it was his vantage point. He clambered up. There was enough light for him to be able to see her when she came across the bridge. One shot would do it, maybe two. It didn't matter. There was no one around. He could fill her full of holes and no one would notice. And she would also sink faster when she hit the water.

He pulled his knees up to his chin, laying his rifle down beside him. He had brought his flask with him and took another drink of whiskey. He was tired and sleepy. His head nodded. It wouldn't hurt to close his eyes for just a few minutes, he decided, and let the drowsiness take him away.

27

Steve could see her.

Diablo was trotting along at a steady pace. He dared not call out to her, for fear she would set the mustang into a run, and she was halfway across the bridge. On the other side were thick woods and swampland. If she galloped across to plunge into them, he might not be able to find her in the dark, and she could get lost among the snakes and alligators lurking there.

But Raven had heard the sound of a horse coming fast behind her and looked around.

Aware that she had spotted him, Steve's instinct was to pull back on Starfire's reins, but he yanked too hard, which made Starfire rear up. And when he did, his mighty forelegs thrashing in the air, Steve feared he was about to fall and struggled valiantly to stay in the saddle.

Raven froze as she recognized Steve, spellbound to

see he was actually riding Starfire, fighting now to bring him under control.

And when he did, she still remained where she was, imprisoned by awe as he approached, Starfire keeping a steady gait.

"You rode him," she said, continuing to be mesmerized. "But how. . . .?"

Steve wasted no time in jerking Diablo's reins from her, lest she ride away. He didn't want to whistle and have the mustang throw her if there was any other way. "I had to. He's our fastest horse, and I had to find you before you got to Mobile."

"And he let you ride him?" She stroked the stallion's neck, temporarily forgetting her pain and anger in the entrancing moment.

"I told him he had to if we were to stop you from leaving us."

She came out of her trance then, realizing Steve had her reins and meant to keep them. "Give those back," she demanded furiously. "It's over. I'm going home."

"You *are* home, Raven." He tried to take her hand, but she snatched it away. "And you have to listen to me. I know what Selena told you. It was all a lie. Lisbeth made her do it, because she found out about you and me and figured she could make you run away if you believed I was Amanda's father."

"No, Steve. *You* are lying. Selena told me how you were—" she twisted her lips in scorn—"*servicing* me to keep your job. But you don't have to worry about me anymore. It will be up to Lisbeth and Julius whether you stay on, because Halcyon is theirs now. It always was. There's no place for me in Alabama. I don't belong here. I never did, only I was too blind to realize it. I thought I could make them like me and want me to be a part of the family." She swiped at a tear with the back of her hand. "But that was only a dream—like you," she added, wishing she hadn't, but telling herself it didn't matter.

When he heard that he dared feel a glimmer of hope. "You do belong here. With me. And I'm no dream. I'm real, if you'll let me be, Raven."

"Listen to me," she cried, fury sweeping through her. "Even if you did care about me, you have a responsibility to Selena and her baby. God knows, I know better than anybody what it's like to feel abandoned by your own father. I could never live with myself if I had anything to do with your abandoning that child."

"But I'm not. Amanda isn't mine. Lisbeth put Selena up to it. You've got to believe that. When I find Selena, I'll get her to tell you everything. The man who got her pregnant died long before the baby was born. He was married. Selena didn't want to hurt his family, so she never told anyone the truth but me. I didn't care if Masson or anybody else thought I was responsible— till now," he added, reaching for her hand again.

Once more she withdrew, but not as quickly. He truly sounded sincere, and with love rocketing through her, she found herself praying that he might be.

"I don't know when it happened, Raven," he went on, misery etched all over his face, "but it did. All of a sudden, I knew I loved you, only you, and I could never want another woman. And not just for the pleasure you bring me, even though I've never known anything so good. I want you for my wife, the mother of my children—*our* children. And I'll never abandon you. With God as my witness, I swear I'll take care of you and love you till my dying breath.

"And God also knows, Raven"—his voice broke as he dismounted and reached for her to pull her down against him, there on the bridge, with the moonlight spilling over them—"I want to spend the rest of my life with you. I want to grow old with you. And when I die, I want to spend eternity with you. I never thought I'd say these things to any woman. Never even knew I could feel this way. But I do. You've got to believe me."

The trembling began deep within her. It came from her heart, then spread all over, inspired by love. And she knew somehow, in that moment, that she could never leave because she did love him, and that awareness, that affirmation, gave her the strength and courage to say, "I do believe you, Steve. And I want everything that you want . . . for always and ever."

"Thank God, sweetheart. Thank God." And with a laugh and a sob of joy, he showered her face with kisses. "I have to tell you I was scared there for a minute Starfire wouldn't let me ride him, but the funny thing is, I think he understood when I told him I only wanted to share his spirit, not break it." He sobered to add, "But even if he'd killed me, at least I would have gone to my grave knowing I tried: for you, for me, for us."

She parted her lips to drink deeply of his sweet kiss, the kiss of avowal for a love not to be denied.

Suddenly a shot rang out.

Even before the whining echo faded away, Steve had grabbed Raven and taken her with him to the ground, rolling on top of her to shield her as he drew his gun, ready to fire back as soon as he could figure out where the shot had come from.

Then they heard a voice cry out in triumph, "I got him. Don't shoot. It's all right. It's all over. I got him."

"That's Julius," Raven said frantically, recognizing his voice as she struggled to get out from under Steve. He let her go, and she was on her feet and running the rest of the way across the bridge, with Steve right behind her.

Julius saw it was her and cried, "Lord, Raven. I didn't know it was you. I just saw him pointing a gun at two people out on the bridge, so I winged him."

She looked down to see Masson Leroux writhing on the ground in agony from a bullet in his right shoulder. "Masson?" She shook her head. It didn't make sense, any of it. Her eyes went from him to the still-smoking six-gun in Julius's hand. "That's no derringer," she said with a little gasp.

"I've been taking shooting lessons," he said, bursting with pride. "I finally realized what an idiot I've been, but I didn't want you to know till I was sure I was good. Today was the day. The man teaching me said I knew everything he did. So I was coming to tell you about it. And also to apologize for how I've treated you. I'd hoped to leave earlier, but I'm learning what it's like to work for a living"—he chuckled—"and I can tell you it's tough, but it feels good when the work is done."

Steve reached around Raven to shake Julius's hand. "I'm glad you were delayed, Julius. You saved our lives, and we thank you."

"But why would he want to kill you?" Julius nudged Masson with his foot. "Tell us, you scalawag."

Raven felt a shiver of alarm and pressed back against Steve. "What if this is also Lisbeth's doing?"

He clasped her shoulders reassuringly. "There's no way she had anything to do with this. She would have told me. It's a mistake, somehow, but we'll get to the bottom of it later. Right now, scalawag that he is, we need to get him back and take care of his wound."

"But what about Lisbeth?" Julius wanted to know. "Is there trouble? I'm going to talk to her."

"That won't be necessary," Steve said. "We'll tell you all about it on the way home."

"Home." Julius breathed the word with pleasure. "That sounds so good. You know, Raven, you were right. Halcyon is big enough for *all* of us. Right, Steve?" He grinned and slapped him on the back. Julius saw where Raven's heart lay, and if Steve became a real member of the family before long, that would suit him just fine.

Steve put his arm around Raven. "That's right, and we're going to see just how big we can make this one."

Raven snuggled against him.

"Then everything is all right?" Julius hung back, watching them as they walked across the bridge.

Raven and Steve looked at each other, smiled, and shared a tender kiss before Raven called back, "Everything is more than all right. It's *simply heaven.*"

Let HarperMonogram Sweep You Away!

Simply Heaven by Patricia Hagan

New York Times *bestselling author with over ten million copies in print.* Steve Maddox is determined to bring his friend's estranged daughter Raven home to Alabama. But after setting eyes on the tempestuous half-Tonkawa Indian, Steve yearns to tame the wild beauty and make Raven his.

Home Fires by Susan Kay Law

Golden Heart Award-Winning Author. Escaping with her young son from an unhappy marriage, lovely Amanda Sellington finds peace in a small Minnesota town—and the handsome Jakob Hall. Amanda longs to give in to happiness, but the past threatens to destroy the love she has so recently found.

The Bandit's Lady by Maureen Child

Schoolmarm Winifred Matthews is delighted when bank robber Quinn Hawkins takes her on a flight of fancy across Texas. They're running from the law, but already captured in love's sweet embrace.

When Midnight Comes by Robin Burcell

Time Travel Romance. A boating accident sends detective Kendra Browning sailing back to the year 1830, and into the arms of Captain Brice Montgomery. The ecstasy she feels at his touch beckons to Kendra like a siren's song, but murder threatens to steer their love off course.

And in case you missed last month's selections . . .

Touched by Angels by Debbie Macomber

From the bestselling author of *A Season of Angels* and *The Trouble with Angels*. The much-loved angelic trio—Shirley, Goodness, and Mercy—are spending this Christmas in New York City. And three deserving souls are about to have their wishes granted by this dizzy, though divinely inspired, crew.

Till the End of Time by Suzanne Elizabeth

The latest sizzling time-travel romance from award-winning author of *Destiny's Embrace*. Scott Ramsey has a taste for adventure and a way with the ladies. When his time-travel experiment transports him back to Civil War Georgia, he meets his match in Rachel Ann Warren, a beautiful Union spy posing as a Southern belle.

A Taste of Honey by Stephanie Mittman

After raising her five siblings, marrying the local minister is a chance for Annie Morrow to get away from the farm. When she loses her heart to widower Noah Eastman, however, Annie must choose between a life of ease and a love no money can buy.

A Delicate Condition by Angie Ray

Golden Heart Winner. A marriage of convenience weds innocent Miranda Rembert to the icy Lord Huntsley. But beneath his lordship's stern exterior, fires of passion linger—along with a burning desire for the marital pleasures only Miranda can provide.

Reckless Destiny by Teresa Southwick

Believing that Arizona Territory is no place for a lady, Captain Kane Carrington sent proper Easterner Cady Tanner packing. Now the winsome schoolteacher is back, and ready to teach Captain Carrington a lesson in love.